THE GULF CONSPIRACY

THE GULF CONSPIRACY

Ken McClure

WINDSOR
PARAGON
THORNDIKE

This Large Print book is published by BBC Audiobooks Ltd, Bath,
England and by Thorndike Press®, Waterville, Maine, USA.

Published in 2005 in the U.K. by arrangement with Allison & Busby Ltd.

Published in 2005 in the U.S. by arrangement with Allison & Busby Ltd.

U.K. Hardcover   ISBN 1–4056–1045–X (Chivers Large Print)
U.K. Softcover   ISBN 1–4056–2036–6 (Camden Large Print)
U.S. Softcover   ISBN 0–7862–7017–9 (General)

The text of this Large Print edition is unabridged.
Other aspects of the book may vary from the original edition.

Set in 16 pt. New Times Roman.

Printed in Great Britain on acid-free paper.

British Library Cataloguing in Publication Data available

Library of Congress Control Number: 2004110763

CHAPTER ONE

Channing House
Kent
November 1990

The moon emerged from behind the clouds to light up the drive of Channing House as a dark Rover saloon swung in through the gates to crunch up the drive and come to a halt. The driver got out and hurried round to open the back door, adopting a concerned expression as the man in the back made an ungainly exit due to the bulk of his overcoat and the fact he was holding a heavy briefcase. He straightened up and told the driver to wait before making his way to the steps leading up to the front door, his gait a little unsteady after the forty-mile drive down from London.

The door was answered by a man-servant, who apologised and requested proof of identity despite seemingly recognising the visitor and addressing him as Sir James.

'Yes, yes,' mumbled the man, feeling in his inside pocket for some ID. 'Let's not carry this nonsense too far, shall we?'

'Colonel Warner's orders, sir,' said the servant, closing the door and taking the man's coat before leading the way upstairs where he opened a set of double doors and announced,

'Sir James Gardiner.'

'Come in, James,' said a man, whose clipped moustache and erect bearing would have marked him out as a military man in any company. 'Good of you to come at such short notice.'

'The tone of your message didn't leave me much choice, Warner,' said Gardiner.

There were three other men in the room. Gardiner nodded to them and took his place at the table.

'I'm afraid I had no alternative,' said Warner.

'Your note said it was serious. Bloody well better be. I was due to dine with HRH and the defence minister this evening.'

'I'm afraid Crowe has some bad news for us,' said Warner. He had lowered his voice and spoke softly like an undertaker dealing with the recently bereaved. 'There's been a bit of an accident, a serious one. It could have potentially disastrous consequences.'

Gardiner looked at Crowe and said, 'If it involves Crowe it must involve Porton Down? We're not all going to get plague or smallpox are we?'

'Nothing like that,' said Crowe. 'It concerns the vaccine being given to our troops before being deployed in the Gulf.'

'What on earth has that got to do with us?'

Crowe, a painfully thin man in his forties with craggy features and a yellowish

2

complexion that suggested old parchment, looked down at the table through tinted spectacles as if gathering his thoughts. He looked up. 'The vaccination schedule is a composite one, comprising a number of component parts—six in all—designed to give protection against a range of diseases—those endemic in the region and those likely to be used as biological weapons.'

'I still don't see what this has to do with us?'

'It's been contaminated,' said Crowe.

'Contaminated,' repeated Gardiner, then when he saw that no more was forthcoming, 'With what?'

Crowe told Gardiner and the others what had happened.

Gardiner's jaw dropped. For a full thirty seconds he did a passable impression of a dead fish. 'You cannot be serious,' he said.

'I wish I wasn't.'

'But how in God's name?'

'One of my team, Dr George Sebring, made a simple mistake. It led to an unfortunate chain of events. As you well know, the nature of our work has required that the Beta Team remain a secret within a secret at Porton. Our real project is known only to a handful of people but we have a cover story inside the establishment itself to satisfy the questions of colleagues. Officially, we have been working on the design of a new vaccine. Ironically, and because of this, a request was made to us for a supply of gene envelopes to assist in the production of the military vaccine. Apparently the manufacturers were running low on a component called cytokines—which boost immune response and make vaccines more effective. They approached us for an alternative. Unfortunately and for whatever reason, Sebring handed over the wrong thing.'

'Not live virus?'

'No, Sir James, not that simple.'

'Bloody hell,' murmured Gardiner, shaking his head as he looked directly at Crowe. 'This beggars belief.'

'It's something we all deeply regret,' said Crowe.

'Surely to God someone on the vaccine production team must have checked out what they were given?'

'I'm afraid the establishment's own security worked against us,' said Crowe. 'Four elements of the vaccine programme have been classified under the Official Secrets Act. The manufacturers were not at liberty to question anything to do with these components or indeed to analyse them in any way.'

'Can't we recall the damned stuff?'

'Too late, I'm afraid; it's already been used.'

'Ye gods,' sighed Gardiner. 'What numbers are we talking about here?' he asked, looking as if he feared the reply.

Crowe looked down at his notes before replying. 'We estimate about fifteen percent of

4

allied forces will have been given the rogue vaccine: this excludes the French who decided against vaccinating their forces.'

'Bloody hell!' exclaimed Gardiner. 'We are talking about thousands of people.'

Crowe's silence confirmed Gardiner's estimate.

A film of sweat had broken out on Gardiner's forehead. He brought out a large white handkerchief and dabbed it away as he asked, 'So what do you damned scientists propose we do about this?'

There was no response.

Gardiner asked, 'What will happen to people who've been given it?'

All eyes turned to Crowe whose stony expression had not varied throughout. 'First of all let me say how sorry I and the team are that this has happened,' he said. 'It's something that Dr Sebring is having particular difficulty in coming to terms with.'

'Please just answer the question,' said Gardiner coldly. He felt irked at Crowe's second attempt at diverting blame from himself. Crowe was the team leader: he should carry the can.

'The nature of our work is such that any reference to precedent is out of the question,' said Crowe.

Gardiner frowned. 'Does that mean that you don't actually know what this thing will do to our troops?' he asked.

'Not in so many words, although we can . . .'

'Guess?' said Gardiner, filling in the blank and making it sound like a dirty word.

'Well . . . informed guess I think it would be fair to say,' said Crowe with an attempt at a smile that just made his face seem more cadaverous than ever.

Gardiner looked at Crowe with a blank expression that might have been concealing contempt. 'Let's just take this one step at a time,' he said quietly. 'Will it kill them?'

'We are pretty sure it won't do that,' said Crowe.

'Incapacitate them?'

'Probably not, although it's very difficult to say in the light of our not having evaluated it to any great degree . . .' Crowe's voice trailed off into embarrassed silence.

Gardiner gave him the same blank look then diverted his gaze while he appeared to think for a few moments. He finally looked at everyone around the table before saying, 'So if they are not going to drop down dead and they are not all going to collapse to the floor coughing and vomiting, what's left?'

Crowe shrugged and said, 'Again, it's really difficult to say. There may well be a range of symptoms occurring over a prolonged period of time . . .'

'But there's no one symptom that would suggest a common agent as being the cause?'

'I don't think so. The nature of the team's

6

brief was to . . .'

'Thank you, I think we are all familiar with the team's brief,' interrupted Gardiner. 'Now let's be quite clear about this, you seem to be saying that it would be difficult to identify the presence of any extraneous agent as being the cause of any illness?'

'I think it would be fair to say that,' agreed Crowe. 'That, of course, was also part of the . . . brief . . . which, naturally, you already know.'

'Well, thank God for small mercies,' sighed Gardiner. 'That at least gives us some leeway. Who knows about this at Porton?' he asked.

'No one,' said Crowe. 'I told the team to say nothing: I would sort it out.'

'Good,' said Gardiner. 'At least that gives us a chance of containing this incident.'

All eyes turned to him, something he interpreted as accusation on the part of the others. 'Well, if no one is going to die and there are no specific symptoms to point people in the direction of the Beta Team and indeed to us, it opens up an alternative course of action, don't you think?' he snorted.

'You seem to be suggesting that we deal with this situation by saying and doing nothing, Sir James,' said one of the others who until this point had been silent. He was Rupert Everley, millionaire property developer and would-be politician who had, so far, failed three times as a Tory candidate at elections. A good-looking man in his early forties with boyish features and a mop of swept-back fair hair, Everley seemed, by general agreement, to take more care with his appearance than with what came out of his mouth. Not regarded as an intellectual giant by the others, they were familiar with a range of facial expressions he was prone to adopt, suggesting among themselves that he had practised them in front of a mirror. At the moment he was doing 'earnest concern'.

'I take it you have a better idea, Everley?' said Gardiner. 'Perhaps you would care to make a public announcement telling everyone that our troops have been inoculated with a contaminated vaccine? Tell them that we haven't a clue what it's going to do to them? Then perhaps you can go on to tell them just what it was contaminated with and where it came from and let's see what the press make of that?'

There was silence in the room. Everley looked crestfallen.

Gardiner stayed on the offensive. 'Have you even considered the effects of telling thousands of our troops that they have been poisoned on the very eve of their going to war? Christ almighty, man, we might just as well send a congratulations telegram to Baghdad and call the whole bloody thing off.'

'You're right, James,' said Warner. 'We need cool heads at a time like this.'

'I suppose when you put it that way,' conceded Everley.

'There's no other way to put it,' said Gardiner. 'We must keep this accident a secret.' Gardiner made a point of establishing eye contact with each man in turn. 'And we are all going to sit here and decide just how we're going to achieve that.'

Dhahran Airbase
Saudi Arabia
20 Jan 1991

'Shit, I'm not sure I want to fight alongside anyone who risks that much on a pair of twos,' said Air Force Corporal Neil Anderson, slapping down three of a kind and reaching across the table with both hands to bring in his winnings. 'Shows a distinct lack of judgement, if you ask me.'

'Don't kid yourself, pal, I saw you waver there for a moment,' retorted fellow corporal, Colin Childs. 'I bloody near had you, sunshine, and just remember: who dares wins.'

'Yeah, yeah,' laughed Anderson.

'Cut the crap and deal.'

Anderson chuckled as he boxed the cards and started dealing. 'I can feel the force,' he joked. 'Lady Luck is not just with me, she's positively taking her knickers down for me.'

Childs was about to say something in reply when the sudden wail of sirens filled the air and both men rushed from the table to their action stations.

'Scud coming in!' yelled Anderson, pointing at the distant night sky as they raced across the dark compound.

'Where the fuck are the Patriots?' complained Childs, trying to look around him and run at the same time.

As if in response, the whoosh of an American Patriot interceptor missile, being launched from the perimeter battery, brought a cheer to their lips.

'Go get that fucker, baby,' yelled Anderson.

'Send it right back up Saddam's arse,' added Childs. There were more cheers and from all over the base when the Patriot made contact with the incoming scud, causing it to spiral out of the sky about four hundred metres from the perimeter fence. In the ensuing silence before ground impact, Anderson and Childs threw themselves flat and covered their ears against the anticipated explosion but none came. Instead, the eerie silence continued until the two men became fidgety. Suddenly, bedlam broke out as the NAIADS (chemical and biological weapon detectors) started wailing all over the base like demented banshees.

'It didn't explode because it's a fucking CB attack!' yelled Anderson as he scrambled to his feet and led the way as both men sprinted over to the clothing store to pull on their protective suits.

'Jesus fuck, this is really it,' murmured Anderson, hopping on one leg as he struggled into his suit.

'Sweet Jesus Christ,' murmured Childs over and over again as he too struggled with the cumbersome fastenings, his fingers all thumbs as fear knotted his stomach and sent adrenalin coursing through his veins. Both men had done this a hundred times before in training but this was for real and Christ, it felt completely different.

For twenty minutes, both men sat quietly with their thoughts. Bravado and banter were things of the past, not that it was ever possible while wearing respirators. They wondered about their position. There was no way of knowing what was in the air and maybe just on the other side of their visors. Nerve gas? A virus? The plague bacillus? All three perhaps?

Anderson remembered training lectures where the Russian tactic of formulating a 'mixed load' for CB weapons had been highlighted as a possible way of countering protective measures against such weapons. He distinctly remembered the instructor pointing out at one stage that Russia and Saddam were big pals. Subconsciously he rubbed the area on his upper arm where he had been vaccinated.

He could see that Childs had his eyes closed. He hadn't known the man to pray before but conceded that now was as good a time as any to start. His thoughts turned to

11

thinking about his wife Jenny and their two children. Claire, the youngest, had been born by Caesarean section a month premature just the week before he'd left for the Gulf. She had seemed so small and vulnerable, a bit like the way he felt at the moment.

The all-clear sounded and broke the eerie silence. Both men felt weak as adrenalin dissipated and feelings of relief took its place. They got to their feet slowly and started stripping off their protective suits.

'Must have been a false alarm,' said Anderson.

'Tell my bowels that,' said Childs. 'Christ, I hate the idea of not being able to see what I'm fighting.'

As they set out to return their protective gear to the storage pods they caught sight of a figure, still wearing his, running across the compound towards them. He was shouting something and waving his arms but his visor was muffling the sound. As he drew nearer, Anderson recognised the man as Gus Maclean, a sergeant and one of the five-man team who operated and maintained the chemical and biological detectors.

'Put them back on!' yelled Maclean. 'It's not over. There's gas all over the fucking place. I'm going to find the stupid fucker who sounded the all-clear and remove his balls.'

Panic returned in an instant and Anderson and Childs struggled back into their suits. A

12

few minutes later the NAIADS sounded again. The base remained in NBC Condition Black (under chemical and biological attack) for the next eight hours.

It was two days before the men saw Gus Maclean again. He was in the canteen, sitting on his own, toying with a meal that he was obviously finding less than appetising.

'So what gives?' asked Anderson, sitting down beside him.

Maclean shrugged and glanced from side to side before saying, 'The official line is that there was no confirmed chemical attack on the base.' He stressed the word 'confirmed'.

'I though you guys confirmed it,' said Childs.

'Every detector on the fucking base was screaming gas attack but the brass are pretending it never happened. What's the point of having the team here if they're not going to believe us? Who else can "confirm" it if we can't for Christ's sake?'

'Fuck me,' said Childs. 'You couldn't make it up, could you?'

'My granddad used to tell me about the fuck-ups the army made in his war,' said Anderson. 'Lions led by donkeys and all that. Some things never change.'

'And what about the all-clear sounding?' asked Childs.

'That's something else again,' said Maclean. 'Nobody's putting up their hands for that one.

13

Hundreds of our guys were exposed to nerve gas unnecessarily and no one's to blame. Apparently it just never happened.'

'Bad enough fighting the Iraqis without our own mob having a go at us as well,' said Childs.

32 Field Hospital
Wadi al Batin
23rd January 1991

Surgeon Commander James Morton watched as the helicopter touched down and sent sand flying up in all directions. As its side door slid open, three field medics ran forward in a crouching run to assist in evacuating the patient from the aircraft. The injured man was a vehicle technician who had been working on an armoured personnel carrier and whose arm had been caught in the half-track when a fellow technician, unaware of his presence, had started up the vehicle and attempted to move off. The man's right arm had been all but severed. Plans to fly him to a proper hospital had had to be abandoned when his blood loss became critical. Wadi Al Batin was the nearest place with the sort of medical facilities that might be able to cope with the situation.

Morton looked at the face of the unconscious man and listened as one of the field medics reeled off a series of statistics as the patient was transferred from stretcher to

14

table. He couldn't be much more than twenty years old. He should have had all of his life before him. 'Blood?' he asked.

'On its way,' replied one of the masked nurses.

'Let's have a look,' murmured Morton as he gingerly peeled away the wad of dressings from the patient's arm. 'What's his name?'

'Jackson, sir. Private Robert Jackson.'

'Well, Private Jackson,' said Morton. 'I'm afraid your soldiering days are over, old son, and I hope to God you're left-handed because this is going to have to come off. Make ready for amputation everyone, will you? How's he doing?'

The question was directed at the anaesthetist, a young RAMC lieutenant who had taken up station at the head of the patient and was taking readings from the monitors he'd been attaching to Jackson.

'Not good. He's very weak.'

'As I see it, we don't have much of an option,' said Morton.

'You don't think it's worthwhile just trying to stabilise him and then transferring him to somewhere with a proper ICU?' asked the lieutenant.

Morton shook his head slowly. 'Much as I'd like to, I don't think I could get him stable with that mess still attached to his shoulder. Apart from that, the chance of infection in this hell-hole increases with every minute that passes.

15

His only hope is a quick amputation, so let's get on with it. Where the hell's that blood?'

'It's here,' replied one of the masked figures as a vehicle pulled up outside the field hospital.

Twenty minutes later Morton paused and stood back to allow the severed limb to be wrapped in gauze and removed from the table. Once again he asked for an update on the patient's condition as he drew together the two flaps of skin he'd deliberately left attached in order to form a neat stump and started suturing them.

'Still iffy,' replied the anaesthetist.

'I'll be as quick as I can.'

Morton's hand jumped as the air raid warnings went off and he cursed as the needle made an inch long scratch on the patient's skin.

'That's all we need,' said the anaesthetist. 'An air raid.'

'Scud attack,' said someone else. 'Listen.'

In the ensuing pause they listened to the sound of the incoming missile.

'I think it's going over,' said an optimist only a fraction before there was a loud popping sound, which made people look questioningly at each other over their masks.

'Oh Christ, no explosion means it's an airburst,' said the reformed optimist.

Morton continued sewing his neat line of stitches, as around him, people shuffled to their feet and looked at each other uneasily over their masks. Then the NAIADS went off and loudspeakers started proclaiming: 'NBC Condition Black. This is not a drill!' It kept repeating, 'This is not a drill.'

'Okay folks, you know what to do,' said Morton, still concentrating on his work and not looking up. 'Everyone into their suits please.'

No one argued but the anaesthetist said, 'I can't just walk away. He'll die.'

'You might die if you don't,' said Morton.

'I'll go when you do.'

Morton smiled under his mask. 'Fair enough.' The procedure was all over in seven minutes but it seemed more like seven hours to the two men. 'Right, you go first and get into your suit,' said Morton, stripping off his gloves. 'Bring up a respirator for him as well, and then you can take over while I get into mine. We'll keep him on the gas for the time being.'

The anaesthetist needed no second bidding.

Three hours later and despite the best efforts of Morton and the team, Vehicle Technician Robert Jackson died without ever coming round. Some two hours after that Morton and the anaesthetist started to feel ill. Both men suffered blinding headaches, stomach cramps and prolonged episodes of vomiting throughout the following night.

'Do they know what it was yet?' gasped

Morton as he found respite for a few minutes after yet another round of vomiting. He asked the question of one of his colleagues who had just wiped the sweat from his face as the sun came up over the base.

'Unidentified chemical attack is all I could get out of the commandant's office,' replied the young doctor.

'How about the monitoring team?'

'The technicians are saying it was Sarin but that has not been confirmed.'

'What does the manual say about that?'

'The only information I could come up with comes from studies they did on volunteers a while back. According to that, you seem to be exhibiting the effects of low level exposure to the gas.'

'Christ, I wouldn't like to find out what high level exposure feels like,' said Morton. 'Do we know what the long term effects are?' he asked.

'There's nothing at all in the manual. The official view seems to be that it's best not to breathe it in the first place.'

'Who would have thought?' said Morton before another bout of stomach cramps made him curl up and cry out in pain. When the pain subsided he lay back on the pillow and took a moment or two to steady himself before asking, 'Surely they must have done follow-up studies on the volunteers?'

'I think they did.'

'Well?'

'You're not going to believe this but the results are classified.'

'Oh, I believe it,' exclaimed Morton. 'The words piss-up and brewery spring to mind.'

Both Morton and his colleague had recovered sufficiently by the following day to attend an official briefing on the scud incident. Chemical attack had not been confirmed, the assembly was informed. Contrary to rumour, the cloud in the sky witnessed by many after the missile had disintegrated had been aviation fuel catching fire. Personnel should pay no heed to rumour. There was absolutely no cause for alarm.

Morton looked at the anaesthetist and the colleague who had looked after him as somewhere behind them a Scottish technician murmured sourly, 'Aye, right.'

CHAPTER TWO

Dhahran Airbase
Saudi Arabia
February 1991

Lt. Colonel James Blamire arrived at the television studio in plenty of time to confer with his American counterpart as they'd previously arranged. A few inches shorter than the gangling Blamire, but broader and with an iron-grey crew cut in contrast to the Englishman's thinning fair hair, Marine Colonel Max Schumacher got up and held out his hand when he saw Blamire come in through the door.

He smiled and suggested, 'Why don't we walk and talk outside?' He picked up his briefcase from the side of his chair.

Blamire, noting the number of people in the room and the noise being made by the technicians as they went about their business of preparing for a press conference, grimaced and nodded his agreement.

The two men made their way to a side exit, stepping carefully over cable lines and easing between satellite broadcasting equipment to leave the studio, pausing only to tell the floor manager who was clutching a clip-board in one hand and gesturing to a man setting up the lighting gantry with the other, that they would return in plenty of time for the start of the conference.

'The word is out that some of the press are going to be asking awkward questions about Saddam's use of CB weapons,' said Blamire.

'I've heard that too and I'm not exactly relishing it. I don't suppose you've any idea what they've got?'

' 'Fraid not. I tried my sources but no joy. Hopefully it's just the stuff of rumour but by God, there's plenty of it going about.'

The two men continued their slow walk in silence until Schumacher broke it by saying, 'Between you and I, 513 Military Intelligence have filed a report of anthrax being found in King Khalid City,' said Schumacher. 'Thought you should know.'

'One of our field labs has identified Plague bacillus at Wadi al Batin,' said Blamire.

'Jesus.'

'But there is to be no change to the official line,' said Blamire.

'Which makes our position about as comfortable as sitting on a barbed wire fence,' said Schumacher.

'Trotting out the same old crap like some military parrot,' said Blamire. He recited, 'There is no confirmed evidence of Saddam ever having used CB weapons intentionally.'

'Note the all-important use of the word, "intentionally",' snorted Schumacher. 'The Iraqis use plague and we use semantics. Still, I guess in some quarters of the UN this would be regarded as progress.'

'If either of these reports has been leaked to the media—despite the fact they're top secret—Joint Intelligence suggests that we point them in the direction of air strikes carried out on Saddam's labs.'

Schumacher smiled and said, 'An unfortunate but unavoidable fall-out carried on the desert wind?'

'Precisely. These facilities posed an

unacceptable threat to the civilised world and had to be destroyed. Any collateral damage due to escaping micro-organisms is to be regretted.'

'Think the media'll swallow it?' said Schumacher.

'Personally I'd prefer if they swallowed the bugs and got off my bloody back. I'm fed up pandering to a bunch of holier-than-thou scribblers so that Joe Public can watch the bloody war on television.'

'Know how you feel,' agreed Schumacher.

'There is one thing that bothers me though,' said Blamire. 'I don't quite understand why we're bending over backwards to pretend that Saddam isn't using CB weapons when he damn well is.'

Schumacher looked at Blamire sideways. 'You're serious?' he said. 'You really don't know?'

'No, I don't,' confessed Blamire.

'We sold him the weapons, James. Uncle Sam supplied him with the bugs less than six years ago and George Bush reckons the American people couldn't quite handle that fun piece of information right now, particularly if our boys should start dying of a plague with stars and stripes written all over it.'

'Oh what a tangled web we weave,' sighed Blamire. 'What exactly did you lot give him?'

'From what I can make out, just about

22

anything he asked for in the mid-eighties. Anthrax, Plague, Clostridia, Brucella, you name it. Oh, and Sarin nerve gas for good measure.'

'Jesus.'

'And d'you know the really cute thing? He was supplied with seed cultures from the American National Type Culture Collection at the rate they charge our research labs at home. Less than sixty dollars a throw.'

'Good God.'

'And the bastard didn't even pay.'

'So now he can grow as much as he wants at any time from these damned seed cultures.'

'Yep,' agreed Schumacher. 'Just thank Christ he can't deliver them properly or we'd be in even deeper shit. These old Scuds are about as useful as wheelbarrows when it comes to actually delivering CB weapons.'

'At least the vaccines seemed to be doing their job too,' said Blamire. 'There's been no outbreak of disease that I've heard about.'

'No,' agreed Schumacher.

'Mind you, the nerve gas could be a bigger problem,' said Blamire. 'I suppose we could have used the same "fall-out from a destroyed lab facility" angle if it wasn't for a couple of well-observed airburst incidents involving Scuds.'

'I heard about that,' said Schumacher.

'And compounded in one case by a fuck-up when they sounded the all clear before the damned stuff had had time to dissipate. You'd almost think that someone wanted to expose the troops to the stuff.'

'You know, it's odd you should say that,' said Schumacher, pausing to light a cigarette, 'I've been worried about these PB pills they've been dishing out to the guys. Do you know what they are?

'They're just pills as far as I'm concerned,' said Blamire, shrugging. 'Not my field, I'm afraid. They're supposed to counter the effects of nerve gas, aren't they?'

'With certain provisos,' said Schumacher. 'One, the substance they contain, pyridostigmine bromide, is toxic itself, especially if you should happen to take too much of it.'

'I take it that's why the troops are instructed only to take them immediately before a gas attack,' said Blamire.

'Correct but it's not clear to me how you can tell when that is exactly,' pointed out Schumacher.

'Good point.'

'So you can understand the temptation to pop these pills every time the guys hear a plane engine come over and that can be dangerous. Nobody knows the long-term effects of PB overdosing.'

'You seem to know a lot about these things.'

'Enough,' agreed Schumacher. 'I spent some time at Fort Dietrich. But you know the

24

really weird thing? PB isn't effective against all nerve gases. In fact, there's one gas where it actually makes the effects worse. Want to take a shot at it?' Schumacher glanced sideways at Blamire.

'Sarin?'

'Yep, Sarin.'

'The one gas we know Saddam has for sure?'

'Exactly. PB works well enough against the effects of Soman and Tabun but when combined with Sarin, it can be a deadly combination. Even tiny concentrations of Sarin in the air can cause problems for someone who's been taking PB pills.'

'Have you said anything about this to anyone?' asked Blamire.

'Are you kidding? I like being a colonel. The uniform of private, first class, wouldn't suit me. No one's supposed to know we gave Sarin to Saddam. Remember?'

'Silly me,' said Blamire. 'So our masters are prepared to have the troops exposed to unnecessary danger in order to avoid any political embarrassment?'

'Seems like it.'

Both men stopped to watch a number of jeeps draw up some three hundred metres away outside the studio building and a number of senior officers get out. Even at a distance the men could see that the bulky figure of General Norman Schwarzkopf was among them.

'Personally I'm counting on Stormin' Norman putting an end to this odyssey of fun and getting all our asses out of here by the end of the month,' said Schumacher.

'Amen to that,' said Blamire. 'We'd better get back; it's almost showtime.'

*   *   *

Blamire and Schumacher took their places at opposite ends of the long table fronting rows of collapsible seats provided for members of the press corps. TV and film cameras were manoeuvred into position and lighting adjusted as General Schwarzkopf took centre stage behind a sea of microphones bearing the logos of their stations. He was flanked by US and British commanders and was the first to be questioned on the progress of the war.

Schwarzkopf handled the press with his usual aplomb and great good humour and the press responded with laughter and even, on occasion, applause. The general was always good copy. He was a tough, straight talking, all action American hero and that was exactly what the folks back home wanted to see on their TV sets—and that went for both sides of the Atlantic. When British commanders were questioned it was as if the lights had been turned out and a speak-your-weight machine had taken over.

26

Blamire was beginning to think that his fears about CB weapons questions had been unfounded when a slight woman with a French accent and wearing fatigues got to her feet and announced her credentials as representing a French radio station. She asked if there was any truth in the rumour that a field laboratory team had recently detected the presence of the anthrax bacillus in Dahran.

Schwarzkopf waited until the hubbub had died down and said, 'I am unaware of any such thing, young lady. How about you Max?'

Max Schumacher shook his head and said, 'No sir.'

'And plague bacillus at Wadi al Batin?' continued the journalist.

Schumacher glanced at Blamire who took his cue and fielded the question for him. 'We are certainly not aware of any deliberate use of any offensive micro-organisms against Allied forces,' he said.

'How about *accidental* use?' asked the woman, picking up on the operative word amidst laughter from the floor. Her accent made the word seem sexy.

'That's really not as daft as it sounds,' said Blamire, using the PR trick of smiling disarmingly as if taking the assembly into his confidence. 'The fact of the matter is that our air crews have been having some success in destroying Saddam's microbiological research facilities.' He paused to allow the journalists to work out what he was going to say next and feel good about it. 'Unfortunately,' he continued, 'it is possible that a certain amount of dangerous fall-out has escaped and although of course, we regret it, the simple fact of the matter is that it's just not possible to contain and destroy everything inside these buildings when high explosive is being used.'

Blamire hoped that the French woman might be satisfied with his answer—as everyone else seemed to be—but she remained standing, small and slim but ramrod straight and exuding the self confidence of someone who saw herself on a mission of truth. Her hair was swept back in a ponytail and the camera lights were reflecting off her frameless glasses. 'So what sort of bacteria can we expect to be in the air around us?' she asked.

'I really don't think that's going to be a major problem,' replied Blamire. 'We would anticipate that any escaping organisms would dissipate to statistical insignificance anywhere outside a radius of two miles from source. As for the identity of these agents, well, of course, that's impossible for us to predict.'

'Is it really, Colonel?' said the French journalist. There was clear doubt in her tone.

For one awful moment Blamire thought that she was about to accuse them openly of knowing perfectly well what organisms Saddam had access to and where he had got them. As fate would have it, however, another

28

journalist got to his feet and said, 'Tom Coogan, NBC News: maybe the rest of us could get a question or two in here?'

The French woman deferred to him reluctantly and sat down. Coogan asked Schwarzkopf if he intended taking his ground forces right on into Baghdad and occupying it.

'I'm a soldier. I do what I'm told. I go where they tell me,' replied the general and good humour returned to the meeting.

Blamire had a few words with Schumacher after the briefing was over. 'It can only be a matter of time,' he said. 'We can't go on like this. That French woman clearly knows what's been going on.'

'It might not be that much of a problem if things go on the way they're doing at the moment,' said Schumacher. 'The bombers have destroyed so much of Saddam's hardware that the Iraqis will be reduced to using catapults by the middle of March assuming they last that long. Once Norman really starts rolling with the ground offensive, they might not make it to the beginning of March, let alone the middle.'

'Something could still go seriously wrong,' said Blamire. 'We're talking about a megalomaniac with his back to the wall. Saddam could still go after the Israelis with CB weapons.'

Schumacher shook his head and said, 'The Israelis have been patient. They've accepted

29

that they have to stay out of this fight or our Arab allies will be hopelessly compromised. They just could not afford to be seen fighting on the same side as the Israelis against a fellow Arab state. But, if what you suggest should happen, it will be out of all our hands. The Israelis will reduce Baghdad to a pile of radioactive dust no matter what anyone says.'

Blamire grimaced at the thought.

'My money is still on Norman kicking Saddam's ass,' said Schumacher. 'Cheer up. We'll all be home by Easter.'

Ministry of Defence
London
September 1991

'The BBC would like us to send someone along to answer allegations that many of our servicemen have been falling ill after returning home from the Gulf, minister. What shall I tell them, sir?'

'Bloody BBC! Whose side are they on? We win a war and all they can do is whinge about a bunch of squaddies who've got flu for God's sake. Whatever happened to pride in one's country?'

'They say the Americans have been experiencing similar problems, Minister,' said the hapless secretary, who had heard it all before. 'They're calling it, Gulf War Syndrome.'

'Poppycock,' retorted the minister. 'Mamby pamby nonsense. For God's sake, what's happening to us? We never read about Agincourt Syndrome in our history books, did we?'

'No sir.'

'Damn right. Nor Crecy Syndrome nor Waterloo Syndrome. Our soldiers were men in these days.'

'Yes sir, shall I tell the BBC no?'

The minister shook his head. 'Oh, I suppose not,' he sighed. 'Ask Jeffrey if he'll go along. Get him to assure them that we are looking at the situation in great detail and seeking the best medical advice available. The welfare of our troops is our primary concern, you know the sort of stuff. Jeffrey knows the form.'

'Yes sir.'

As the secretary left the room, the minister took out a file from his desk and flipped it open. It was headed, *Top Secret, Gulf War Syndrome.*

Channing House
Kent, England
18 Sept. 1991

'England in the autumn, eh Warner? Our England. Who'd want to be anywhere else?' said Sir James Gardiner. He was looking down from the bay window of a first floor room at the trees in the garden. 'Season of mists and mellow fruitfulness and all that. So sad, don't you think? Another year of our lives gone, but with such a beautiful requiem.'

Warner grunted his agreement. 'If only more people realised it. Maybe they'd be less inclined to sit back and let the country go to the dogs.'

'With a bit of luck our success in the Gulf War might put some backbone into them,' said Gardiner.

A bonfire of leaves, lit in the early afternoon, was still smouldering and sending tendrils of smoke up into the still evening air. The smell of burning leaves was everywhere.

'Let's join the others,' said Gardiner.

As was usual at such meetings, Gardiner took his place at the head of the table.

'I thought it best we meet in view of the press coverage being given to something I understand is being called Gulf War Syndrome,' said Gardiner. 'Does this have anything to do with what happened at Porton a year ago? And if so, just how much of a problem we can expect?'

The question was addressed to Dr Donald Crowe, leader of the Beta Team at Porton Down Defence Establishment.

'I think we have to face the fact that the accident may have something to do with it,' said Crowe. 'But there are a great number of other factors to be considered which, if I may say so, tend to work in our favour.'

'Explain.'

'Veterans of the war have apparently been coming down with a wide range of symptoms.' He read from his notes. 'Chronic fatigue, intermittent fever, night sweats, headaches, skin rashes, abdominal bloating, diarrhoea and so it goes on: the list seems endless. This in itself should prevent these symptoms from ever being assigned to any one particular condition.'

'But in reality, all these things are due to contamination of the vaccine?' asked Gardiner.

'Far from it,' replied Crowe. 'Saddam did us a favour with his primitive attempts to use CB weapons in the war. Inadvertently and most obligingly, he created a very convenient smoke screen.'

'You mean that some of the illness may be due to the effects of these weapons rather than our agent?'

'Almost certainly.'

Gardiner appeared to relax a little and others took their cue from him.

'Our American friends also did their bit by not being entirely explicit about the use of PB as an antidote to nerve gas attack,' said Cecil Mowbray. The speaker was a dapper man in his early fifties, whose intelligent but cold eyes and propensity to listen rather than speak in company marked him out as a natural for a career in intelligence. He had worked for MI5 for some twenty-five years, ever since leaving Cambridge with a First in classics. 'Quite a number of forces personnel suffered the effects of over-dosing and unfortunately a small number suffered the combined effects of Sarin gas and PB ingestion.'

'More smoke,' said Warner.

'It's a pity of course, that the Iraqi use of CB weapons can't be made public,' said Crowe. 'For obvious reasons.'

'There's public and then there's public,' said Warner. 'Rumour was rife in the Gulf. The tales of conspiracy and cover-up that our dear friends in the media are so fond of will keep them chasing their tails rather than come sniffing at anything closer to home.'

'I anticipate the fact that the Americans supplied Saddam with these weapons will become public knowledge over the next few years but, by that time, the war will be something of a distant memory in public consciousness and therefore this will not be such an issue,' said Mowbray.

'You seem to be suggesting that we have nothing to fear from Press interest in this Gulf War Syndrome thing and that we're in the clear?' said Gardiner.

'I believe that to be the case,' said Mowbray.

'I agree,' said Crowe.

'I'm not sure that congratulations are in order, Crowe: this should never have happened in the first place, but I suppose it could have turned out much worse. I take it that none of the personnel affected by the accident will suffer any long-lasting effects?'

There was a long pause before Crowe, picking his words carefully, said, 'We would sincerely hope not, Sir James. It was a very early version of what we were working on so we didn't assess it in any great detail at the time but I really think we can put this affair behind us.'

'Good. All's well that ends well eh? I take it no embarrassing questions were ever asked at Porton and you cleaned up behind you, so to speak?'

Crowe cleared his throat as if taken by surprise by the question. 'The project was abandoned and everything destroyed as you directed,' he said. 'No questions were asked.'

'What about the people on your team?' asked Gardiner.

'Dr Sebring had great difficulty in coming to terms with the accident. He felt responsible— as indeed he was.'

Gardiner diverted his eyes momentarily from Crowe to hide his distaste at Crowe once again distancing himself from blame.

'He had to seek medical help,' Crowe continued. 'He was on sick leave for some considerable time and when he eventually did return he decided that he no longer wanted to do the same kind of work and left our employ. It was probably for the best really.'

'And the others?'

'One other man left; the remaining two have been reassigned to different projects.'

'I take it they all understood the full implications of the Official Secrets Act?'

Crowe was about to offer assurances when Mowbray interrupted. 'I don't think we need have any worries on that score. Low-level surveillance has been kept on them ever since the break-up but everything seems fine. Sebring has been taken on as a lecturer at the University of Leicester. Michael D'Arcy is currently employed by a pharmaceutical company here in Kent while Lowry and Rawlings are, of course, still at Porton.'

'Working on malaria,' added Crowe.

'Good,' said Gardiner.

'Obviously, there may be financial implications for HMG if the numbers of sick veterans continues to grow,' said Rupert Everley, adopting his grave concern expression. 'That in itself might well keep this so-called Gulf War Syndrome in the public eye.'

'Cries for compensation, you mean?' said Gardiner sourly. 'Let's hope HMG takes a strong line on that. Give it to one and they'll all be after something for nothing.'

'Come, that's a bit harsh, James,' said Warner. 'After all that went on in the Gulf, some of these soldiers are genuinely ill.'

'The state already makes provision for people who are genuinely ill,' retorted

36

Gardiner. 'There's no need to recognise a whole new syndrome, especially one that doesn't actually exist. When you take the Queen's shilling, you take your chances. That's the way it's always been.'

'When the guns begin to shoot, my lad, when the guns begin to shoot,' said Warner. 'Mind you,' he added, smoothing his moustache with thumb and forefinger, 'We usually just had to fight the other side . . .'

'We've just been assured that there will be no lasting effects from this damned thing,' snapped Gardiner, bristling at the remark.

'I sincerely hope and believe that to be the case,' said Crowe, realising with some obvious concern that he was the source of assurance Gardiner was referring to. 'Of course, there's no way of being absolutely sure . . .'

CHAPTER THREE

Downing Street
London
February 1997

'It is almost six years since the Gulf War ended,' declared the Prime Minister with an obvious sense of frustration. 'And yet Gulf War Syndrome is still an issue. Why hasn't this matter been resolved long ago?'

'With respect, Prime Minister,' replied one of those present from the Department of Health, 'it's much more complicated than it seems. It has of course, been the government's position all along that no such syndrome exists—a decision only taken after extensive consultation with the medical authorities, I have to say—and yet the number of people claiming that there is and seeking recompense keeps on growing.'

'What numbers are we dealing with here?' asked the PM.

'Estimates put the figure at approximately fifteen percent of the returning allied forces having complained of health problems, which they ascribe to having taken part in the conflict,' said the DOH man.

'And in real numbers?'

'Something in the order of quarter of a million, Prime Minister.'

'I take it we are talking in terms of all the allied forces?'

'Yes sir.'

'And deaths?'

'Ten, perhaps as many as twelve thousand.'

There was a long silence before the PM said softly, 'That many?'

'With respect, Prime Minister,' said the Defence Minister, 'hysteria has played no small part in inflating these figures. Any tommy sniffing a hint of compensation has been turning up at his GP looking for a ticket to easy street.'

'And the dead? Are they malingering too?'

'As you yourself pointed out, it has been six years since the war. A lot of things can happen in six years to all of us and people do tend to die for a whole variety of reasons. It has always been quite clear that the huge range of symptoms appearing on medical reports must preclude any one single cause as being responsible for illness among veterans.'

'And yet the veterans seem more adamant than ever,' said the PM. 'I've been looking through submissions from their various associations and they have become an organised and articulate lobby.'

'The facts remain the same,' insisted the Defence Minister.

'I need hardly remind you that we are only months away from an election,' said the PM. 'Put bluntly, on top of everything else, we cannot afford to be seen fighting the sick.'

'Would the Treasury consider softening its attitude on compensation perhaps?' suggested a man from the policy unit.

The Department of Health man shook his head and said, 'Apart from the sheer numbers involved, we would need some method of appraising the condition, some guidelines as to how we decide whether or not symptoms could be ascribed to the war. You don't need to be clairvoyant to see that this would be an enormous stumbling block which would in turn lead to a sense of injustice in those denied and the consequent setting up of appeals panels and so on and so forth. It has all the makings of a bureaucratic nightmare, if I may say so.'

'Of course it has. It's an absolute non-starter,' said the Defence Minister. 'Frankly, I don't think the Press will be too hard on us over this issue simply because of the enormous range of illnesses. Even a fool can see that they can't all be right.'

'So you would suggest that we do nothing and ride out the storm, should it come to it?' asked the PM.

'I honestly don't think that it will,' said the Defence Minister. 'The public have grown bored with it.'

'One odd thing that struck me as I was reading through the submissions from the veterans,' said the PM, 'was an assertion by some that their condition was infectious. They claimed that their wives and children were being affected. It sounded quite extraordinary.'

'Ridiculous,' said the Defence Minister. 'Only goes to prove what I've been saying all along. Every time an ex-squaddie wakes up with a hangover it's down to service in the Gulf War.'

'What sort of illness were they talking about, Prime Minister?' asked the policy unit man.

'It was all a bit vague,' replied the PM.

'Chronic fatigue, increased susceptibility to colds and flu, that sort of thing.'

'God in heaven,' snorted the Defence Minister. 'That's all we need, infectious yuppie flu!'

'Does sound a bit implausible, I must say,' said the PM.

'Stuff and nonsense,' said the Defence Minister. 'There is one thing we might try however, if you think that these veterans' associations might actually succeed in making this an election issue. We could leak it to the papers that Saddam *did* actually use chemical and biological weapons in the conflict.'

'A number of them have already tried running with that story over the years,' said the PM. 'One paper in particular has taken particular delight in pointing out on several occasions just where Saddam actually got these weapons.'

'Without attracting much attention, as I recall,' said the Defence Minister.

'Thankfully no,' agreed the PM.

'Yesterday's news,' said the policy unit man. 'Today's chip wrapper.'

'Despite that,' said the Defence Minister, 'I still think it might well be the way to go simply because it's the way these associations seem to be heading. Only last week in the Lords the Countess of Mar asked if the MOD had any documentary evidence of chemical warfare in the Gulf conflict.'

'What did Howe say?'

'He simply stated that research carried out by the MOD did not indicate any confirmed use of chemical warfare agents during the conflict. It was actually that which made me think that if we were to make an official leak— if that's not an oxymoron—about Saddam having used such weapons, the nationals might run with it and conveniently divert attention from HMG at a critical time,' said the Defence Minister.

'Considering that Saddam has been building up his arsenal of such weapons ever since the end of the Gulf War, that's not at all a bad idea,' said the PM. 'The prospect of him becoming a problem again might even work in our favour come election time, considering our track record in the Falklands and the Gulf.'

'Good point, Prime Minister,' said the policy unit man. 'There's a good chance the voting public won't want a bunch of left-wing appeasers at the helm should Saddam get restless again.'

'Offering asylum and counselling to all and sundry no doubt,' snorted the Defence Minister.

'Then we are agreed,' said the PM. 'We do not alter our stance on Gulf War Syndrome and we use PR to combat any attempt to make it an election issue.'

'Perhaps we could plant a suggestion that Saddam be made to pay compensation to affected personnel because of his use of CB weapons?' suggested the policy unit man.

'Why not,' agreed the PM.

Channing House
Kent
March 1997

'We have to face it, Warner, our worst nightmare is about to come true,' said Sir James Gardiner to his host, Colonel Peter Warner. The two men had just had dinner and were taking port by the fire.

'You don't think there's any chance of a last minute swing among the electorate?' asked Warner. 'Better the devil you know?'

Gardiner shook his head with a wry smile. 'Not unless either Blair or Brown are caught with their pants down—and preferably in the company of each other—between now and next month. It's shaping up to be a bloody landslide.'

'God, it makes me so angry,' said Warner. 'To think grubby little men with their brown paper bags filled with cash and their inability to keep their trousers up in the company of tarts who can't keep their mouths shut have brought the party to this.'

'It's not just the party,' said Gardiner. 'It's the country we have to think about. Evolution is about to go into reverse. Just mark my words. Survival of the fittest is about to

43

become a thing of the past. The weak and the halt and the lame are about to inherit the earth. Everyone will be a winner because no one will be allowed to lose.'

'And what about us?' asked Warner. 'What do we do now?'

'What can we do? We bide our time, Warner. We keep our eyes and our ears open and we bide our time. Our priority at the moment is to make sure we're secure from the prying eyes of an incoming hostile administration.'

'We're always been careful about who came on board,' said Warner. 'You don't think we're vulnerable, do you?'

'There is one thing I have some concern about,' replied Gardiner. 'That business at Porton and the mistake that was made.'

'Ah, the vaccine problem?' said Warner. 'I thought Crowe sorted all that out. I thought he handled it well.'

'It's not Crowe I'm worried about; he's one of us. It's more the people who were working on the project at the time, the team. They were under the impression that their work was government-sanctioned when, strictly speaking, it wasn't. Funding of the team was a bit of a grey area because of politicians not wanting to inquire too deeply in what goes on at Porton. It was accounted for as "special projects" money.'

'Ah,' said Warner. He reached over to refill

44

Gardiner's glass from the crystal decanter that sat on the small table at the side of his chair. 'New blood at the MOD and new faces at Porton might start asking awkward questions.'

'Mowbray will keep an eye on the situation; he's kept surveillance on the team ever since that damned cock-up, nothing too obtrusive but if any of them suddenly gets the urge to write their memoirs we'd have to do something about it. There's never been any sign of anything like that but it's still a niggling little worry.'

'But they all signed the Official Secrets Act. They knew that everything they did at Porton was top secret,' said Warner.

Gardiner smiled wryly and said, 'I've noticed that in recent times the Official Secrets Act doesn't quite exert the same hold over people it once did.'

'You mean, if the money's right . . .'

'Another sign of the times, damn it. But apart from that, if these people should ever find out that what they were doing had not quite been officially sanctioned and that HMG were never actually informed about the problem with the vaccine then all bets would be off. Sebring, the chap who Crowe went to great pains to tell us actually made the mistake, is not one of us, remember. He's a worry.'

'So what do you think we should do about it?' asked Warner, looking over the top of his glass as he took a sip.

'Maybe I'll have a word with Mowbray. Tell him of our concern. Ask him to keep a special eye on Sebring, should there be any kind of a shake up at Porton or awkward questions coming out of MOD about special budgets.'

Warner nodded. 'Do you see these Gulf War Syndrome people as any kind of threat?' he asked before getting up out of his chair to put another log on the fire. 'They were on television again this morning.'

'Our eyes and ears at MOD have told me in confidence that HMG will not change its line on it and it seems solid enough to me. There's no such thing as far as they're concerned.'

'What about the incoming lot with their bleeding hearts and regiments of social workers?'

'The bleeding hearts won't make it to the cabinet room,' replied Gardiner. 'Politicians will and they're much more predictable. There won't be any sudden handouts. It's my bet they'll stick to Tory spending limits so they can blame everything on the outgoing administration for a while. As regards the Gulf War lobby, they'll point them at the BMA who've always maintained that there's no such thing as Gulf War Syndrome.'

'But still these people keep coming back, demanding investigation after investigation,' said Warner.

'Maybe, but I think we're safe enough,' said

46

Gardiner. 'We were lucky that there were just so many screw-ups in that damned war there was no real need to create red herrings; the bloody Gulf was awash with them.'

Warner put his head back on the leather cushion of his armchair and looked into the flames of the fire. 'Five bloody years in the wilderness, not a happy prospect.'

'It might well be more than five,' said Gardiner.

'D'you really think so?'

'Pity Blair wasn't a Tory. He seems to be everything that Major isn't. Major will have to go before the next election of course, but for the life of me I can't see his successor.'

'A bit like looking for a virgin in a whorehouse,' agreed Warner.

'So what do we do in the meantime?' asked Warner as the clock on the mantelpiece struck eleven.

'We bide our time. We dig the dirt on the incomers, and throw it when we can. There will be plenty. Rest assured. They're politicians.'

The Cenotaph
London
November 1997

Ex-RAMC sergeant Angus Maclean rested his hands lightly on the top bar of the steel crowd barrier and watched impassively as the Guards slow-marched up Whitehall to the haunting strains of Albinoni. The colour of the soldiers' greatcoats matched the sky. In fact, everything seemed grey except for the blood red of the poppies. The colours of sadness, thought Maclean as he surveyed the scene through dark, haunted eyes.

The great and the good were about to remember the fallen on behalf of the nation. They would don their chosen uniforms of the day and salute solemnly while lesser ranks stared unseeingly, at attention, into the middle distance. They would lay their wreaths and bow their heads.

Maclean prepared himself mentally for what he felt he had to do. He was glad it was raining because raincoats bestowed a convenient and welcome anonymity on their wearers. The loose fitting nature of waterproof gear also made it easier to conceal things. In Maclean's case this was a 500ml glass bottle full of anti-coagulated blood and a large, folded banner with the words, 'Bloody Hypocrites! Justice for Gulf War Victims,' written on it. He had already spent three hours standing at his chosen spot, adjacent to a convenient join in the barriers, for he didn't want to have to manoeuvre his way through crowds of people when the moment came. He needn't have worried; the crowd wasn't as dense as in past years thanks to the inclement weather and a growing sense of cynicism among the young.

When the new Prime Minister, Tony Blair, stepped forward to lay his wreath, he would pull the barrier back a little and slip out through the gap to run across to the Cenotaph itself. He would launch the bottle so that it smashed on the granite, splashing blood all over it while he unfurled his banner out along the base for the benefit of the cameras. It would be risky. There was a chance he might get shot, probably not by the soldiers but more likely by one of the plain-suited men guarding the House of Windsor and its new government. But he was counting on there still being a few moments of indecision, just enough time to complete his mission. After all, there wasn't a gun culture in the UK and armed police still thought twice before pulling triggers. And if he should get shot? Well, it didn't matter. Nothing mattered much any more except that these bastards be made aware of his anger and that of others like him.

The bagpipes of the massed pipes and drums made their traditional hesitant start and the strains of *Over the Sea to Skye* filled the damp air with yet more melancholy while drizzly rain settled on the Guards' bearskins.

Maclean took his right hand off the barrier and slipped it inside his plastic raincoat to grip the neck of the bottle, which he'd hung on a string loop from his belt. The poster was folded across the front of his chest inside his jacket and then tucked into his belt. His fingers, wet and cold from gripping the steel barrier for so long, fumbled to release the bottle from the string and he suddenly became aware that he was attracting suspicious glances from the couple standing next to him, especially the woman, a short, dumpy figure with badly dyed blonde hair and a sullen expression, who was clearly wondering what he was doing with his hands inside his raincoat.

Perhaps it was agitation inspired by the woman's disapproving glances or the slight numbness in his fingers from having stood in the cold for so long but just as he succeeded in releasing the bottle from the loop, it slipped from his grasp and fell to the ground to smash on the pavement, creating a large, growing red puddle round his feet.

'Oh my God, it's blood!' screamed the woman, clutching at the arm of her companion and pointing downwards. The immediate crowd shrank back to leave a space around Maclean just as several more women started to scream and cries went up for the police to come. A man with a cockney accent exclaimed loudly, 'What the fuck?'

Gus stared down at the puddle, mesmerised for a moment, his plans in ruins and his mind in turmoil. When he looked up again there were hostile faces all around him. He had lost the visual impact that his prop would undoubtedly have had but he hoped it might still be possible to display his banner. It wouldn't be nearly so dramatic as splashing blood on the Cenotaph but maybe the cameras of some of the press would at least catch the message. He tugged desperately at the barrier to widen the gap but it proved more difficult to budge than he'd anticipated. He gave up and tried to squeeze through the small gap he had managed to open but got stuck half way. He was struggling to free himself when two burly policemen arrived, intent on smothering the incident as quickly as possible.

The crowd melted back to allow the policemen to manhandle Maclean out through their numbers rather than parade him along the front of the barriers where he might detract from the ceremony and possibly be photographed. Maclean was forcibly bent over as his arms were twisted painfully up his back. He couldn't see the crowd—only their feet—but he could hear them.

'Fuckin' loony.'

'Christ! They're everywhere these days.'

'He was gonna kill the Queen, the bastard.'

Maclean felt someone take a kick at his leg and cried out in pain.

'He had a fuckin' gun,' exclaimed someone else.

'You don't understand,' gasped Maclean. 'I'm one of you . . . I went to war . . . I served my country . . . Don't let them fool you . . . These bastards over there don't give a shit . . . They don't give a shit about any of us . . . All that praying and saluting . . . It's just a fancy-dress party for them . . . They're pretending, the lot of them. They don't care: they just don't bloody care.'

This only made the policemen twist his arms further up his back, making him cry out again before being thrown bodily into the back of a police van and driven off.

Maclean found it a relief when the cell door was closed behind him and he was blissfully alone again. It was infinitely preferable to being pushed and pulled around by police who had treated him as an object from the outset and steadfastly refused to acknowledge anything he'd said or asked. He'd felt like the invisible man, only with the proviso that no one could hear him either.

Maclean lay down on the bare bunk and stared up at the ceiling. He had failed in his mission to make his point at the Cenotaph and he felt dreadful. It was such a pity because he felt sure that the blood would have made such a strong impact, but, looking on the bright side, he might still get his chance to get his message across in court. He started planning what he would say to the magistrates and hopefully, to the Press in the gallery. He got no inspiration at all from the graffiti of despair on the walls.

An hour later, after having been examined by a police doctor and declared sane and lucid, Maclean was formally questioned.

52

'Tell us about the blood,' was the opening gambit from the interviewing officer.

'It was horse blood,' said Maclean.

'Horse blood,' repeated the policeman mechanically, as if humouring the village idiot.

'We use it in the lab to make blood agar plates,' said Maclean matter of factly. 'To grow bacteria on,' he added by way of explanation and in response to the look on the officer's face.

'Silly me,' said the officer. 'Maybe we can just go back a few steps here. Who exactly are you and what's this all about?'

'Gus Maclean, I'm a technician in the bacteriology department at Princess Louise Hospital in Glasgow.'

'Now we're getting somewhere. What exactly did you intend doing with the bottle of blood?'

'Ideally I would have liked to have rammed it up Fatty Soames's arse but I was going to make do with smashing it on the Cenotaph to draw attention to the victims of Gulf War Syndrome.'

'Fatty Soames?' asked the policeman.

'Ex Defence Minister,' said a colleague.

'So your beef is with the MOD?'

'Among others.'

'What did they ever do to you?'

'Not just me,' replied Maclean. 'Thousands of us came back from the Gulf War sick and these bastards have been pretending that

53

there's fuck-all wrong with us.'

'You fought in the Gulf War?'

'Sergeant, 1st Field Laboratory Unit,' replied Maclean. 'The secret team,' he added, as if he thought it a bad joke.

The policeman raised his eyes. 'Secret team? What's that all about?'

'We weren't supposed to exist,' said Maclean. 'We're on nobody's list. Forty of us in eight five-man teams. We operated out of Porton Down.'

'The defence establishment?'

'Yeah, right,' said Maclean sarcastically. 'We were deployed in the Gulf to detect the presence of chemical and biological weapons and then to identify them.'

'If this is true, should you be telling us this?' said the policeman. 'Official Secrets Act, I mean.'

'Fuck the Official Secrets Act,' said Maclean.

The policeman thought for a moment before saying to the uniformed constable standing by the door, 'Take him back to his cell.'

Maclean was brought back to the interview room two hours later. The police deferred to two men in plain clothes and left him alone with them. One asked Maclean, 'Do you know who we are?'

'Spooks,' replied Maclean. 'I've been expecting you.'

'You do realise that you contravened the Official Secrets Act in this police station two hours ago?'

'Yup,' replied Maclean. 'So charge me.'

'So you can put on your one-man show in court? I don't think so.'

'So I'll go on contravening the Official Secrets Act,' said Maclean.

'It's one thing saying something, Maclean, quite another getting anyone to listen to you. Look at you, for God's sake. London's full of unemployed Jocks with stories to tell. No one gives a shit.'

'I'm not unemployed,' said Maclean, stung by the comment. 'I'm off sick.'

'In the head.'

Maclean looked down at the floor. 'There's nothing wrong with my head,' he said through gritted teeth.

'Your kid died of leukaemia three years ago. Last year you lost your wife to a brain tumour and . . .'

'I killed them,' said Maclean.

'What are you talking about?'

'I killed them. The thing I brought back from the Gulf, the thing that's making me ill, that's what killed them.'

'That's just plain daft,' said the Special Branch man, although his tone softened somewhat and his voice took on an edge of pity. 'They died of very different things. It was just bad luck, man. You weren't to blame.'

Maclean looked at him, his eyes now burning. 'Like I say, it was that that killed them and some of these bastards at Porton know all about it. I won't rest until they come clean.'

The officer could see that he was getting nowhere with advice. 'Go back to Scotland, Gus,' he said, 'rebuild your life. Stop tilting at windmills. You can't win. Believe me; the odds are stacked against you.'

'You're not going to charge me?'

'You're free to go.'

CHAPTER FOUR

St James's Park
London
April 2002

'You know, Warner, all my life I've looked forward to the springtime but not this year,' said Sir James Gardiner as he and Peter Warner sauntered slowly through the park in the pale yellow sunshine of a spring afternoon. 'It should have been obvious to me that I was getting old but for some reason it's come as a bit of a shock.'

'We all have days like that, Jimmy,' said Warner.

'No, I'm serious,' said Gardiner. 'I've had to

face up to my own mortality and come to terms with the fact that it's just not going to happen.'

'What's not going to happen?'

'Our dream, man. Our dream of making England a place fit to live in again, an England where brains and initiative are rewarded, competition is encouraged and courtesy and manners are the norm. It's just not going to happen. The party's still a mess; they've had five bloody years to get their act together and they've still blown it with their continual squabbling and manoeuvring. They've ended up with all the credibility of a used-car salesman. It's quite clear Blair's going to get in for another five years.'

Warner offered no argument.

'Well, that's going to be an end to it as far as I'm concerned. By the time the next parliament's over, or maybe the one beyond that if I'm still around to see it, our future will be entirely in the hands of a whole generation of foul-mouthed, nose-picking louts with degrees in media studies and social work from toytown universities that couldn't even teach the buggers to read and write. They'll sit on their arses and expect to be pampered as their right because they always have been. When they find out that isn't going to happen, there's going to be anarchy but by that time there'll be nothing worth saving anyway. New Labour, the patron saint of mediocrity, the guardian of all that is worthless, shallow and banal will have pissed away our entire heritage against the wall.'

'It's not like you to be so negative, Jimmy,' said Warner. 'I've never heard you speak like this before.'

'I'm not used to losing,' said Gardiner. 'It's a bitter pill to swallow but our England has gone, Warner, it's just a memory. I want you to call a meeting of the others. I'm going to disband the group and the organisation.'

They walked another ten paces in silence before Warner said, 'I won't insult you by asking if you've really thought this through because you obviously have but I really must ask you to reconsider, James. Surely at a time like this our country needs people like us more than ever?'

'As a soldier, Warner, you know better than most that you don't get into a fight you can't win and we cannot win this one. We need the party to be in power for us to make a difference. We need a sympathetic infrastructure and that isn't going to happen. The Tories are spiralling down the toilet in a vortex of their own making. You'd almost think they had a death wish. What ever possessed them to make that idiot schoolboy leader?'

'He'll go after the election, Jimmy and then we'll get a more credible hand at the tiller. Word is it's going to be Ken Clark. He'll give

Blair a run for his money at the despatch box.'

'He'll split the party right down the middle over Europe,' said Gardiner. 'Then we'll be back to square one.'

'I still think you should reconsider.'

'No, my mind's made up. I want you to call a meeting as soon as possible. We'll clear up any loose ends and that'll be that.'

'What will you do?'

'Alice and I have a place in the Highlands of Scotland where, thank God, it's still possible to lead a civilised life without demands for wheelchair access and signs in Urdu.'

'And only the Gordons are gay,' added Warner with a smile.

'Being called a nation of shopkeepers was bad enough,' said Gardiner. 'But God help us, we've become a nation of bent hairdressers. Just set up that meeting, will you?'

'If your mind's made up I'll try for next Friday.'

Princess Louise Hospital
Glasgow
April 2002

George Drummond, the lab manager, looked up from his desk and smiled as he saw Gus Maclean come in through the door of the bacteriology department. Maclean was wearing the same navy duffel coat that he seemed to have been wearing for decades. He watched him hang it on his peg by the door and then asked, 'How did you get on at the weekend?'

'Quite well,' replied Maclean, donning his lab coat. 'The MOD has agreed to look at the position again and come back to us with a new report before the end of the year.'

'Well done. I'll say this for you guys, you certainly don't give up easily,' said Drummond.

'Damn right we don't,' said Maclean with a conviction that even Drummond, who had known Maclean for over twenty years, found chilling. He saw in his friend and colleague the same obsession he'd seen in certain relatives of those who had died in the Lockerbie air disaster. It was as if their lives had been frozen at a moment in time.

'We even managed to get a commitment from them to make enquiries as to what was going on at Porton just before the war started,' said Maclean.

'Good,' said Drummond, not at all sure that he meant it. He would much rather his friend had gotten over the tragedy that had struck at his life with the death of his wife and daughter and returned to being something more like the man he had known when they were younger, the man he had gone climbing with every weekend in the Highlands, the bloke who had played the dame with side-splitting success in the hospital pantomime, the bloke he had got drunk with on his stag night and ended up explaining to the police why he happened to be tied to a lamppost wearing a nurse's uniform at four in the morning. But that Gus had gone. They were still friends but there was no place in Gus's life for fun any more. The Gulf War had put an end to that. The veterans' association that Gus led was now his sole reason for being.

'It looks as if George W is determined to have another go at Saddam,' said Drummond.

'So I see,' said Maclean, without giving anything away.

'And taking us in with him if the papers are to be believed.'

'Where the master goes the poodle must follow,' said Maclean.

'That's pretty much what the papers are saying too,' agreed Drummond.

'They've probably got teams of writers working on condolence letters as we speak,' said Maclean bitterly. 'Rest assured your boy did not die in vain, Mr and Mrs Smith. He died fighting for democracy, freedom, human rights and any other high-sounding crap they can come up with. Bastards. These buggers have no idea what war is really like. They pretend they do but they haven't. And what's more, they haven't even begun to deal with the thousands of guys they maimed in their last little expedition to the desert sands.'

Drummond nodded. 'Well, let's hope it

doesn't come to that,' he said, anxious to steer the conversation away from Maclean's favourite hobby-horse. 'There seems to be quite a strong body of opinion that says nothing should be done without the agreement of the United Nations.'

'Aye, right,' said Maclean, making clear his lack of any high regard for the UN organisation.

'Mary has called in sick,' said Drummond. 'Maybe you could cover for her in serology this morning? Make sure her juniors know what they're doing.'

'Will do,' said Maclean.

'Oh, and Ward Seven phoned earlier. They'd like confirmation of the menigococcus that you reported finding in patient, Robin Chester's CSF last night as soon as possible. I take it you were called out?'

'At three this morning,' said Maclean. 'Just when I was getting into a deep sleep.'

'Always the way,' said Drummond.

Channing House
Kent
26th April 2002

There was silence round the table as Sir James Gardiner sat down after telling of his intention to disband the group.

Peter Warner said, 'I can see everyone here is as stunned as I was when Sir James told me last week. Believe me, I've tried persuading him to change his mind, but without success.'

'We simply must be pragmatic, gentlemen,' said Gardiner. 'We are sitting here on the eve of an election that's going to see Labour in power for another five years. With our own party still in disarray and unlikely to be even able to mount a credible opposition, we have become an irrelevance. We cannot hope to change things under these conditions.'

'Sir James,' began Donald Crowe; he sounded polite but looked angry. 'I know that you have always regarded the scientific input to this group with a scepticism bordering on contempt and, it might be argued that you had some reason to after what happened at Porton, but if you will hear me out. We have spent over ten years building up our organisation. We have people, like-minded people, in just about every sphere of modern life. This is not the time to throw this all away. It is tantamount to a betrayal of them and what we believe in. If we can't change things using the ballot box, we should at least start considering other means.'

'I think I agree,' said Mowbray.

'I think I do too,' said Rupert Everley, clearing his throat in deference to the fact that he was daring to disagree with Gardiner, a man so clearly his intellectual superior. 'Our country needs us more than ever if we're to stop the rot.'

Gardiner had a face like thunder. 'What

other means did you have in mind?' he growled.

'Nothing specific,' said Crowe. 'I just think we should take time to consider our position and perhaps apply a little more lateral thought to our situation.'

'It wouldn't do any harm to delay a little, James,' said Warner.

'We really should explore every avenue,' said Mowbray.

In the face of general agreement from the others, Gardiner looked down at the table in front of him. 'Very well,' he said. 'I'll delay informing our people of the disbandment for six months but when we meet again I expect to hear concrete proposals for action—within the law.'

When Donald Crowe left the house he found Cecil Mowbray standing beside his car. 'We need to talk.'

He and Mowbray started to walk slowly along the path leading to the rose garden. 'Never been that fond of roses myself,' said Mowbray. 'Fine when they're in bloom but a mess at any other time. God, that was a close call in there.'

'You can say that again,' said Crowe. 'Disbanding now would scupper everything. We need another few months. The agent's ready but we're going to need the help of one or two people in setting up the trial.'

'Is a trial absolutely necessary?' asked

Mowbray.

'There's no deal without it,' said Crowe. 'They demand a successful demonstration before they'll pay.'

'Have they stipulated any conditions?' asked Mowbray.

'They have,' said Crowe.

Mowbray noted a reluctance to answer in Crowe's voice. 'And?' he asked.

Crowe told him.

'You can't be serious?' exclaimed Mowbray.

'We either do that or we wave goodbye to twelve years work and twenty million dollars.'

'It sounds as if you haven't dismissed the idea out of hand,' said Mowbray as they continued walking.

'It can be done,' said Crowe. 'I've had a think about it and it can be done but we need money and reliable key people. Money means Everley. How do you feel about taking him on board?'

'The man's an idiot,' replied Mowbray. 'But a vain and predictable one. If we can convince him that joining us is the way to his dream of a seat in parliament I'm sure he'll cough up without too much trouble. Leave that to me. What do you need in the way of people?'

'We don't need many but we do need specialists. I'm relying on you for the derring-do input and I'll have a look at the group's database for the others. I've already come up with a couple of key people but we have to get

65

them on board before Gardiner pulls the plug. Time is not on our side.'

'There's something else we have to worry about,' said Mowbray. 'Intelligence says that Bush has set his heart on another Gulf War within a year. He'll go through the motions with weapons inspectors and the like and try for UN support for military action but the smart money is saying he's going to go it alone if that doesn't happen.'

'So?' said Crowe.

'Blair will back him and take us in with him.'

'Where is this leading?' asked Crowe.

'Plans are already in place to have the troops vaccinated against biological attack.'

Crowe felt an icicle move up his spine as he thought he saw where Mowbray was going. 'My God, you're going to tell me that they're going to use the same vaccine as last time?'

'They've enough left over for five thousand men. They plan to use that up first. Financial prudence, I think they call it.'

'Hell and damnation,' said Crowe.

'I didn't say anything inside because I felt sure James would have insisted that we immediately come clean about it and confess all,' said Mowbray.

They had come to the lily pond at the end of the rose garden where they turned round to look back at the lights of Channing House behind their reflection in the stagnant water.

'Can't you find some way of destroying the

old stocks?' asked Crowe.

'Destroying stores of vaccine would require some explanation, I fear,' said Mowbray.

'But some of your people are sympathetic, aren't they? That's the sort of thing they do, isn't it. James Bond stuff and all that?'

'None of them know about the accident twelve years ago. They didn't need to, so I never told them.'

'I see,' said Crowe.

Mowbray continued hesitantly. 'If it should prove necessary to call on them for some other reason in the near future I'd rather not involve them in anything else beforehand.'

'I understand,' said Crowe. 'But we have to do something to stop them using that damned stuff.'

'I've been thinking,' said Mowbray. 'Many of the '91 Gulf War veterans maintain that the vaccine they were given was to blame for their symptoms. If we were to let it be known openly that HMG were planning to use up old vaccine stocks on today's troops there will almost certainly be an outcry. With a bit of luck HMG will be forced to back down over the issue and destroy the old stuff.'

Crowe shivered against a chill that had crept into the night air. 'And no need for us to be involved,' he said, starting to walk again. 'That sounds attractive.'

'I think it will work,' said Mowbray. 'We know all the leaders of the Gulf War veterans' associations so we can quickly make them aware of what's going on and make sure the papers get on to it too. But there is still one fly in the ointment.'

Crowe gave him a look that suggested that there always was.

'When the story gets into the papers, the original Beta team at Porton are going to start wondering just why HMG was going to use a vaccine they knew to be faulty. And if any of them should work out . . .'

'That HMG didn't actually know that to be the case,' completed Crowe.

'Exactly,' said Mowbray.

'The last thing we need right now is for a scandal to break out over a twelve-year-old accident. Do you think you can deal with any problems that might arise?'

'I think so,' said Mowbray.

Crowe gave a cursory nod and said, 'Good.' He rubbed his arms. 'God, it's getting cold.'

As he opened the door of his car, Mowbray turned to Crowe and said, 'We'll talk again soon.'

CHAPTER FIVE

Glasgow Airport
Scotland
June 3rd 2002

Dr Steven Dunbar, senior medical investigator
with the Sci-Med Inspectorate, settled back
into his seat on the British Airways shuttle
flight and noted as he fastened his seat belt
that the flight was almost full. He recognised a
couple of faces passing by as belonging to
those of Westminster politicians, one of whom
he'd seen on television the night before being
interviewed about the potential costs of
another Gulf War. As with most conversations
involving politicians, no straight answer had
been forthcoming.

Steven had been called back from Scotland
where he had been spending—or had hoped to
spend—a long weekend with his young
daughter, Jenny, who lived there with his
sister-in-law and her husband and their own
two children. Jenny had lived with them since
Steven's wife Lisa had died some four years
before.

The summons had come in the form of a
text to his mobile phone from the duty officer
at Sci-Med; it said simply that John
Macmillan—the head of Sci-Med—required

him back in London at his earliest convenience. Steven had managed to get himself on board the first plane to London from Glasgow Airport on Monday morning after having driven the sixty miles or so from the village of Glenvane in Dumfriesshire where Jenny lived.

'Good weekend?' enquired the passenger, smelling strongly of aftershave, who eased into the seat beside him. He was a fat, loose-jowled man with a ruddy complexion. He wore a striped business suit that was too small for him, as was the collar of the Bengal striped shirt that trapped his fleshy neck, causing it to bulge over. A heart attack waiting to happen, thought Steven.

'Fine thanks,' he replied, a bit surprised at the question coming from a complete stranger but assuming that this might well be normal for the Monday morning shuttle with many Scots who worked in London returning after spending the weekend at home. 'You?'

'Daughter got married,' said the man. 'Cost me a bloody fortune. Don't like the bugger much but there's not a lot you can do these days, is there? Kids are a law unto themselves. Do as they damn well please, whatever you say.'

'Times change,' said Steven.

'Damn right they do. If I'd spoken to my father the way she speaks to me . . .'

It was a familiar theme that Steven had no

wish to hear enlarged upon. He gave a sympathetic nod and pointedly turned to reading his newspaper. He was allowed to read in peace until a communal groan broke out an hour later when the captain announced that they were now in a circular holding pattern while waiting for permission to land at Heathrow.

'The all-elusive "slot",' sighed the man in the seat beside him. 'Heathrow's version of the holy grail. If I had a fiver for every time I've circled Watford or West Drayton I'd be a bloody millionaire by now.'

They landed only ten minutes behind schedule and Steven took the Heathrow Express into Paddington and then a taxi to his flat where he stopped off to shower and change. He had gone to Scotland wearing casual gear—leather blouson and chinos—so he thought he would get into 'uniform' before seeing Macmillan. John Macmillan didn't make a big issue of such things but he had let it be known that he subscribed to the sloppy dress = sloppy mind school of thought.

Now wearing a dark blue suit and Parachute Regiment tie, Steven glanced out of the window to check on the weather while lightly brushing the shoulders of his jacket. His flat on the third floor of an apartment block wasn't quite on the waterside—he couldn't afford that—but he could see the passing traffic on the Thames through a gap in the buildings opposite. Checking his watch, he went downstairs and walked the couple of blocks necessary to reach a main thoroughfare before hailing a taxi and asking to be taken to the Home Office.

Steven exchanged a few words with Rose Roberts, John Macmillan's secretary, while he waited in the outer office for Macmillan to see him. As usual their conversation took the form of Rose asking after his daughter and he inquiring about her singing—Rose was a member of the South London Bach Choir. When the pleasantries finally petered out, Rose got on with her work and Steven took to idly looking out of the window at the world. It was something he'd done many times in the past while waiting to be briefed on a new assignment and he was aware that the feeling in his stomach was still the same—a mixture of anxiety and excitement. It wasn't an altogether unpleasant sensation. In fact, it was a feeling he had courted for most of his life if truth be told.

He had first experienced it in his youth when climbing in the mountains of the Lake District—he had been brought up in the small village of Glenridding on Ullswater. Youthful exuberance and a lack of forethought had on occasion taken him into situations it might have been wiser to avoid but he and his friends had learned much about themselves and each other on these occasions and Steven had been smitten with the buzz that danger brought with it. He had re-acquainted himself with it on many occasions when serving with the military and had noticed that it could become as addictive as a drug—something to which many fighter pilots and racing drivers would testify. There was something about being on the edge of disaster that heightened human senses to otherwise unattainable levels. As one fellow soldier had once put it, you don't know what being alive is until you're very nearly not.

But there were downsides to chasing the buzz. Not only was there the prospect of an early death but even if that was avoided, it could lead to an inability to ever fit in again to the nine-till-five existence of 'normal' life. This, in turn, could lead to marriage difficulties and even conflict with the law as Steven had seen happen to a number of ex-SAS colleagues.

Steven had qualified as a doctor but had never practised medicine, deciding that he had no real vocation for it and not wishing to become a second rate practitioner if his heart wasn't in it. Like many children of middle class parents, he'd done medicine at university in order to please them and perhaps ambitious schoolteachers as well—former pupil medical graduates always looked good on the school record. Unlike many before him, however, he had faced up to the problem before drifting too far into a career he wasn't suited to. He completed medical school and served out his obligatory registration year as a hospital houseman before joining the army where, after basic training, he had served with the Parachute Regiment before being seconded to Special Forces.

As a tall, strong, naturally athletic man, military life had suited him down to the ground and he had enjoyed the challenge and camaraderie of it all. His service had taken him all over the globe and placed him in situations where his every faculty had been tested to the limit, something that most men would never experience throughout their entire lives. Although they might not realise it, these men would live and die without ever really knowing themselves. They might imagine that they were heroes; they might even end up singing 'My Way' down the pub and believing it, but, without ever having been tested, it simply wouldn't be true.

Steven knew that the most unlikely people could turn out to be heroes under pressure and, conversely, those who'd been champions on the sports field could equally well prove to be craven cowards when life's contests were played out for real and the stakes were infinitely higher.

Steven had been sad when it came time for him to leave the army—the operational life of an SAS soldier not being much longer than that of a professional footballer. During his service he had become an expert in field medicine and had acquired many military skills but little to commend him or equip him for a life as a civilian other than his original medical degree. The prospect of life as an in-house physician with some large corporation had been looming when he had been rescued from what almost certainly would have been a life of structured boredom by John Macmillan, who had offered him the job of medical investigator with the Sci-Med Inspectorate.

Sci-Med was Macmillan's brainchild: it operated as a small independent unit within the Home Office, its remit being to investigate potential problems and possible wrong-doing in the hi-tech worlds of science and medicine, areas where the police had little or no expertise. This was no reflection on them. These areas of modern life had just grown to be too complicated for the scrutiny of outside observers. Accordingly, the small team of investigators recruited to Sci-Med were graduates in either science or medicine and with a range of experience acquired in pursuing other careers before coming to Sci-Med—post-graduate degrees from the university of life, as Macmillan termed it.

From the outset, Steven had fitted in perfectly to Sci-Med. He found the job challenging, exciting—even if, on occasion, downright dangerous—but his background of having had to use his initiative while under great stress in the deserts of Iraq or the jungles of South America had served him well and he had proved himself over the intervening years to be the investigator that Macmillan would place most trust in.

For his part, Steven had the greatest respect for John Macmillan, who, on many occasions in the past, had needed to fight his corner against heavy odds in order to maintain the independence of the Inspectorate. It was inevitable from time to time that Sci-Med would come across something that perhaps another arm of government—often a far more powerful one—would rather be kept under wraps but Macmillan would not be swayed. In his book, truth was not to be compromised on any political altar. He was also unfailingly loyal to his people on the ground, something that Steven had had cause to be grateful for on more than one occasion when he had trodden on the toes of the powerful.

Although John Macmillan did not behave like a Whitehall mandarin—in that he did not display any of the signs of Machiavellian philosophy that a life close to politics almost inevitably breeds—he did look like one. He was tall, erect, with swept-back silver hair and a smooth, unlined complexion that belied his years.

'Sorry to keep you waiting,' he said, replacing the telephone as Steven entered. 'Your colleague, Scott Jamieson's, exposure of an incompetent surgical regime at that hospital down in Kent hasn't exactly gone down well with the Department of Health.'

'I didn't suppose it would,' said Steven.

'Good God, the figures spoke for themselves,' said Macmillan. 'A blind butcher with a penknife could have achieved a higher success rate. If the management had faced up to this a couple of years ago the hospital wouldn't have the press camped at their gate right now and there would be a lot more space left in the local cemetery. Why on earth didn't his colleagues say something?'

'Maybe they just didn't want to see what was there in front of them,' said Steven. 'It's a common enough phenomenon. Apart from that, whistle-blowing isn't exactly encouraged in the medical profession. You can end up practising in New Zealand.'

'Well, I can't see any such conflict arising in this instance,' said Macmillan, pushing a photograph across his desk towards Steven.

Steven picked up the A4 size print and grimaced at the sight of a man, lying spread-eagled, face-down beside a stretch of still water. Chequered tape at the scene suggested that a police photographer had taken the picture.

'Dr George Sebring,' said Macmillan. 'Thirty-eight years old, a lecturer in molecular biology at Leicester University. The police pulled his body from a canal three days ago

77

after a man walking his dog found him lying in a reed bed. You know, I sometimes think that if people stopped walking their dogs the police might be out of a job. Dog-walkers seem to turn up more dead bodies than anyone else on the planet.'

'Good point,' said Steven. 'What's our interest?'

'Sebring joined the university ten years ago. Before that he worked at Porton Down.'

'Our microbiological defence establishment,' said Steven.

'He was quite a high-flier but he suffered some sort of nervous breakdown in the early nineties and had to give up his job.'

'Defending get too much for him?' said Steven, tongue in cheek.

Macmillan, unsmiling, looked over his glasses at him and said, 'There's a school of thought that says if you go up against Goliath with a slingshot in the real world, you'll end up with it inserted in your nether regions— sideways.'

'Point taken,' said Steven. 'We have to be as bad as each other. Only the philosophy behind it varies.'

Once again Macmillan fixed Steven with a stony stare. 'Sometimes I admire your idealism, Steven,' he said. 'At others . . .' He let Steven fill in the blank and he responded with, 'Sorry.'

'At first the Leicester police didn't see

78

anything suspicious in Sebring's death. They were inclined to treat it as suicide rather than an accident because of his medical history but his wife insisted that her husband had not been suicidal, although she did admit that he had appeared to be very troubled of late. She believed it had been an accident.'

'So who was right?'

'Neither,' said Macmillan. 'The police pathologist rained on everyone's parade. Apparently he's a young chap and new to the job, bright-eyed and bushy-tailed, you might say.'

Steven had difficulty in ascribing this description to any pathologist he personally had ever come across. Morose, cynical, alcoholic or even downright weird, yes, but bright-eyed and bushy-tailed?

'He established that Sebring did die of drowning,' continued Macmillan, 'but he then showed that the water in Sebring's lungs was not canal water but Leicester tap water.'

'So he was murdered?'

Macmillan nodded. 'Drowned, probably in a domestic bathtub, and then dumped in the canal to make it look like an accident or suicide.'

'Motive?' asked Steven.

'The police have drawn a blank. He seems to have been a popular lecturer with the students and a respected colleague among his peers. Everyone liked him.'

'Except the man who held his head under the bath water until he drowned,' said Steven.

'Quite so,' said Macmillan, managing to convey that he wouldn't have put it so bluntly himself.

'Did his wife say what had been troubling him?' asked Steven.

'Good question,' said Macmillan. 'She said a man came to see him a few weeks ago, an ex-soldier who'd served in the Gulf War. She thinks his name was Maclean, although she couldn't swear to it, but she is pretty certain he was Scots because of his accent. Apparently he knew Sebring when he worked at Porton Down.'

'What was a soldier doing at Porton Down?' asked Steven.

'Something for you to find out,' said Macmillan. 'She said that Maclean seemed angry about what he called Gulf War sickness and seemed to be under the impression that her husband knew some secret—something that could help him in his campaign. Sebring wouldn't tell her anything when he'd gone. She didn't press him because she knew that his work at Porton was classified but she's sure his change in behaviour stemmed from that day.'

'So we have a dead scientist, an ex-soldier and maybe something that happened at the time of the Gulf War,' said Steven. 'That was quite a while ago.'

'It's beginning to look as though we might

80

be about to fight it all over again,' said Macmillan.

'Pity they didn't finish the job last time,' said Steven.

'As I remember, people were throwing up their hands in horror at the very idea of marching into Baghdad,' said Macmillan. 'Television pundits delighted in pointing out at every opportunity that the allied mandate was to free Kuwait, nothing more.'

'I remember well enough,' agreed Steven. 'So what would you like me to do about Sebring?'

'Have a root around, will you? The police have more or less admitted that they have nothing to go on although they are trying to find the mysterious Scotsman, Maclean. If Sebring's death really had anything to do with his time at Porton and what he was working on there, the police are going to hit the wall. We might be able to help out and take it a stage further. See what you can come up with. Miss Roberts will give you what little information we have on Sebring.'

Rose Roberts looked up when Steven emerged from Macmillan's office and held out a thin brown foolscap envelope. 'Not much, I'm afraid,' she said. 'Dr Sebring's work at Porton was secret so we have to go through the usual channels to get information and that, as you know, might take time. If you think you really need to know what he was working on

81

let me know and I'll see what I can do to speed things along.'

Steven accepted the envelope and said, 'Thanks Rose; I think maybe we should start pushing about Sebring's time at Porton right away. I've a feeling it might well be relevant.'

'I'll get the application in to the MOD this afternoon and mark it top priority,' said Rose Roberts. 'I'll let you know when we get something back but don't hold your breath. They do like holding on to their secrets.'

Steven decided to spend what was left of the afternoon in the library. He needed to do some background reading on the Gulf War so that he had more of a feel for it. His knowledge at the moment was painfully thin. First though, he read through the file that Rose Roberts had put together on the dead man.

Sebring, the son of a Church of England vicar, had studied medical sciences at Edinburgh University, graduating with a first class degree in the summer of 1985 before moving to the University of Oxford where he had spent the next three years working for a D.Phil. on the cloning of viral pathogenesis genes. He started work as a post-doctoral research associate in the labs at Porton Down in January 1989 but left in June 1991 after suffering a nervous breakdown. He made a tentative return to work but decided to resign. He went on to make a complete recovery however, and was appointed to the teaching staff of Leicester University in October 1991 as a lecturer in molecular biology; had been there ever since. He was married to Jane Manson, a teacher, whom he met in 1993 and married in May 1994. They had no children although they had recently applied to be considered as adoptive parents. Steven copied both home and school addresses into his notebook.

He put away the file and started to work his way through a succession of articles on the Gulf War and issues arising from it. It wasn't something that he had thought about in a long time, although he had been aware of an ongoing battle between government and war veterans over the existence or non-existence of Gulf War Syndrome. After a couple of hours he had to admit to having some sympathy with the establishment view that there could be no such thing. No one single condition could possibly have so many differing symptoms. On the other hand, he was taken aback at the sheer number of soldiers who had come down with illness after service in the Gulf—and the number of deaths among them was nothing short of alarming. He felt sure that there had to be some middle ground.

It seemed to him that the troops had been subjected to a number of different but nonetheless harmful factors, all of which had caused illness and which had combined in the minds of sufferers to give the impression of a syndrome linked to war service in the Gulf.

If nothing else, Steven felt that his appetite for knowledge had been whetted by his afternoon in the library. He resolved to continue his search for information at home on the internet. By nine in the evening he had amassed a pile of print-outs that would keep him going for the rest of the evening and probably through all of the following day.

Steven had downloaded documents from a wide variety of sources including official Ministry of Defence sites as well as those run by Gulf War veterans' associations and from individuals who felt they had something to say on the subject, usually posting some personal experience of their time in the Gulf on the web. He noted that many of these personal depositions related to bad treatment or even a complete lack of treatment since returning home and falling ill.

Steven made notes as he went along, hoping that when he'd finished he would be able to put them together and gain a better understanding of claims and counter-claims and what lay behind them. It had gone four on the following afternoon before he felt ready to draw conclusions:-

Saddam *had* used both chemical and biological weapons against allied forces in the Gulf.

These weapons *had* been supplied to Iraq

by the United States—probably the reason for the continued denial of the above by official sources as several web-sites had pointed out.

Many of the troops had reported adverse reaction to the vaccines they had been given. The Ministry of Defence had been less than candid about what the vaccines had contained, having declared some components to be 'classified' although there seemed to be disagreement about just how many 'classified' components there had been. The Surgeon General, Admiral Revel's account to the Parliament's Defence Committee seemed at variance with what the Ministry of Defence had replied in response to outside questioning.

The use of an antidote to nerve gas, pyridostigmine bromide, seemed to have been a mistake when Sarin was the gas being used by the Iraqis. An American website pointed out that this compound actually heightened the effects of the Sarin rather than countered them. Not only that, it was toxic in its own right and many troops had suffered accidental overdose through pill-popping instigated by feelings of panic when the sirens had gone off.

Individual tales of blunders and misunderstandings that had led to troops being exposed to unnecessary danger were legion.

It seemed likely to Steven that a number of allied troops had suffered the effects of Sarin nerve gas and/or its antidote. Many had reacted adversely to vaccines given to protect them against viruses and bacteria. Some had been subjected to attack by such biological agents. Some had been the victim of mistakes made by those in command and were exposed unnecessarily to toxic compounds.

Satisfied with his work, Steven rubbed his eyes and stretched his arms in the air. He was stiff from sitting in the same position for so long and his eyes felt as if they had sand in them from staring at his computer screen, but it now seemed much clearer to him why Government and representatives of the Gulf War veterans had been at each other's throats for so long. To him as an outside observer, it seemed probable that both parties were right in their assertions. There was indeed no such thing as Gulf War Syndrome but on the other hand a whole lot of troops had fallen ill because of their service there. The only thing that hadn't become any clearer was why George Sebring had been murdered.

CHAPTER SIX

Steven left early next morning for Leicester. He wanted to find out if Sebring's wife could elaborate on what she had referred to as her husband's 'troubled state of mind'. He also wanted to find out if she could remember any more about the Scotsman who had called on him and upset him. Although Jane Sebring had told the authorities that her husband had never spoken about his work at Porton, Steven reckoned that there was a possibility that she would have said that anyway—almost as an automatic response to the question. Like most partners of people whose work was secret she would almost certainly have picked up more over the years than she was letting on.

Before he questioned anyone about anything however, he would make himself known to the Leicester police who were dealing with the enquiry. He knew from past experience just how sensitive police forces could be when they felt an outsider was intruding on their patch. If he didn't get off on the right foot he might well find himself tip toeing through a minefield of fragile egos for the foreseeable future should Sci-Med's interest in the case continue.

If push came to shove, he had every right to expect—even demand—police cooperation but he preferred not to go down that road. Until he was sure that there really was a reason for Sci-Med to be involved in the case, he would present himself as little more than a Home Office observer, willing to give any help and advice he could. He saw from the road signs that he was entering the outskirts of Leicester and the car radio had just told him it was 10am. He made directly for Leicester police headquarters.

Detective Chief Inspector Glyn Norris, the officer in charge of the Sebring murder investigation, gave Steven a world-weary nod when he was shown into his office.

'Take a pew,' said Norris, handing back Steven's ID, which had been brought through to him by way of introduction. 'A little bird told me at the weekend that you lot were taking an interest in the case. She just omitted to say why.'

'It's no big secret,' said Steven. 'Sebring once worked at Porton Down. If his death should turn out to have anything to do with that fact we'd like to know about it and for the same reason you might just find your investigation a little hard going.'

'You mean, no bugger would tell us anything,' said Norris.

'More or less,' agreed Steven.

'So you're here to help,' said Norris as if he didn't believe a word of it.

'In a way,' said Steven.

Norris settled an owl-like stare on Steven. 'What makes you think that Sebring's work at Porton Down had anything to do with his death?' he asked.

'Nothing apart from the visit from a mysterious Scotsman that you must know about,' said Steven. 'His wife got the distinct impression that they had met at Porton Down and as he seemed to be the only suspect on the horizon . . .'

88

'He's no longer a suspect,' said Norris.

'You've traced him?'

'Didn't take long,' said Norris. 'He's known to the police. He's been a Gulf War activist for a long time. He's pulled several stunts over the years to draw attention to what he sees as his cause. Ex-army sergeant, lives in Glasgow, works as a lab technician in one of the hospitals.'

'But not a suspect?'

'He was in Glasgow at the time of the murder; he could prove it beyond doubt.'

Steven nodded. 'Did you ask him why he went to see Sebring?'

'He thinks the boffins at Porton know more about Gulf War Syndrome than they've ever let on. His latest tack has been trying to call on them individually, hoping they'll admit as much.'

'How did he manage to find out who they were?' asked Steven. 'I shouldn't think it's something they go out of their way to advertise.'

'He claims he was a member of something called the 1st Field Laboratory Unit during his Gulf War service and that he and the others had actually been trained at Porton Down. He claims he knew several of the scientific staff from his time there.'

'Did it check out?' asked Steven.

Norris shook his head. 'Ministry of Defence say they've never heard of Maclean or the 1st

Field Laboratory Unit.'

'So Maclean's lying?'

'One of them is,' replied Norris. 'And Maclean is no doubt as to who the "lying bastards", as he put it, are in this instance.'

'You sound as if you believe him,' said Steven.

'He was very convincing. He rhymed off names, times, dates, places, says there were forty of them, split into teams of five, all medics and technicians who were trained to detect evidence of chemical and biological attack in the Gulf War.'

'So why would the MOD deny it?' said Steven.

'I think it's something to do with the ruling classes,' said Norris, pushing the loud pedal on a working class accent as emotion got the better of him. 'They're taught at public school to deny everything. It's their way of preventing others finding out what a bunch of screwed-up, anally retentive fuck-wits they actually are.'

'It's obviously not working too well in your case,' said Steven. 'You seem to have found them out.'

Norris seemed to wonder for a moment or two how he should take Steven's comment then he said, 'My brother-in-law fought in the Gulf. Tank commander, he was. He was invalided out of the army within six months of coming home.'

'I'm sorry. What happened?'

'Absolutely nothing, according to the MOD. There's no good reason at all for my sister now being the only breadwinner in that family. The fact that her husband now weighs four stone less than he did when he went to war and can't walk the length of himself without falling down exhausted is all in his mind according to them.'

'I've come across more than a few stories like that in the past few days,' said Steven.

'Well, whatever,' said Norris. 'Maclean's no longer in the frame for George Sebring's murder. He was on duty in a hospital in Glasgow at the time. Staff and patients testified to that.'

'So where does your inquiry go from here?'

'Unless we can come up with a secret double-life for Sebring—and between you and I, I don't think we're going to—it's going to hit the wall,' said Norris. 'It's the worst possible scenario for an investigating force; murder by a stranger without motive.'

Steven nodded sympathetically and got up to go. 'Well, I won't take up any more of your time,' he said. 'Best of luck.'

'Back to London?' asked Norris, coming out from behind his desk to see him to the door.

'I'll have a word with Sebring's wife first.'

'She's busy,' said Norris.

Steven looked at him questioningly.

Norris looked at his watch and said, 'She's burying George at noon.'

'Damn, I should have thought,' said Steven.

'It's not been that long since the death.'

Out in the car park, Steven looked up the location of the cemetery in the map of Leicester he'd picked up at a service station on the way in. It was less than two miles away and it was five minutes to twelve. He was still thinking in terms of speaking to Jane Sebring today if he could, but first he thought he would drive to the cemetery and get a feel for the situation. If it looked as if the widow might be too distressed, he would put things off until another day and go back to London.

It wasn't until he had parked the car and walked over to the cemetery gates with the sun warm on his face that Steven realised what a nice day it was. The early cloud had cleared away and the birds were singing as he approached an internal road junction in what appeared to be a large but well-kept municipal cemetery. He looked left and then right to see if he could spot the Sebring cortege.

At this time in the year, the trees were in full foliage and it was difficult to get a clear view in either direction so he left the path and climbed a grassy knoll some twenty metres away, which he thought would afford him a better angle of vision. He caught sight of a funeral group about two hundred metres to the left and quickly returned to the path to hurry towards it. He didn't want to disturb the proceedings so he veered on to the grass again and circled round behind a clump of yew trees where he could see that his final approach would be masked by a number of large granite monuments from another—probably Victorian—age.

From his vantage point Steven saw that some fifty people had assembled at the graveside where a clergyman in white robes set off by a purple stole was reading the burial service. He couldn't help but feel that this was the way to take your leave of life. England was doing George Sebring proud. The blue of the summer sky, the lush green of the newly-mown grass, the black worn by the mourners, the weeping willows; all combined to paint the perfect farewell scene. He could imagine it hanging on the wall of some gallery. Steven could remember so many funerals where foul weather had stolen centre-stage, where the earth had turned to mud underfoot and the valediction had been snatched away by the wind. This was better: this was how it should be.

It was easy for him to pick out Jane Sebring because she had presence. Although slight in stature and lace-veiled under a broad-brimmed black hat, she seemed to stand out from the others. She was flanked—presumably by relatives—but none touched her or supported her in any way as if such a gesture might not have been welcome. Instead she stood alone and erect, hands clasped together in front of her, head slightly bowed. When her husband's coffin was lowered into the ground she accepted a single yellow rose from a man at her side and after a slight pause, threw it down lightly on to the lid. She exchanged a few words with the vicar then turned to walk without falter towards the waiting cars. The other mourners followed suit.

Steven decided that he would try to speak to Jane Sebring. He would follow the official cars to see where the journey took him and then make plans accordingly. He had just come out through the cemetery gates—the last to do so—when he felt a hand on his shoulder and a rough voice told him to 'stop right there'. He turned to find a thickset man wearing a light grey suit with a yellow shirt and a black tie that looked more suited to being worn by a young boy: it seemed so short and narrow. He was fumbling for something in his inside pocket and Steven noticed he smelt of sweat.

'Who are you?' he asked Steven.

'I might ask the same of you,' replied Steven.

'Police. Just answer the question,' said the man finally finding his warrant card and holding it up in front of Steven.

Steven took out his own ID and flipped it open.

His questioner's demeanour changed in an instant. 'Sorry sir,' he said. 'We've been on the lookout for strangers turning up at Sebring's funeral. The boss thought his murderer might put in an appearance. Apparently it's not uncommon.'

Steven nodded but thought otherwise. It might have been at one time, he acknowledged, but since TV detectives had started pointing this out every other week you'd have to be some kind of mental defective as well as a murderer to turn up at your victim's funeral these days. He left the policeman and ran to his car, having noted that the cars had turned left at the end of the road and hoping he wasn't going to lose them.

The road seemed quiet so Steven gunned his MGF down past the cemetery gates and up to the end of the road where his tyres squealed as he threw it into a tight left hand turn. There was nothing up ahead. 'Damnation,' he muttered as he accelerated again up to the first junction where he was just in time to see the back end of a dark blue Mazda make a right turn off the road to his left. He remembered such a car belonging to one of the mourners. Another brief sprint and he was sure it was the same one. The official limousines were a few cars up ahead.

When the convoy finally turned into a pleasant crescent of large, 1930s detached houses with bay windows and Virginia creeper much in evidence, Steven deduced that they were headed for Jane Sebring's home rather than one of the local hotels, which 'catered respectfully' for the funeral trade. This would make it more difficult for him to mingle with the mourners. He had a decision to make. Should he gate-crash the wake or should he go away and come back later?

Steven gambled on attaching himself to the mourners, a decision encouraged by the fact that nearly everyone who had been at the cemetery seemed to have come back to the house so he shouldn't stand out like too much of a sore thumb unless, of course, they all knew each other intimately. He noted as he walked up the path behind a black-clad group of four that the house was called 'Vermont'.

Now that she was no longer wearing her veil, Steven could see that Jane Sebring was a very good-looking woman, somewhere in her mid-thirties, he reckoned, with fair hair, blue intelligent eyes that gave nothing away and such poise and self-control that he could not help but imagine what she might be like if she ever let her guard down. Although she did have an air of sadness about her, she was clearly not the kind of person to parade her grief in public and busied herself enquiring after the health of ageing family members and generally thanking people for coming as well as making sure they had enough to eat and drink.

'You know, I reckon old George was a spy,' said one of the men in the group Steven had loosely attached himself to. He'd gathered that the man was one of Sebring's colleagues at the

96

university and had already pigeonholed him as belonging to the 'all brains and no sense' branch of academia.

'It's always the quiet ones that have a past,' continued the man. 'George never spoke much about what he did before joining us, a sure sign if you ask me.'

'He's right,' said another. 'He was very cagey about that. So you reckon it was the KGB that did for George then?'

'Or some such outfit. There was that chap who fell foul of the Bulgarians, if you remember; they got him with a poisoned umbrella tip.'

'Didn't strike me as the James Bond type,' said another man. 'I mean, he was a member of the university choir for God's sake.'

Steven detached himself from the group and joined an elderly lady who was looking out of the window at the garden. 'Everything's looking nice,' he said.

'George hated gardening,' said the woman, without looking at him. 'Jane does it all. She's good at it but then she's good at most things. Were you one of George's colleagues, Mr . . . ?'

'Dunbar, Steven Dunbar, a long time ago,' lied Steven. 'And you?'

'I'm his mother.'

'I'm so sorry, I didn't realise,' said Steven, feeling embarrassed and even a little ashamed of the circumstances. 'It's a tragedy,' he said.

97

'No mother should live to see her son buried. It must be an especially cruel kind of grief.'

The woman turned and looked at him for the first time. Steven was aware of her giving him an appraising look before she said, 'It is. Pardon me for saying this but you sound as if you've had more than a passing acquaintance with grief yourself?'

'My wife,' said Steven. 'Cancer. We'd only been married two years.'

'Another special kind of grief.'

Steven didn't say anything. It had been the worst time of his life.

Up until he'd started to speak to Sebring's mother, Steven had kept watch on where Jane Sebring was in the room. He wanted to avoid making contact with her until the others started to leave. His lapse in concentration was brought home to him when a pleasant voice at his elbow said, 'Can I get you two anything?'

Steven turned to look directly at Jane, feeling immediately that she could see right through him with her deep blue eyes. 'I'm fine, thanks,' he said. He had been nursing the same glass of sherry since he came in.

'I don't think we've . . .' began Jane.

'Mr Dunbar was a colleague of George's once upon a time,' said Sebring's mother before Steven could say anything.

'It was nice of you to come, Mr Dunbar,' said Jane. 'Where would that have been?'

'Porton Down,' said Steven.

'Ah, someone else from those days,' said Jane, starting alarm bells in Steven's head. 'You must know Donald Crowe over there then?'

Steven followed Jane's line of sight to a tall, gaunt, cadaverous-looking man who seemed to be preoccupied with examining book titles on the shelves along the back wall of the room. 'I don't think so,' he said, having to think quickly. 'Our times mustn't have overlapped.'

'I see,' said Jane Sebring. 'So you're not here to help him make sure George didn't leave any secrets behind. That's why he's really here.'

Jane moved off before Steven could respond: her comment had come out of the blue. Sebring's mother beside him said, 'Jane's a remarkable woman. It would be a silly man who thought he could fool her.'

'Quite so,' said Steven. He didn't dare look at her.

'Why don't we walk in the garden? It seems such a shame to be indoors on such a glorious day,' suggested Sebring's mother.

'If you're sure Jane wouldn't mind?' said Steven.

'She won't.'

Steven sensed that Maud Sebring—as he now knew her—needed to talk about her dead son so he was happy to let her. Apart from anything else, it kept him away from potentially embarrassing situations and, from the garden, through the french windows, he could see what was going on inside. He was interested in when people were going to start leaving.

Maud was telling him about a family picnic of long ago when he saw a large group inside begin to move towards the front door. Jane was accompanying them. She paused by the side of the door and was kissed on the cheek by each in turn. Steven could see the herd instinct take over among the remaining mourners and they all started to file out, uttering last condolences as they did so.

'So this is where you've got to, Mother,' said Jane when she finally came out into the garden. She was smiling at them.

'We couldn't resist the sun, dear,' replied Maud. 'I was just telling Mr Dunbar here about the time George decided he was going to live up a tree like Tarzan and then got stuck.'

'The stuff of family legend, Mr Dunbar,' said Jane, then, turning to her mother-in-law, she said, 'Mother, Jimmy says he'll give you a lift home now if you're ready to go. It'll save you getting a taxi later on.'

'How very kind,' said Maud Sebring. She disappeared indoors to find her coat, leaving Steven and Jane alone in the garden.

Jane Sebring turned to Steven and said, 'You didn't know my husband at all, did you, Mr Dunbar?'

'How did you know?' asked Steven.

'Donald Crowe was my husband's boss at Porton; he still works there. You couldn't have failed to have come across him had you been there yourself at any time when George was.'

'Well spotted,' said Steven. 'I apologise for the deception.'

'Who are you?'

Steven showed Jane his ID.

'So, it's *Doctor* Dunbar,' said Jane. 'From another government organisation full of spies and secrets that must never be revealed, no doubt.'

'Not really,' said Steven. 'We're usually quite open about things. We just tend to help out when the police might be out of their depth.'

'And why should they be that in George's case?'

'It did seem possible that his death might have had something to do with his time at Porton Down, Mrs Sebring. The visit you had from the Scotsman, Maclean, seemed to suggest that, although the police no longer think that's the case.'

'They found Maclean?'

'Apparently he's a well-known Gulf War activist. He was at home in Glasgow when your husband died.'

'The war was all such a long time ago,' sighed Jane. 'But Mr Maclean seemed so angry about everything—as if it happened yesterday.'

'Did you get the impression that your husband knew him when he turned up on your doorstep?' asked Steven.

'Oh, yes,' said Jane. 'They'd clearly met before.'

'They argued?'

Jane nodded. 'From what I overheard, Mr Maclean seemed to think that my husband had been involved in something untoward during his time at Porton. He kept insisting that he should come clean. George insisted that he was imagining things but Mr Maclean accused him of lying.'

'Did your husband say anything afterwards?' asked Steven.

'Nothing. He refused to discuss it.'

'I take it you personally have no idea what George worked on at Porton.'

'As I told Donald Crowe earlier, none at all.'

'What made you think Crowe was here to check up on things?' asked Steven.

Jane gave an involuntary laugh. 'He told me to my face,' she said. 'He asked if he could go through George's papers to make sure there was nothing there of a "sensitive nature" as he so delicately put it.'

'You don't like Crowe,' said Steven.

'He gives me the creeps. You'd find more humanity in a bar of soap.'

'Did he find anything?'

Jane shrugged and said, 'I've no idea. I just

told him to help himself.'

'You told the police that there was a change in your husband after Maclean's visit. He seemed worried? Angry?'

Jane smiled wanly and said, 'George wasn't really a man who ever got angry. He was extremely . . . even-tempered.'

Steven sensed that there was much more lying behind Jane's choice of words but— although he was interested—it was not the right time to ask. 'Worried then?'

'Alarmed would be a better word,' said Jane. 'He had trouble sleeping after Maclean's visit. I was worried about him but he wouldn't open up to me. That was George.'

Jane looked at Steven in what he found a very strange way. He imagined there was some kind of debate going on inside her head. Eventually she said simply, 'He called a newspaper, the *Guardian*. I know because I listened in. He asked to speak to a journalist who had done a number of stories on the Gulf War over the years. His name's Martin Hendry.'

'I know the name,' said Steven.

'He wasn't there but George left word saying that he had a major story for him and that he should give him a call back. Hendry did call back, about two hours later. I answered the phone. I heard George make arrangements to meet him the following day.'

'George didn't tell you face to face?' asked

Steven.

Jane shook her head. 'No,' she said.

Steven saw the hurt in her eyes. He said, 'As you say, he was very upset at the time.'

CHAPTER SEVEN

Steven drove back to London reflecting on his day. A lot had happened since the meeting that morning with Norris at Police Headquarters. He had parted company with the policeman, almost convinced that Sebring's death had nothing to do with his work at Porton Down after the elimination of Maclean as a suspect, but now, after talking to Jane Sebring in the garden of her home, he had started to believe otherwise. In a practical sense there was only one lead to follow and that was Martin Hendry, the journalist Sebring had contacted at the *Guardian*. He sighed as he realised that getting anything out of a journalist about his source was going to be about as easy as getting information out of the Ministry of Defence about Sebring's past work—or blood out of a stone. He'd have to push the murder inquiry button pretty hard to make Hendry budge.

When he phoned the paper Steven was told by the receptionist that Martin Hendry was not in the office and was asked if he'd like to leave a message. He said not and instead asked to speak to the editor. He persisted through the series of obstacles that people who answer phones seemed duty-bound to erect until he finally reached the ear of a deputy editor. 'I really do have to speak to Martin Hendry,' he said.

'Me too,' replied the man. 'Believe me, it's not a case of him avoiding you. He really isn't here. He had a story to deliver yesterday morning with a noon deadline but no show and believe me, I'm as pissed off as you are.'

'You've no idea where he is?' asked Steven.

'Well, yes. I know exactly where he's supposed to be. He told us he was going up to Scotland to work on his story. He said he had to talk to a man in Glasgow to get some details straight and then he was going to his place in the Highlands to produce the final draft. But as I say, he was due to produce it yesterday and didn't.'

'Would you say this was unusual?' asked Steven.

'No,' replied the deputy editor matter-of-factly. 'Happens all the time. Sometimes I think that editing a paper is like juggling with one hand tied behind your back.'

'Do you know where in the Highlands he was going to?' asked Steven.

'No, it's his own place and somewhere he's always regarded as his bolthole. It's where he goes to escape the cares of the world or when

105

he's feeling put-upon. He's never been keen on telling any of us where it is, presumably in case we arrive on his doorstep armed with fishing rods and cases of lager. It's become a bit of a joke in the office. They talk about Martin going up to Balmoral. I think he inherited the place from his parents, nothing too grand, just a hut up in the hills I think.'

'He must have a mobile phone?'

'He's not answering. I'll give you the number if you like but he's probably switched it off while he's working. I don't think the muse cares for "Fur Elise" going off every ten minutes.'

'How about the man he went to see in Glasgow. Do you know anything about him?'

'No to that too, I'm afraid.'

'If he gets in contact will you tell him I have to speak to him?' said Steven. 'It's important.'

'Of course, leave me your number.'

Steven left his mobile number and rang off. He immediately rang Sci-Med to ask if they'd managed to get anything out of the Ministry of Defence.

'Nothing yet,' replied Rose Roberts. 'I did mark it urgent but then . . .'

'I know,' said Steven. 'Keep at them, Rose.'

Steven realised that he was hungry; he hadn't eaten properly since breakfast time. There had just been no time for lunch although he'd managed to grab a couple of sandwiches at Jane Sebring's place after the funeral. He found he had nothing in the flat in the way of the tinned or packet food he depended on—he'd never really got round to learning to cook—so he went out to The Jade Garden, his local Chinese take-away where he was a regular at least once a week and picked up some hot food. He came back and watched the news on television while he worked his way through lemon chicken and special fried rice.

He learned that George W Bush seemed determined to extend his supposed war on terrorism by going to war with Iraq and Tony Blair still seemed solid in his support of US policy—as indeed he had been since the destruction of the twin towers—but convincing other countries of the justification of a new initiative against Saddam was proving problematical. Nothing was ever going to be quick or easy once the United Nations became involved, thought Steven. He recalled the adage of a camel being a horse designed by a committee. He turned off the TV as the news ended and put the Stan Getz album, *Jazz Samba*, on the stereo while he considered what he should do next with the Sebring investigation.

If Sebring really had given Martin Hendry a story about the Gulf War and Hendry had gone to Glasgow with it, you didn't have to be a rocket scientist to work out that there was a good chance the man was the activist, Angus Maclean. According to DCI Norris, Maclean now worked in a Glasgow hospital as a lab technician.

After wondering for a moment if it would be worth his while going up there to speak to Maclean he concluded that he had nothing to lose by doing so and maybe everything to gain. He would fly up to Glasgow in the morning but before setting off, he would call Norris in Leicester to get some more details about Maclean and his place of work.

*   *   *

Steven's flight into Glasgow touched down a little after ten and he took a taxi to the Princess Louise Hospital. As both the airport and the hospital lay out to the west of the city it only took fifteen minutes. He followed the signs to the microbiology laboratories through a maze of corridors and waited in line at the Reception counter while a nurse in front of him delivered a series of clinical specimens she'd brought up from one of the wards.

'Jeeez-O!' said the young male technician behind the counter. 'Is this national-swab-your-nose-week or something?' He was looking at the three dozen or so plastic swab tubes lying on the desk in front of him. 'This is the fifth lot this morning.'

'Blame the TV news,' said the nurse. 'They did a scare story on MRSA last night so the powers that be thought it would be a good idea to swab the whole hospital just in case the press come to call. Image is everything.'

'Better cancel my summer holiday then,' said the technician. 'In fact, I'll be lucky to make it home for Christmas at this rate.'

The nurse smiled and turned away leaving Steven to ask if he could have a word with Angus Maclean.

'Can I ask who's calling?' said the technician.

'Dr Dunbar.'

The technician pressed one of the numbered buttons on the intercom beside him and said, 'A visitor for you, Gus. It's a Dr Dunbar.'

'Never heard of him,' came the gruff voice from the speaker.

The technician looked embarrassed.

'He doesn't know me,' said Steven and the technician relayed this information.

'Send him through,' said the voice.

The technician released the electronic lock on the doors leading to the main labs and said to Steven, 'Room nine; it's on your right.'

Steven entered and immediately noticed the smell he associated with medical labs the world over, a mixture of organic solvents and disinfectant with undercurrents of noxious substances he'd rather not think about. He knocked on the frosted glass door to Maclean's lab and was invited to enter with a solitary, 'Yup.'

109

Maclean, a short, slightly-built man with an unfashionable crew cut and round shoulders that suggested possible chest problems was seated with his back to the door, peering down the binocular eyepiece of a microscope. 'Be with you in a moment,' he said.

Steven reassured him there was no hurry and took in his surroundings while he waited. A Bunsen burner was alight on the small bench to the left of where Maclean was seated, a platinum inoculating loop propped up on its base. Beside it lay a plastic Petri dish filled with a medium that Steven remembered from times past as blood agar and next to that, a box of microscope slides and a pack of coverslips. It was clear that the bacterial colonies growing on the blood agar were the subject of Maclean's scrutiny.

Maclean finished his examination and removed the glass slide from the microscope stage to drop it into a beaker of disinfectant before jotting down his findings on the report form beside him. He turned and said, 'What can I do for you?'

Steven showed him his ID and said, 'I'm making inquiries connected with the death of Dr George Sebring; I understand you knew him?'

'I thought the police did that sort of thing,' said Maclean. 'I've already told them all I know. I've no idea who killed the bugger.'

Steven nodded, deliberately making an

effort to remain calm in the face of Maclean's aggression. He said, 'I'm not so much concerned with the criminal aspects of the case as the scientific ones, particularly where they might provide motive.'

'What does that mean?' said Maclean, affecting a scowl and dropping his head slightly to look over the top of his glasses.

'I think we both know that Sebring once worked at the Porton Down Defence Establishment,' said Steven. 'I'm trying to establish if his time there might have had something to do with his death.'

'Well, there's irony for you,' said Maclean with a smile that lacked any vestige of humour. 'You're wondering whether his work had anything to do with his death and I'm bloody sure it had everything to do with that of my wife and daughter.'

'How so?'

'I don't know how so,' replied Maclean. 'That's what I've been trying to find out for Christ knows how many years. Bloody place. Defence establishment, my arse.'

'How come you know so much about it?'

'I was trained there when I was in the army,' said Maclean. '1st Field Laboratory Unit.'

'That's what you told the police,' said Steven. 'The MOD says they've never heard of it.'

'Lying bastards,' said Maclean.

'Why should they lie?' asked Steven.

111

'Christ knows!' said Maclean, spreading his hands. 'God knows why they even went to the bother of setting us up in the first place,' he said. 'They recruited us from all over the country: they trained us to monitor and detect the use of chemical and biological weapons in all sorts of situations and then they threw away every report we ever made. Now they've taken to denying we ever existed.'

'Bizarre,' agreed Steven. 'I take it you're absolutely convinced that Saddam used these weapons?'

'Christ man, I was there. I saw it with my own eyes. I ran the tests. I isolated the bacteria. I'm not JK Rowling. I didn't make the whole thing up. None of us did.'

'So why blame Porton?' asked Steven. 'Surely Gulf War Syndrome should be put down to the Iraqis and the CB weapons you say they used?'

'Some of the problems are due to that,' conceded Maclean. 'But there was something else going on. Saddam's CB weapons and the allied fuck-ups helped disguise it but there was definitely something else going on.'

'And you think Porton were behind it?' said Steven.

'I know they were,' said Maclean. 'I saw it in Sebring's eyes when I talked to him.'

'His wife told me he was very upset after your visit,' said Steven.

'He was upset when I arrived,' said

112

Maclean. 'Now he's dead, like my family.'

'I can understand your bitterness,' said Steven.

'Can you?' snapped Maclean. 'It's absolutely amazing the number of people who can "understand my bitterness" when they know hee-haw about it.'

'I lost my own wife,' said Steven. 'Cancer.'

The comment stopped Maclean in his tracks. There was a long pause before he said, 'I'm sorry but I bet it wasn't from anything you gave her.'

'What makes you think your wife died from something you gave her?'

'I just do,' said Maclean.

Steven gave him a look that suggested this answer wasn't good enough and Maclean said, 'First it was me when I got back from the Gulf. I picked up every infection that was going; it was just one thing after another, cold, flu, bronchitis, food poisoning, you name it. And then the same thing started happening to my wife and daughter, only they weren't so lucky. They died, God love them, one from a brain tumour, the other leukaemia and don't tell me they're not infectious conditions or try to tell me it was just bad luck. I've heard it all before. I know. Believe me; I just know it was down to me.'

'Have you ever heard of a man named Martin Hendry?' asked Steven.

'He's a journalist. He came to see me.'

Steven was pleased to hear he'd made the right call. 'What about?' he asked.

For a moment Maclean looked as if he might tell Steven to mind his own business but his hard expression changed and he said simply, 'Gulf War Syndrome, he wanted to "know my thoughts". He particularly wanted to know about infectious conditions reported by vets of the war.'

'Did he say why?'

'What reason did you have in mind?'

'Did George Sebring's name come up?'

'No, why should it?'

'According to his wife, Sebring contacted Hendry after you'd been to see him and told him he had a story for him. They arranged to meet.'

'Well, well, well,' murmured Maclean, smiling for the first time.

'Apparently Hendry has a particular interest in the Gulf War. He's done a number of stories about it over the years.'

'I know,' said Maclean. 'I've read them all. Social conscience of the nation sort of stuff, high on morals, low on practicalities, typical *Guardian* stuff.' Maclean looked thoughtful for a moment before appearing excited at the prospect. 'Maybe Sebring decided to come clean after all these years?' he said. 'It would explain Hendry's line of questioning. He wanted to know all about the symptoms I and my family had, every little detail. Do you know

114

when the paper's going to run it?'

'When I find Hendry I'll ask him,' said Steven. 'But I'm having trouble. I don't suppose you've any idea where he went when he left here?'

'He told me where he was going,' said Maclean. 'Like most of the scribblers I come across, he tried to gain my confidence through small talk so that I'd be lulled into telling him what he wanted to know. He went on about how much he liked Scotland and how he came up here as much as he could. He said he had a place in the Highlands and that's where he'd be going to work on his article when he left me.'

'Did he say where?'

'A stone's throw from Blair Atholl, that was how he put it.'

'Nothing more specific?'

'Nope.'

'You've been a great help,' said Steven, getting up to leave.

'Don't mention it,' said Maclean, moving from the microscope stool to the one at the bench to start preparing his next sample for examination.

'You're a medical microbiologist,' said Steven as a thought struck him. 'Did you ever try finding the infectious agent you believe you passed on to your family?'

Maclean gave Steven a look that questioned his basic intelligence. 'Of course I bloody did,' said Maclean. He pulled open the top drawer of an under-bench filing cabinet and brought out a blue A4 folder. He held it up in his right hand saying, 'Analyses of sputum, blood, urine, faeces, gastric lavage, skin scrapings, the lot. I must be about the most well-characterised human being in microbiological terms on the face of the planet.'

'Sorry,' said Steven. 'I suppose it's obvious you would have screened yourself. I take it you didn't find anything?'

'Nothing pathogenic,' said Maclean, replacing the folder. 'And no, that does not change my mind. It just means that these bastards at Porton were clever bastards.'

Steven nodded and prepared to leave. 'Thanks for talking to me,' he said.

'Will you let me know when Hendry's story's coming out?' asked Maclean.

'Will do.'

By the time he reached the front doors of the hospital Steven had made the decision to hire a car and drive up to Blair Atholl. He felt sure he could find Hendry's place by asking at local businesses, especially if as the editor had said, his parents had owned the place before him. He glanced at his watch and saw that it was twelve thirty. If he got a move on he should be there before they started to close. He used the WAP facility on his mobile phone to find the nearest branch of Hertz and took a taxi there.

It started to rain as he finally escaped the gravitational pull of Glasgow's traffic and headed north-east, first to Stirling and then on to Perth. It was coming down in torrents when he negotiated the last of a series of roundabouts and joined the A9 north to Pitlochry and Blair Atholl. For the most part here the road was no longer dual carriageway or motorway and he was not long in finding out that the rented Ford he was driving fell a long way short of his own car's performance when it came to brisk overtaking. An angry blare of the horn from an oncoming truck driver when he took too long to pass a bus reminded him to assume that he was towing the QE2 the next time he considered such a move.

After drawing a blank at the first two places he asked about Martin Hendry—a petrol station and a small craft shop—he decided that the local hotel might be his best bet, based on the assumption that journalists and alcohol went together like love and marriage. He found the bar busier than he'd expected with tourists and day-trippers but this was because of the weather. It was still raining cats and dogs outside. He waited patiently while a man from Yorkshire, judging by the accent, placed his family's order for food and drink. The man finished by asking, 'Is it always like this up here, luv?'

'Mostly,' replied the girl behind the bar as

117

she started pulling a pint. Steven reckoned she was a student working her vacation. 'It keeps the grass green.'

'It's a wonder you Scotties don't have webbed feet,' said the Yorkshireman, breaking into laughter and turning to share it with Steven. 'I brought a caravan; I should have brought a bloody boat!'

Steven smiled and said, 'Maybe it'll be better tomorrow.'

'You sound like the bloody wife!' exclaimed the Yorkshireman. 'The sun will come out tomorrow,' he half sang as he picked up his tray of drinks, changing it to a tuneless whistle as he headed for his table.

'What can I get you?' the girl asked Steven.

He ordered a pint of Stella and then said, 'I'm looking for a friend of mine. He has a place up here. His name's Martin Hendry.'

'Doesn't mean anything I'm afraid,' said the girl.

'He's a journalist.'

'Maybe Peter will know him,' said the girl. 'I just work the holidays. I'll ask him when I get a chance.' She gave a meaningful look at the queue forming behind him.

Steven found a seat and sipped his beer while he took in his surroundings. It was just before four in the afternoon and they had the lights on because of the dark clouds outside, yet it still seemed gloomy. It was noisy too because of bored children being allowed to run

118

around and people playing the electronic games machines. Two television sets, mounted high up on wall brackets, were switched on although their sound had been turned down and the air was heavy with the smell of wet clothing and fried food. At a table next to Steven, two Germans, wearing leather biker gear, had spread a road map and were planning the next leg of their journey. They were going to Inverness and then on to Loch Ness.

Steven saw that, for the moment, there was no queue at the bar. He managed to catch the girl's eye and jog her memory. She smiled and disappeared through the back for a few moments. She returned with a short bald man wearing an apron and they both looked in Steven's direction. He went over to the bar.

'You're looking for Martin Hendry, I hear,' said the man.

'Do you know him?' asked Steven.

'Comes in quite a lot,' replied the man. 'Comes up here to work on his novel. Going to be the next John Grisham, he tells me.'

Steven was unaware of this but inwardly conceded that it would not be an unusual ambition for a journalist or maybe it was just bar room bullshit. That would not be unusual either. 'That's him,' he said. 'Have you seen him lately?'

'He was in two or three nights ago,' said the man.

'So he's still up here?'

'As far as I know. He usually says cheerio when he's going back down south and he didn't say anything the other night.'

'Thanks,' said Steven. 'Can you tell me how to get to his place?'

'He's got a cabin over on Tulach Hill.'

Steven looked blank and the man beckoned. He moved along to the end of the bar and came out from behind to lead Steven to a framed map of the area hanging on the wall. 'Over here to the west,' he said. 'You can't miss his cabin. It's called *Garry Lodge*. It's the only one on that side of the hill.'

Steven thanked the man and left, running across the car park to get in out of the rain as quickly as possible. He followed the man's directions, finally stopping at a rough track leading uphill. At first he was unsure as to whether this was the right one—there seemed to be so many farm tracks leading off the road—but he found reassurance when, through the semicircles of the screen being cleared by the wipers, he caught sight of the small board nailed to a tree saying *Garry Lodge*. He nursed the Ford up the steep slope, its wheels scratching unsurely at the wet stones, until the cabin came into view and he saw to his relief that the lights were on and there was a car parked at the side.

Steven brought the car to a halt right in front of the cabin—something he did

120

deliberately so that Hendry should be aware that he had a visitor. With a bit of luck he wouldn't have to stand too long outside in the rain. However, the cabin door remained firmly closed as Steven ran up the five steps to it and knocked. He tugged his collar up against the rain while he waited but it still found the back of his neck.

'C'mon, c'mon,' he murmured as the seconds ticked by with no response from inside. He knocked again, this time harder and longer but with still no answer.

Feeling loath to just turn round and drive away after coming so far, Steven tried the door and found it unlocked. 'Hello, anybody there?' he called out as he stepped inside.

The only sound to be heard inside the cabin was that of the rain on the roof. Steven moved through it slowly, looking into each of the rooms in turn. It didn't take long; there were only two and a small shower cubicle. Hendry, dressed in cream chinos and a blue denim shirt, was lying on top of the bed, an empty glass resting lightly in his right hand, a two-thirds empty whisky bottle sifting on the bedside table

Thinking that Hendry was in a drink-induced sleep, Steven was about to rap his knuckles against the door when he noticed the dark brown pill bottle lying on its side beside the whisky and understood its significance.

'Oh, shit,' he murmured as he moved

121

towards the bed. 'What brought *you* down cemetery road, my friend?'

Steven touched Hendry's cheek and found it icy cold. 'And through the gates.'

He checked for a carotid pulse but it was little more than a gesture. The man was dead—and had been for some time.

Seeing that Hendry was about the same age as he himself, Steven felt a lump come to his throat. There had been a time in his life when he had looked down the same road and found it attractive. It had been one option in ending the tide of sorrow and pain that engulfed him after Lisa's death. Only thoughts of his daughter, Jenny, had stopped him but it had been a close-run thing. He knew nothing about Hendry's personal circumstances but it was obvious that he had not found anything as strong to cling to. 'They call it the easy way,' said Steven softly. 'But we both know that ain't so.'

Steven brought out his phone to call the police, all too aware that he would be starting off a train of events which would lead to hurt, sorrow, bemusement and even anger among Hendry's nearest and dearest. This was always the way with suicide deaths. The 'if only' complex kicked in. If only he had said something . . . If only he had talked to me about it . . . If only he had asked for help . . .

Steven was assuming that Hendry *had* nearest and dearest but there was no reason

122

not to. He had been a first rate journalist who had earned the respect of his colleagues over many years. He would bet on a wide circle. His fingers hovered over the phone buttons but he hesitated when he thought about why he'd come here in the first place. Hendry's death was a tragedy but it had to be kept in perspective. A dead man could tell him nothing so he was left with a problem. He would have to find another way of discovering what George Sebring had been so anxious to confess. If, as Gus Maclean had suggested, Sebring had decided to 'come clean' about some awful secret concerning Porton Down, he had to know about it.

Hendry had come to Scotland to work on the story so there was a good chance that it must be somewhere in the cabin—either in hard copy or . . . His gaze fell on a Sony Vaio laptop sitting on the table in the room that doubled as living room and kitchen. It looked like the best bet. He turned it on and waited for Windows to open with its familiar jingle before accessing the documents list. It was empty. Not so much as a letter. He clicked on Windows Explorer and scanned the contents of the hard disk for data files. There were none.

Steven cursed under his breath. The hard disk had been wiped clean of everything but the operating system. Why should a man about to take his own life go to the trouble of erasing all the data files on his computer? The lack of any logical explanation made him uneasy but on the other hand, he had to admit that he had no idea why Hendry had taken his own life either.

There was an external Zip drive attached to the laptop by cable. He pushed the eject button on the front but no disk appeared. Steven was puzzled. Such a back-up drive would be useless without one but he couldn't see it lying around anywhere. Feeling that this was important, he searched the cabin thoroughly—right down to emptying out the rubbish bin—but there was still no sign of the disk. Steven went back to the laptop and checked the floppy drive. There was no disk in that either. 'Well, well,' he murmured. 'Do I detect that old familiar smell of . . . rat?'

While it was conceivable that Hendry could have wiped all the data off his computer and could also have erased any back-up material on a Zip disk, had it been there for him to check, *it wasn't.* Someone else had been in the cabin. They had removed the disk from the drive and taken it away. The same someone who had wiped the hard drive, perhaps? The same someone who had . . . Steven felt a strong sense of foreboding as he returned to the bedroom to take another look at Hendry's body. He felt he had to review the suicide scenario in the light of what he'd just learned.

He found no suspicious marks on Hendry's

head or neck and found himself murmuring apologies to the corpse as he unbuttoned the dead man's shirt to examine his torso. Again, he drew a blank. He was beginning to think— maybe hope—that he'd let his imagination run away with him, when he rolled back the cuffs of Hendry's denim shirt and saw the very slight marks on both wrists. They were faint and very narrow—as if thin wire had been used—but consistent with the man having been tied up. The rain continued to beat relentlessly down on the roof as Steven called in the police.

CHAPTER EIGHT

Steven closed down Martin Hendry's laptop while he waited for the police to arrive. He disconnected the various cables before packing everything away in its leather carry case and taking it out to his car. His thinking was that if the person who had wiped the data had simply deleted the files it might still be possible to recover them although he suspected that they would have known this too and over-written them. Still, as someone—he couldn't quite remember who—used to say about every idea that was mooted, it was worth a try. With the computer safely concealed in the boot of the Ford he called Sci-Med and spoke to the duty-officer.

'I want to call a code-red on the Sebring investigation,' he said.

'I'll set things in motion,' replied the man. 'Would you like me to inform Mr Macmillan?'

Steven said that he would. Calling a code-red was the way Sci-Med investigators signalled that a situation they had been asked to appraise should now be regarded as an official Sci-Med investigation. It was not something they were encouraged to do lightly and certainly not without being sure that there was some particular aspect of the case that Sci-Med should concern itself with. Once this was agreed, the authorities in all relevant areas would be made aware of the situation and be required to comply with any request for information or assistance that might come their way. In addition to smoothing the way locally, Sci-Med would also provide a full range of back-up services ranging from financial—through the issue of two credit cards—to the supply of a weapon should this be deemed necessary.

As Steven expected he might, John Macmillan phoned him back within the hour, asking for details. Steven explained where he was and of the circumstances that had prompted him to call a code-red, in particular the link between the dead journalist and George Sebring.

'Have you any idea what Sebring told him?' asked Macmillan.

'Only that it concerned the Gulf War.'

'That in itself does not make it Sci-Med's concern,' Macmillan reminded him.

'I'm pretty sure Sebring's work at Porton Down comes into it,' said Steven. He told Macmillan what the Leicester police had discovered about Sebring's Scottish visitor and of the conversation he'd subsequently had with Maclean in Glasgow.

'I think Sebring was suffering pangs of conscience about something he'd been involved in at Porton. It's my bet that he confessed all to Martin Hendry and now they're both dead.'

'I see,' said Macmillan. He said it as if he was already thinking one step ahead. 'How . . . unfortunate.'

'I'm sure they'd agree,' said Steven, mildly irked by Macmillan's use of establishment understatement, something he had a particular dislike of.

'I was actually considering who might have wanted to keep them quiet,' said Macmillan, leaving Steven wishing that he hadn't been so hasty. He now saw what Macmillan was getting at. There was only one clear candidate for having a vested interest in the men's silence and it looked terribly like Her Majesty's Government.

'Have the MOD come up with anything yet?' he asked.

'No,' said Macmillan. 'But if you're intent

on calling a code-red I'll speak to the Defence Secretary personally. In fact, in the circumstances, I think I'd better had anyway . . .'

'I don't think you should say anything about Hendry's death being murder. The police haven't called it that yet,' said Steven.

'Very well. Anything else?'

'You could ask the secretary about something called the First Field Laboratory Unit,' said Steven.

'Ask him what?' said Macmillan.

'Does it exist?' said Steven.

Steven told the police when they finally arrived, in the form of an inspector and a sergeant sent up from Perth, that Hendry was someone—one of a number of people—he had been seeking to question in connection with an ongoing investigation. He hadn't known the man personally or anything at all about him, other than the fact that he was a journalist. He'd found him dead on arrival at the cabin and had immediately called the police. He neglected to mention anything about the marks he'd found on Hendry's wrists. He thought he'd let the police medical examiner do that in his own good time. For the moment, an apparent case of suicide meant that he would get away from the cabin much quicker.

'Well, Inspector, if you don't need me any more . . .' said Steven, preparing to leave.

'Why do they do it?' mused the inspector, a

short, portly man, who exuded the air of a park-bench philosopher. He was standing by the bed, reading the label on the empty pill bottle.

Steven shook his head.

'England daein shite in the World Cup wouldn't have helped,' said his sour-faced sergeant. Then looking at Steven, he added, 'Nae offence like.'

Steven considered staying overnight at the hotel in Blair Atholl but suspected that the only topic of conversation in the bar would be Hendry's death, something that would quickly become public knowledge if Blair Atholl were like any other village. Instead he drove south to Pitlochry and booked into a small hotel where he felt he could be anonymous. After a few gin and tonics he opted for early bed and spent a restless night, plagued by bad dreams of a man being tied to a chair while whisky and pills were forced down him. He was glad when morning came and he could drive down to Glasgow Airport to catch a flight back to London.

When he picked up his e-mail at the flat, Steven learned that Macmillan wanted to see him at two that afternoon 'should he find it convenient'. He smiled at Macmillan's turn of phrase—he'd never known the man to be anything other than polite. He phoned Rose Roberts to say he'd be there.

It was such a nice day in London that

129

Steven decided to walk to the Home Office. The pavements were crowded but he was in no hurry and it was good to feel part of summer in the capital for a little while. Scaffolders whistled at pretty girls who self-consciously ignored them while tourists photographed and videoed just about everything in sight. Policemen were in shirt-sleeves and ice cream cones melted in the hands of children.

Steven found John Macmillan looking thoughtful. He waited until Rose had placed a tray with two coffees and a plate of biscuits on his desk before saying, 'I spoke to the Defence Secretary last night.'

'And he told you to pull the investigation,' said Steven. 'He said it wasn't in the national interest?'

Macmillan took a moment before saying, 'I'd ask you what makes you so cynical about our political masters if I didn't know already,' said Macmillan. He was referring to a previous Sci-Med investigation in which Steven had been asked to take a look at problems connected with the planting of a genetically modified maize crop. He had succeeded in opening up a can of worms which had brought him into conflict with a dark side of government that he hadn't even realised existed and it had nearly cost him his life. He survived but the affair had jaundiced his view of the establishment. His previous conviction that he worked for the 'good guys' had been seriously questioned.

'No such request was made,' said Macmillan. 'Nor would it have been complied with if it had. Sci-Med is and always has been independent—something maintained at no little cost to myself over the years, I must remind you.'

'I'm sorry,' said Steven and meant it. He knew very well how often Macmillan had gone to war within government to keep Sci-Med free of the influence of other bodies. It was also widely believed to be the reason why he was still plain 'Mr' instead of 'Sir John'.

'The minister was responding to my earlier request for information,' said Macmillan. 'During his time at Porton Down, George Sebring was assigned to a research group who were working on a vaccine against AIDS. Sebring was an expert on the antigenicity of viral proteins, whatever that means.'

'Antigens stimulate the production of antibodies in the body,' said Steven. 'If you can separate out a few key proteins from a virus you can stimulate the production of antibodies against them which in turn will attack the whole virus.'

'Thank you,' said Macmillan.

Steven thought for a moment before saying, 'But Sebring had a nervous breakdown.'

'What's your point?' asked Macmillan, seeing that nothing more was forthcoming.

'Working on a vaccine against AIDS is going

131

to get you a round of applause in any company,' said Steven. 'Possibly even a Blue Peter badge and a front-row seat in heaven. Why on earth should he have a nervous breakdown while he was engaged on something so noble? Why should he suddenly decide he had to up sticks and work elsewhere?'

'Well, who's to say,' said Macmillan, looking down at his desk as if forced to agree but unwilling to acknowledge the fact. 'There may have been other factors going on in his life at the time, things we don't know about.'

'And we can't ask him now because somebody murdered him to keep his mouth shut,' said Steven.

'I don't believe the Defence Secretary was lying,' said Macmillan.

'I'm not suggesting that he was,' said Steven. 'But he may have been "advised" wrongly. We both know that cabinet ministers are at the mercy of career civil servants when it comes to getting information. There's a lot they don't know and a lot perhaps—when it suits them—they don't even want to know.'

Macmillan appeared to concede the point. 'So what do you want to do?'

'I don't suppose the minister said who the other members of Sebring's group at Porton were?' asked Steven.

'Only that it was led by a chap named Dr Donald Crowe,' replied Macmillan. When he

132

saw a slight smile appear on Stevens face he added, 'Did I say something amusing?'

Steven said, 'Crowe turned up at Sebring's funeral. Sebring's wife told me he was there to make sure that Sebring hadn't left anything about his work at Porton lying around.' He added, 'I suppose you wouldn't want any important information about a vaccine left lying around . . .'

'I think you've made your point,' said Macmillan.

Steven took a sip of his coffee before asking, 'Did you ask the minister about the 1st Field Laboratory Unit?'

'It doesn't exist,' said Macmillan.

Steven replaced his cup in the saucer. 'Really?' he said.

'But he concedes that it did,' continued Macmillan. 'Apparently it was conceived as long ago as the First World War but was then disbanded until the time of the Gulf War when they re-commissioned it. It comprised a team of forty men who were used in teams of five to monitor the potential use of chemical and biological weapons. They were known officially as "The Secret Team". Each member was sworn to secrecy under the terms of the Official Secrets Act and it wasn't and isn't government policy to acknowledge their existence.'

'I don't suppose the minister explained why the government of the day ignored every report the unit ever made?' asked Steven.

'Indirectly, I think he did,' said Macmillan. 'A great deal of pressure was forthcoming from our American allies at the time. Because of that it was decided that Saddam's use of CB weapons should be . . . underplayed, I think was the minister's word.'

'Because the Americans had supplied them to him?'

'Regrettably and embarrassingly, yes.'

'That fits with what I've heard,' said Steven. 'Angus Maclean, the Scotsman who called on Sebring before his death, maintains he was a member of the unit although, of course, the MOD denies it.'

'Well, it was a secret organisation,' said Macmillan. 'By rights he could be prosecuted under the act for even revealing that fact.'

'I think that's why he keeps telling people,' said Steven. 'He wants to be prosecuted so he could say what he has to say in open court. He's convinced that his wife and daughter are dead because of something that Porton did, something that Sebring was involved in, something that Sebring may even have confessed to Martin Hendry.'

'I see you're determined to get your teeth into this,' said Macmillan.

'Code-red?' asked Steven.

'Code-green,' replied Macmillan, giving his assent. 'Be careful and keep me informed.'

Steven left the Home Office and walked

down to the river to enjoy what remained of the afternoon sunshine. He was pleased that he had been given the go-ahead but with Sebring and Hendry both dead it was difficult to see how he should proceed. The only other name he had was that of Donald Crowe, who had been head of Sebring's group at Porton and who still worked there. It didn't seem at all likely that Crowe was going to admit to anything illegal, immoral or embarrassing when his sole purpose in attending Sebring's funeral had been to make sure that nothing had been left lying around.

He supposed it was still possible that Jane Sebring might know more than she'd told him or that Martin Hendry had left a copy of his story or maybe some notes at another location—his home in Manchester, for instance. As for the other members of the group, they might be a better bet than Crowe but they would still be subject to the Official Secrets Act. Apart from that he didn't know their names and suspected that Crowe might be less than helpful should he request them. Doing that would also alert the establishment to what he was up to and that might be a bad idea in the present circumstances. It occurred to him that Gus Maclean might know who the other group members were. He might even have spoken to them in his personal quest to discover the truth. Maclean would be an unofficial source and he was certainly no

135

friend of the establishment. He settled on the idea of asking Maclean.

Steven decided that he would travel north in stages. First he would pay another call on Jane Sebring: she had already been helpful in putting him on to Martin Hendry. He also had an excuse for doing so because he had promised to keep her informed about how he was getting on. If he didn't learn any more from her he would go to Manchester to investigate Martin Hendry's home circumstances. He would ask Sci-Med to find out his address, marital status and so on and get them to arrange with the Manchester police for a search warrant. If he still hadn't come up with anything after that, he would go back to Glasgow to speak to Gus Maclean again.

A Thames river launch, water creaming from its bow and crowded with laughing tourists, passed by as he paused for a moment to look at the river. Three girls standing near the stern, dressed in summer frocks and straw hats, waved to him and he waved back. It made them giggle and made him think how happy and carefree they looked. He felt envious.

Contentment was a state of mind that had moved beyond his grasp since Lisa's death and reminders of this had a habit of popping up at odd moments, whether in observing the lives of others or seeing the girls on the boat.

But was it really because of Lisa's death that

he felt this way, he wondered as he looked down at the muddy water. If he were being honest he would have to admit to being the type of person who, when he was here, wanted to be there, and when he was there, wanted to be here. His time with Lisa may have provided a respite from this because he had been truly happy with her, but his restless side had always been present. It had just resurfaced after her death. There was no real fundamental reason for it; it was just the way he was.

Coming close to death on a number of occasions had encouraged him to adopt a live-for-today policy rather than one based on any long-term plans but he'd come to recognise that this had more merit as an excuse than a philosophy. Tomorrow wouldn't always take care of itself and he had a daughter to consider. He'd done his best to take this responsibility seriously in recent times: he would now think twice before putting himself in dangerous situations, reminding himself that Jenny would benefit more from having a living father than a dead hero to remember.

He phoned his daughter twice a week to be updated with what she was doing and tried to get up to Scotland as often as he could to take her out and about. But despite this, he knew in his heart that she had come to regard his sister-in-law, Sue, and her husband, Richard, as her real parents. This was no bad thing for Jenny because she was obviously a perfectly happy little girl but it had left him with feelings of regret over what might have been.

Steven had had enough of self-analysis. What he wanted right now was a beer. He would have a pint of Guinness at a riverside pub and start thinking about more practical matters.

Redford Mansions
South Kensington
London

'I thought you weren't coming,' said Donald Crowe. 'It's almost midnight.'

'Just taking precautions,' replied Cecil Mowbray. 'It's probably just professional paranoia but I thought I was being followed when I left the flat.'

Crowe looked alarmed but Mowbray waved away his concern. 'I've been in the business too long,' he said. 'I like to err on the side of caution. I moved back and forth across the city changing taxis until I was quite sure there wasn't a problem.'

'Why should anyone want to follow you?' asked Crowe.

'No reason at all,' replied Mowbray, looking Crowe in the eye. 'Unless of course, you know different?'

'I haven't said anything to anyone,' said Crowe, hearing accusation in what Mowbray had said.

'But?' asked Mowbray, thinking he detected a slight hesitation in Crowe's voice.

'A man named Steven Dunbar turned up at George Sebring's funeral,' said Crowe. 'He steered clear of me but I knew him. He's an investigator with the Sci-Med Inspectorate. He's sent stuff to Porton for analysis in the past and even asked for advice on occasion although not from me personally.'

'I don't think we should read too much into it,' said Mowbray. 'Sci-Med's computer would have picked up on the fact that Sebring had been murdered and that he'd worked at Porton Down at one time in his career. Actually, that murder verdict was down to a bit of bad luck: any other pathologist would have been happy to put it down as suicide.'

'What about Sebring talking to that journalist?' said Crowe.

'I don't think Sci-Med know anything about that,' said Mowbray.

'How did *you* find out about it?' said Crowe.

'His phone,' said Mowbray. 'We've been keeping tabs on all the Beta team since the papers broke the story about government plans to use up the old vaccine.'

'Sci-Med asked the MOD about Sebring's work at Porton,' said Crowe. 'The MOD got on to our director and he asked me to respond.'

'As it should be,' smiled Mowbray. 'I take it you told him he was working on a vaccine

139

against AIDS?'

Crowe nodded. 'Of course.'

'No need to worry then,' said Mowbray. 'I had lunch with Everley yesterday. He's getting restless: thinks we're not keeping him in the picture.'

'He makes me nervous,' said Crowe. 'I'm still not sure asking him was a good idea.'

'We needed his money,' said Mowbray. 'But I know what you mean. I don't see him as a problem. He's a type. He's made a mint in business and then discovered money wasn't enough; he wants power; he wants public recognition. He's deeply in love with himself and wants others to share his fascination. He'd give his eye teeth to become an MP and probably his balls to become a minister. He sees us as his best chance.'

'Why do you think he failed before? A three time loser, isn't he?'

'The party kept putting him up for seats he couldn't possibly win,' said Mowbray. 'I think they had reservations about him too but like us, they saw the attraction of his cash.'

'He's going to expect a return on his investment this time,' said Crowe.

'True,' agreed Mowbray. 'I've done my best to convince him that he's going to finish up as the honourable member for somewhere or other but if he starts being a problem he has more skeletons in the cupboard than a medical school—and I've got the negatives.'

'You have a file on him?'

'Are you serious?' said Mowbray. 'A multi-millionaire businessman with political ambitions? We've got a small novel.'

'Well, you seem to have thought of everything,' said Crowe.

'How are things with you?'

'I've been in touch with a few names on the group database and they've given me the information I need to make final plans. It's looking good.'

'Excellent.'

'I don't suppose you caught *Newsnight*?' asked Crowe.

'I was in a taxi,' Mowbray reminded him. 'Why?'

'The government have given in to demands that old military vaccine stocks should be destroyed. The troops will be given all new stuff.'

'Only right,' smiled Mowbray.

CHAPTER NINE

Steven called Jane Sebring from home and asked if he could come and see her on the following day.

'You've seen Martin Hendry?'

'Yes.'

'Did he tell you anything?'

'He couldn't; he was dead.'

'Oh my God. How? What happened?'

'It looked like suicide,' said Steven, thinking that this really wasn't a lie. It did. The Scottish police, as far as he knew, had not yet stated that they were treating Hendry's death as murder so he couldn't openly suggest otherwise. He had an ulterior motive in that he had no wish to scare Jane Sebring into silence by telling her that another person had been murdered over something her husband had been involved in.

'So you are no further forward in finding out who killed George or why?' said Jane.

'I'm afraid not.'

'Then I don't understand why you want to see me again,' said Jane.

'I just thought if we talked for a while you might remember something that you hadn't thought of as being important before,' said Steven.

'You're driving up from London?'

'Yes.'

'Come for lunch.'

Steven thanked her and agreed to be there by one o'clock. As he put down the phone, he found that he was very much looking forward to seeing Jane Sebring again.

*   *   *

The woman whom Steven remembered

142

dressed in black and behaving with such poise and dignity at her husband's funeral opened the door wearing jeans, sandals and a halter neck blouse. Her long fair hair was hanging loose and she pushed it away from her face as she said, 'The bloody cat's just been sick on the floor. Come on in; I'll be with you in a moment. Help yourself to a drink.'

Steven was left alone in the room they had all been in after Sebring's funeral. It seemed much bigger now that it was empty of mourners and smelt of leather and furniture polish rather than the heady mix of perfume and flowers. There was a tray sitting on a walnut dresser with a number of drinks bottles on it so he poured himself a gin and tonic. He considered shouting through to ask if his hostess would like something but, as he couldn't hear any nearby sounds, he decided that she was probably out of earshot. He sipped his drink and looked out at the garden where he had walked and talked with Sebring's mother.

'Sorry about that,' said Jane as she returned. 'It's dry food for Moggie from now on. He can turn up his nose all he wants to but that's what he's getting. Nice to see you again.'

'You too,' said Steven, shaking hands with her.

'I thought we might eat outside,' said Jane. 'It would be a shame to waste a day like this. What d'you think?'

'Sounds good,' said Steven.

'You can either wait here or give me a hand in the kitchen. What would you prefer?'

'I'll help but I warn you, I know nothing about cooking,' said Steven. He followed Jane through the house to a bright, modern kitchen with open patio doors leading out into the back garden.

'We're having lasagne and salad,' said Jane. 'You can do the dressing.'

'I wouldn't know where to begin,' said Steven.

'You'll find a small bowl in that cupboard above the sink,' said Jane with a wave of her hand, clearly used to taking charge. 'You'll find balsamic vinegar and virgin olive oil among these bottles on the island.'

'Now what?' asked Steven after finding them.

'Two tablespoons of each into the bowl and mix thoroughly. When you're happy with it, drizzle it over the salad.' She pushed a large bowl of salad towards him. 'That's all there is to it. Easy huh?'

'Absolutely,' agreed Steven, feeling absurdly pleased to have mastered a new skill.

'If you take it outside, I'll bring out the lasagne,' said Jane, putting on oven gloves and bending down to open the door of the Aga.

'Yes ma'am,' said Steven, taking the bowl outside and putting it down in the middle of the round wooden table sitting on the patio.

'We'll need knives and forks,' Jane called to him from inside. 'Third drawer from the end on your left as you come in.' She made another vague gesture with her arm. Steven collected the cutlery and returned to set the table.

'Well done,' said Jane with a smile as she arrived carrying the lasagne.

'Why, thank you,' said Steven slightly tongue in cheek.

'Oh dear, you think I'm bossy, don't you?' said Jane.

'Yes,' replied Steven matter-of-factly.

'Sorry,' said Jane with a grin.

'I'm not complaining,' Steven smiled back.

'I'm a teacher,' said Jane. 'I tend to treat everyone like class 4b.'

'What do you teach?'

'English. This salad dressing is perfect by the way,' said Jane, picking up a piece of lettuce with her fingers and popping it in her mouth. 'You're a natural.'

Steven laughed out loud and pointed out that he had only mixed A plus B as directed.

'That's probably enough to get your own TV show these days,' said Jane. 'How come you never learned to cook?'

'Old fashioned family,' said Steven. 'Mum did all the cooking. I tried when I was at university but it always turned out a complete disaster so I tended to live on bacon and egg and beans and toast then I joined the army— so once again someone else did the cooking.'

145

'You were an army doctor?'

'Sort of.'

'What does that mean?'

'Field medicine.'

'Ah,' said Jane. 'You were an operational medic and you've no intention of telling me any more about your daring exploits. Right?'

'You could say.'

'Why is it the men I meet always have secrets to keep?' asked Jane.

'Maybe all men have secrets,' said Steven.

'You know what I mean,' said Jane. 'Real secrets, government secrets, military secrets.'

'I can see it must have been very difficult having a husband with a secret past,' said Steven.

'I don't know that difficult is the right word,' said Jane. 'But it was certainly something that was always there between us. I'd see his mood change and not know why but it was because he was thinking about something that I couldn't ask about, or if I did, something he couldn't tell me.'

'Maybe he should have,' said Steven.

'You clearly didn't know George,' said Jane.

'No I didn't,' said Steven. 'Tell me about him.'

'George was an everything-by-the-book sort of a man. Rules and regulations were the cornerstones of his life,' said Jane. 'A more honest, dependable, loyal, dutiful employee never walked this earth. If George's superiors

146

said something was secret then George would carry that secret with him to the grave.' Jane winced at her own mention of the word grave as if she'd suddenly realised that that was exactly where George was.

Steven was afraid that she might change the subject so he said, 'But he did decide to talk to Martin Hendry?'

'Yes he did,' agreed Jane distantly. 'After all these years and all that his damned past had done to us he finally chose a complete stranger to unburden himself to. A certain irony there, don't you think?' She paused and re-charged Steven's wine glass before pouring what remained of the bottle of Riesling into her own.

'Pudding?' she asked.

'Er, yes,' said Steven, unprepared for Jane's sudden change from wistfulness to concerned hostess.

'I've made a lemon tart and, although I say it myself, it is spectacular,' she said, getting up from the table and disappearing inside. She returned with two large portions of lemon tart and a jug of cream.

'You weren't joking!' exclaimed Steven as he tried a mouthful. 'This is wonderful!'

'Told you,' said Jane, making him smile.

When they'd both finished, Jane suggested that it might be more comfortable if they sat on the garden swing—a chintz-covered couch mounted on a metal swinging frame beneath a

147

canopy of the same material and positioned between two silver birch trees.

'That was a delicious lunch,' said Steven as he settled down on to it.

'I'm glad you enjoyed it,' said Jane, sitting down beside him. 'God, this weather's so nice,' she said, leaning back and closing her eyes. 'If only it was like this more often. I think we bought this swing two years ago and used it about four times in all.'

'Makes you appreciate it all the more when it happens,' said Steven. 'We'd get bored if it was like this all the time.'

'Do you really believe that?' asked Jane.

'No,' replied Steven and they both laughed.

'You mentioned something earlier about what George's secrets had done to you?' Steven said gently. 'What did you mean by that?'

Jane kept her eyes closed and remained silent for a few moments. Steven watched the sunlight flicker on her eyelids as the swing moved slowly to and fro. He suspected she was considering whether she should say any more or not.

'When I first met George he told me that he'd worked at Porton Down some years before—I must say I hadn't even heard of the place at the time—and that he'd suffered a nervous breakdown. He told me that he'd recovered but that he was prone to bouts of depression. I felt it was no big deal and

148

thought I knew what to expect. I suppose like all women in love I thought I could change things. I could make him happy and everything would be fine but, of course, I couldn't and it wasn't. George was moody: he had nightmares. He couldn't—or wouldn't—tell me why or what about so I just had to assume that it had something to do with his secret past. Gradually he lost interest in . . . well, in the physical side of our married life so we ended up having separate bedrooms.'

'I see,' said Steven.

'Don't get me wrong, George was the kindest, most gentle man when he was well and we loved each other . . . in our own way; a bit like brother and sister I suppose in the last few years.'

'You were going to adopt a child,' said Steven.

'We thought—I thought—it might help.'

'Compensate for not having any of your own?'

'I suppose. The frustrating thing for me was that there was nothing physically wrong with George. It was all psychosomatic. He just seemed to be on the mother and father of all guilt trips. He could just never relax enough to . . .'

'Make love to you?' said Steven softly, turning his head to look at Jane's closed eyes. She opened them and turned to face him. 'Yes,' she said.

At that moment every other thought in Steven's head gave way to an overwhelming desire to kiss Jane Sebring and he did, very gently. It was every bit as beautiful as he thought it might be, her mouth was warm and inviting and the fact that she did not draw away made it all the more exciting.

'I always knew drinking at lunch time was a bad idea,' said Jane as they moved apart.

Steven kissed the side of her neck.

'This is silly,' murmured Jane. 'I hardly know you . . . and George has only been dead for . . .'

'Several years by the sound of it,' said Steven. 'That was sheer selfishness on his part. He shouldn't have made his guilt yours. You are a beautiful woman; it's a perfect summer's day and my only secret is that I want to make love to you.'

'The really awful thing,' murmured Jane as Steven continued to kiss her neck and run his tongue across her ear lobe, 'is that I want you to.'

'Upstairs?'

After a moment's hesitation, Jane took Steven by the hand and led him up to her bedroom where sunshine was streaming in through the open window and the smell of fresh linen and newly-mown grass was heavy in the air. She lay down on the bed and turned to look at him, the look in her eyes giving him all the invitation he needed. He knelt astride her

150

and removed her jeans and top before taking off his own clothes. He lay down beside her to run his hands over the curves of her body while his mouth sought hers. He unhooked her bra and moved down on her to suck on her nipples and tease them with his tongue, becoming increasingly aroused by the groans of pleasure that were coming from her.

Jane reached down and took his erect penis in her hands. She altered position to take it into her mouth and it was Steven's turn to gasp with pleasure. He caught a glimpse of dust motes dancing in a sunbeam as he turned his head on the pillow, willing the minutes to become hours. Jane released him and swung her right leg over his to sit up astride him and look down at him. 'I told you, I'm used to being in charge,' she said.

'We'll see,' replied Steven, gripping her buttocks firmly and pulling her up higher on him. She laughed and reached behind her to grip his penis with both hands while he cupped both her breasts in his hands and squeezed.

'God, you really are beautiful,' he murmured.

'Why thank you, kind sir,' said Jane.

Steven brought Jane up on him until she was sitting on his chest. She was still wearing her panties so he moved the silky crotch to one side to seek out her clit with his tongue.

'Oh sweet Jesus,' murmured Jane, reaching out in front of her with the palms of her hands

151

to steady herself against the wall. 'That is . . . is . . . bloody wonderful.'

At length Jane, sweat running down her face and breathing heavily, looked down at Steven and said, 'Much as I'm learning to love your tongue, I think something more substantial is called for.' She rolled over and spread her legs, taking Steven's penis in her hand and guiding him into her as he rolled on top.

'Now that is good,' she gasped as he filled her up. 'Very good.'

'Bloody wonderful,' murmured Steven, thrusting into her in a slow rhythmic grind.

'I'm going to feel so guilty . . .'

'Fuck feeling guilty,' whispered Steven.

'No . . . fuck me,' gasped Jane.

At length and without withdrawing from her, Steven reached down and pulled Jane's left leg across between them so that she was turned onto her right shoulder.

'What are you doing?' she giggled.

'Something I always do to bossy women,' he replied. 'Fuck them sideways.'

Jane giggled.

*   *   *

As they lay together in complete calm with the birds singing outside in the garden and the leaves rustling in the soft summer breeze that played with the curtains, Jane whispered,

'That was outrageous.'

'Was it that bad?' murmured Steven.

'Don't be obtuse,' said Jane, poking him in the ribs. 'You know damn well it wasn't. But now comes the guilt. We really shouldn't have.'

'Don't look forward and don't look back. Live life as it happens.'

'A philosopher,' said Jane.

'More disillusioned realist,' said Steven.

Jane rolled on to her front and traced circles on Steven's chest with her forefinger. 'Well, Dr Dunbar, I suppose your interview is now at an end?'

'Do you want it to be?'

'No,' said Jane softly.

'Then let's shower, dress, go walk in the sunshine and find a place by a river that'll serve us strawberries and cream under a weeping willow.'

Jane looked at Steven's smiling face and recited wistfully, 'When he came in she was there. When she looked at him, he smiled. There were lights in time's wave breaking on an eternal shore . . .'

Steven ran his fingers gently through her hair.

'Bet you don't know who wrote that?' said Jane.

Steven looked at her as if he were about to agree then he said, 'There were fathoms in her too, and sometimes he crossed them and landed and was not repulsed.'

153

'Oh my God,' exclaimed Jane, resting her head on Steven's chest. 'A literate lover. Now I know there is a God.'

Jane returned from the shower with a white towel wrapped round her. It emphasised her smooth, tanned shoulders. She was carrying another towel, which she tossed to Steven saying, 'Your turn.'

When he returned Jane had put on a summer frock and was trying on a large brimmed sun hat. He thought she looked like a figure from a French impressionist painting.

'What d'you think?' she asked. 'Over the top?'

'Beautiful,' he replied, coming towards her and circling his arms round her from behind.

'We've done that bit,' she said, holding up her hands. 'If we start that again we're never going to get out of here.'

'Would that be so bad?' said Steven, coming closer.

'No,' murmured Jane. 'But I do love strawberries . . .'

*   *   *

It was well after six in the evening before they got back to the house. 'That was a wonderful afternoon,' sighed Jane as she slumped down into a chair and kicked her shoes off.

'I enjoyed it too,' said Steven, sitting down opposite her and smiling at the way she was

154

sitting in the chair, arms and legs akimbo. 'If 4b could only see you now.'

'Bugger 4b,' replied Jane, looking up at the ceiling. 'What now, Prince Charming?'

'We sit in the garden with our eyes closed and listen to the birds herald the end of the day, then we shower, get changed and go out to dinner at a good restaurant, which you will choose. We'll sip chilled wine from crystal glasses and tell each other things that we've never told anyone else before.'

'Before your regiment marches at dawn . . .' said Jane.

'No regiment,' said Steven.

'Oh day that I have loved . . .' said Jane.

*   *   *

The sky was overcast next morning and there was a threat of rain in the air. It seemed to match their mood as they sat together having breakfast in the kitchen. The looks that passed between them said more than the small talk.

'So how will you go about finding out what George worked on at Porton?' asked Jane.

'I already know,' replied Steven. 'At least I know the official version.'

'You do?' said Jane, sounding surprised.

'He and the team he was assigned to were working on a vaccine against the HIV virus. That's what the Ministry of Defence told my boss.'

155

'A vaccine?' said Jane. 'Why would anyone have nightmares about making a vaccine?'

'My thoughts too,' said Steven.

'Then you don't believe them?'

'Not a word of it.'

'So what can you do?' asked Jane.

'I know you think it was Gus Maclean's visit that pushed your husband over the edge and into making contact with the press but I've spoken to Maclean about that and he seemed to think your husband was already uptight about something when he arrived. He agrees his visit might have made things worse but he doesn't think he was the root cause of the problem.'

'I just remember it as being one shit awful day,' said Jane. 'Maybe Maclean's right. It's possible that George was having one of his days.'

'This is really important,' said Steven. 'If something else happened to upset your husband that day, I have to know about it.'

'I can understand that,' said Jane, trying to think back. 'But it's hard to think what. He didn't go out at all and no one else came to the house that day before Maclean.'

'No telephone calls?'

'None that I remember.'

'E-mail?'

'He always picked these up in his office at the university and the postman just brought a couple of bills I think. I remember he was

156

absolutely fine at breakfast. He planned to spend the day marking essays at home. I had the day off because I had been supervising a school trip the previous weekend so we thought we'd have lunch together at the local pub. When the paper-boy brought the morning paper I remember he made a joke about reading some facts before changing to fiction. He was sitting reading the paper and drinking coffee at the kitchen table when I left to go down to the local shops for some odds and ends.'

'So you went out?' said Steven.

'Only for ten minutes or so,' said Jane, then she added more thoughtfully, 'But you're right. I remember it now. His mood had changed when I got back from the shops. I asked him if he was feeling all right because he seemed very pale but he said it was nothing and went off to his study to start his marking.'

'Did you go out to lunch as planned?' asked Steven.

'No we didn't, come to think of it,' said Jane. 'When I asked him about it he said he'd changed his mind and didn't feel like it after all.'

'It was the paper,' said Steven.

'The paper?'

'Something he read in the paper upset him,' said Steven. 'You said he was reading the paper when you left.'

'But what?' said Jane.

'Can you remember the date?' asked Steven.

'It would be . . . Monday the 28th,' said Jane.

'Time for a trip to the local library,' said Steven. 'What paper do you get?'

'The *Guardian*.'

'Want to come?'

'Of course, this is fascinating.'

Jane gave Steven directions and they drove to the nearest public library where Steven used their computer reference facility to access back issues of the *Guardian*. He brought up the edition for June 28th and after a few moments said, 'There it is. It has to be this.' He read out, 'Gulf War Veterans slam Ministry of Defence over plans to use up old vaccine stocks.' He paused to read it fully before saying, 'The government were planning to use up old stocks of vaccine on the troops being put on alert for a new conflict in the Gulf. The veterans' associations are up in arms because they believe that the vaccines were faulty in some way.'

'Do you think one of them could have been the vaccine that George was supposed to have been working on?' asked Jane.

Steven said not. 'There would be no call to vaccinate the troops against AIDS,' he said. 'Apart from that, no one's succeeded in coming up with such a vaccine as yet. The troops would be given the WHO recommended

158

vaccines for the region: they would also be given protection against bacteria and viruses likely to be used as weapons—anthrax, plague and the like.'

'So why should a story about using up old vaccine stocks have George running to the newspapers after keeping quiet for twelve years?'

'Good question,' murmured Steven. 'But I'm pretty sure that it did.'

'I suppose this would fit with the phone calls I heard George making immediately after Maclean's visit,' said Jane. 'He kept asking the people he was calling why the government were doing something that he clearly thought they shouldn't. He seemed to be getting more and more angry and frustrated about it all,' said Jane.

'This was before he called Martin Hendry at the *Guardian*?'

'Yes.'

'So George clearly did think that using old vaccine stocks was a bad idea.'

'Surely it must have been something more than that to have made him go to the papers,' said Jane.

'A *very* bad idea?' suggested Steven.

'But why?' said Jane.

'Why indeed?'

CHAPTER TEN

'What do you think?' asked Jane as they drove back to her house.

'I think the vets' associations were probably right. There was something wrong with the vaccine and George knew it. But if that were the case why would the government even consider using it again?'

'Maybe they didn't know?' suggested Jane.

'Now there's a thought,' said Steven. 'The government didn't know but your husband and Donald Crowe did?' After a few moments he dismissed the idea. 'But they were a research outfit; they wouldn't have had anything to do with anything the troops were being given.'

'Maybe they really were trying to design a new vaccine and wanted to try it out on the troops?' suggested Jane.

'Giving soldiers an untried and untested vaccine along with other inoculations, you mean? Highly unethical,' said Steven.

'Might explain George's nightmares,' said Jane as they swung into the drive. 'Especially if there was something wrong with it?' she added.

Steven shook his head and said, 'Even if that were true and they had experimented with a new vaccine there would be no question of them doing the same thing all over again

160

almost twelve years later, so why was George so alarmed at the story in the paper?'

'There must have been something wrong with one of the other vaccines,' said Jane.

'That only George and the research team knew about?' added Steven.

'Yes,' said Jane.

Steven thought then shook his head again. 'We're still not there,' he said. 'Doubts about the vaccines the troops were given have been expressed many times,' he continued. 'They must have been subjected to the most rigorous scrutiny over the years and nothing has ever been found to be wrong with them.'

'Mmm,' said Jane.

'On the other hand . . .' Steven paused as he thought about Gus Maclean and his efforts to find the cause of his illness and the thing which, according to him, had caused the death of his wife and daughter. He'd come up with nothing but his conviction remained undimmed. 'I wonder,' he said.

'You're having second thoughts?' asked Jane.

'I was just thinking that there's no evidence for life anywhere else in the universe but that doesn't mean to say . . .'

'That there isn't any,' said Jane.

'Right. It just means that we haven't found any.'

'So you think it's possible that there was something wrong but they just haven't yet

161

found out what?' said Jane.

'I have to phone Sci-Med,' Steven said.

'I'll make some coffee,' said Jane, leaving Steven alone.

Steven used his mobile and had to wait a few moments to be put through to the admin officer assigned to his case.

'I've got some news for you,' said a woman with a pleasant Irish accent who introduced herself as Maureen Kelly when she came on the line. 'Someone re-formatted the hard disk on the laptop you left with us. We couldn't retrieve any files, I'm afraid.'

'I feared as much,' said Steven. 'Any news from the Scottish Police about the post mortem on Martin Hendry?'

'Strangely, they still seem to be treating his death as suicide. What do you want to do about that?'

'Nothing at the moment,' replied Steven.

'You're sure it was murder?'

'There were slight marks on his wrists consistent with having been tied up,' replied Steven.

'Maybe the pathologist put them down to something else?'

'Or maybe someone leaned on the pathologist,' said Steven.

'As a matter of interest, did you find any software for the laptop in Hendry's cabin?' asked Kelly.

'No, why?' asked Steven.

'When the killer re-formatted the disk, he or she would have wiped everything off it—including the standard software—and yet it had Windows XP and Microsoft Office on it, and appeared to be a normal laptop that just hadn't been used for anything recently.'

Steven saw what the girl was getting at. 'You mean the killer must have re-installed the software to hide the fact the disk had been wiped—and therefore the motive for murder?' he said.

'And then removed the software disks along with the ZIP disk you said was missing. If it's of any use we can tell the exact date and time they carried out the re-install procedure. Maybe the police would be interested in that.' The comment sounded like a mild rebuke.

'I'd rather you didn't tell them for the moment,' said Steven. 'It suits me to have the opposition think that I know less than I do.'

'It's your call.'

'Did you get the stuff on Martin Hendry I asked for?'

Kelly read out an address in Manchester and Steven wrote it down.

'He lives—lived—with his partner, a girl named Lesley Holland. The Manchester police have been informed of our interest. They've arranged for a search warrant to be made available to you if you request it. Anything else?'

'I need to talk to someone at Porton Down

about the vaccines used on Gulf War troops.'

'Last time or this time?'

'Last time, and not some PR person; I need to speak to someone who knows what they're talking about.'

Steven found Jane sitting at the kitchen table. He sat down opposite and she poured out his coffee without making eye contact. He thought she seemed quiet and said so.

'I was just thinking,' she began hesitantly. 'If George was murdered because he was going to tell all about this vaccine business, surely it must mean that . . .' She paused as if having difficulty saying it. 'That the government were responsible for his death?' Her eyes were now as wide as saucers.

'Scary thought,' said Steven.

'You're supposed to say, "No, Jane, that's ridiculous."'

'No, Jane, that's ridiculous,' said Steven in a flat monotone.

Jane looked at him and said in a small quiet voice, 'But it isn't, is it?'

'There's a level of government that operates without the knowledge of government,' said Steven.

'What on earth does that mean?' demanded Jane.

'I only discovered this myself when I came up against it a couple of years ago.'

'They tried to kill you?'

'"They" did but who "they" actually were is

still a matter of some conjecture,' said Steven.

'I don't think I understand,' said Jane.

'Let's see,' said Steven. 'It goes something like this. Man A at the top tells man B—a subordinate—that he has a problem. Man B tells man C and man C says he'll see what he can do. Man C mentions it to man D who in turn employs man E, whom none of the others have ever heard of or he of them, to solve the problem on the understanding that if anything goes wrong he's on his own. Man E does the job and is paid from slush funds. The problem goes away and man A at the top is very happy but, of course, has no idea how it all came about.'

Jane looked aghast. 'But that is immoral in the extreme!' she exclaimed.

'Moral is not an adjective that often finds itself beside government,' said Steven.

'So you think that some man E killed George?'

'It's possible,' said Steven. 'But it could have been a disaffected Gulf War veteran out for revenge. There are plenty of them out there.' He did not mention that the murder of Martin Hendry had more or less ruled out that possibility.

Jane shivered slightly and said, 'I know this sounds silly and I feel ashamed to say it but I'm frightened. I feel really scared. I just want it all to stop. I just want to get on with my life. I need all this to go away.'

165

Steven took both her hands in his and squeezed gently. 'Does that mean you want me out of your life too?' he asked.

Jane looked as if she were fighting an inner conflict. She took a moment to steady herself before saying, 'You are part of this . . . nightmare. But no, if I have a choice, I don't think I do want to lose you.'

Steven kissed her hands. 'Good,' he said. 'Because there's no way I'm going to go voluntarily.'

A tear ran down Jane's cheek and she wiped it away angrily as if seeing it as a sign of weakness. 'Promise me you won't lie to me,' she said. 'Promise me you'll tell me everything you're doing and exactly what's going on at all times?'

Steven looked doubtful.

'Promise me?'

'If you're really sure that's what you want,' he said.

Jane nodded and said, 'Starting right now.'

'Very well,' said Steven. 'Martin Hendry did not commit suicide. The police don't seem to know it yet but he was murdered. All traces of the story he was working on were wiped from his computer and I think the story is the reason he was killed.'

Jane looked for a moment as if this might be a step too far but she recovered her composure and said, 'Man E again?'

'Looks like it,' said Steven.

'How will you find him?'

'I'm more interested in stopping him,' said Steven. 'I can only do that if I can find out what it is they've been covering up. Once that happens, the game's up. In the meantime the police can deal with the monkey; it's the organ grinder I'm after. I'm going up to Manchester to see if Hendry left anything lying around in his flat about what he was working on.'

'Please be careful,' said Jane.

'I'll call you.'

* * *

Steven was in Manchester by three. He had called the Manchester police before leaving Jane's to say that he was coming and that he would like the search warrant for Hendry's flat. He drove straight to police headquarters where he spoke with an officer who introduced himself as DI Lawrence.

'I don't suppose you're going to tell me what it is you're looking for?' said Lawrence.

'Anything that might be connected with my enquiry,' said Steven.

'Fair enough,' smiled Lawrence.

'I understand Hendry had a partner?' said Steven.

'I was the one who had to break the bad news to her,' said Lawrence, looking rueful. 'Nice kid.'

'Is she still living there?'

167

'As far as I know,' said Lawrence. 'We've had no occasion to go back.'

Steven accepted the warrant and said thanks.

'Need some uniforms?' asked Lawrence.

'I don't think so.'

There was no answer to his knock on the door of Hendry's apartment on the third floor of a modern block of flats about three miles from the city centre. After his third knock a neighbour, a woman in her seventies opened her door and volunteered, 'I don't think anyone's living there any more. Mr Hendry died recently.'

Steven turned to the elderly woman and said, 'Yes, I heard. It was very sad. It was actually Lesley I was looking for.'

'I think Lesley's gone too. She certainly wasn't here when the men from the gas board came the other day.'

'The gas board?'

'Apparently there was a gas leak and they had to gain access to the flat,' said the woman.

'Just this flat?' asked Steven, pointing to Hendry's front door.

'Yes,' replied the woman. 'Is something wrong?'

'No, no,' replied Steven, not wishing to alarm her. 'Tell me, how did they get in if Lesley wasn't at home?'

'Oh, they had a key,' replied the woman. 'They said the Gas Board had them for emergency use. I must say, they were very nice gentlemen, very polite, so different from so many people today.'

'Good to hear,' said Steven. 'Did they find the leak?'

'Oh yes,' replied the woman. 'They came and told me afterwards and said there was nothing for me to worry about. They had found the problem and fixed it.'

'Good show,' said Steven. 'I don't suppose you know where I could find Lesley, do you?'

'I'm afraid not,' said the woman, shaking her head. 'Although I do know that she's a teacher. She teaches at Green Street Primary, if that's any help. My granddaughter goes there: she says Lesley's a very kind teacher. It's so important for children to like their teachers, don't you think?'

Steven agreed that it was and thanked the woman for her help. He waited until she had closed her door before calling DI Lawrence. 'I should have taken up your offer of uniforms,' he said. 'I need a forced entry here.'

Steven was surprised when Lawrence himself turned up with two uniformed officers.

'Call me an interested observer,' he said. 'What exactly is the problem for the sake of the record?'

Steven told Lawrence about the supposed visit from the Gas Board. 'If they were from British Gas I'm from the planet Zog. They had a key, and a neighbour I spoke to hasn't seen

Hendry's partner for some time.'

Lawrence nodded to the two constables and they made short work of gaining entry. The noise of splintering wood brought the neighbour to her door again and Steven had to try to assure her that there was nothing for her to worry about.

'I thought the police would have had a key as well,' she said.

'We think that the men from the gas board weren't all that they seemed,' said Steven. 'The police think they should check out the flat just to make sure everything's all right.'

'I must say they've got a funny way of going about it,' replied the woman, eyeing the splintered door jamb with alarm.

'Don't you worry, madam,' said Lawrence. 'We'll make everything as good as new when we're finished here.'

'Please see that you do,' replied the woman, retreating indoors. 'I think I preferred the Gas Board men.'

Steven found pretty much what he expected to find when he walked through the flat. The 'Gas Board' men had gone through it with a fine-tooth comb. The contents of every drawer and cupboard had been tipped out on to the floor and even the floorboards had been taken up in several places.

'Workmen these days . . .' said Lawrence, tongue in cheek. 'Looks like someone beat you to it?'

170

'Afraid so,' said Steven. 'What worries me now is how they got the key. If no one has seen Hendry's partner for a while—'

'Oh dear,' sighed Lawrence. 'Do you think . . . ?'

'I think we'd better check it out,' said Steven. 'The neighbour says she's a teacher at Green Street Primary.'

Lawrence looked at his watch. 'The schools are on holiday. I'll try and get an address for her from the education authorities.'

Steven continued to look through the flat while Lawrence made his call. He always hated the feeling he got when circumstances forced him to intrude in other people's lives. He went through the motions of sifting through everything, but knowing full well that he was not going to find anything useful.

When Lawrence joined him he said, 'The authorities just have this address down in their records but I managed to contact the head teacher at Green Street and she told me that Lesley has been back staying with her parents since Martin Hendry died. Want to give it a try?'

Steven said that he did and Lawrence told the two uniformed men they were on their way to 21, Paxton Avenue. He told them to stay put until the flat had been made secure.

Steven and Lawrence presented their IDs to the man working in the front garden of the neat bungalow in Paxton Avenue. He looked like everyone's idea of a bank manager—short, plump, bald and bespectacled—so they were taken aback by his immediately aggressive response.

'Hasn't my daughter been through enough from you insensitive bastards?' the man demanded. 'She doesn't know anything about what Martin was doing or why he took his own life. Isn't that enough for her to cope with, for Christ's sake?'

'I'm sorry your daughter has been upset, Mr Holland,' said Steven. 'But we really do have to speak to her. It won't take long and we'll be gentle, I promise.'

Holland muttered something about dogs chasing their own tails as he tugged off his Wellington boots before going indoors in his diamond-patterned socks to go upstairs.

'Who is it, Sam?' inquired a woman's voice.

'The bloody police again for our Lesley,' replied Holland. 'No wonder they never catch any burglars.'

When Holland returned he was accompanied by a small fair-skinned girl with a bank of freckles across the bridge of her nose and upper cheeks and whose blonde hair was tied back with a pink ribbon. She looked as if she hadn't slept for some time. There was an expression in her eyes that was easy to read—fear.

'Miss Holland? I'm Dr Steven Dunbar,' said Steven gently. 'This is DI Lawrence. Is there

172

somewhere we can talk?'

A look of blank resignation crossed Lesley Holland's face as she indicated that the men should follow her inside.

'I don't know what Martin was writing about. I've told you people over and over again. I don't know,' said Lesley Holland as she sat perched on the edge of an armchair, hands clasped between her knees. 'You can threaten me all you want to but I can't tell you what I don't know.'

'Who threatened you, Miss Holland?' asked Steven.

'The two men from Special Branch, they said they knew perfectly well what Martin had been up to and that he must have told me all about it. They said I would be charged and go to prison for up to fourteen years if I didn't tell them everything. But I couldn't tell them. I didn't know anything. Martin was just doing what Martin did, working on a story. He didn't tell me anything about it but they wouldn't believe me. They just went on and on . . .'

'Did you give them the keys to your flat?' asked Steven.

Lesley nodded. 'They forced me to. I've been back staying with Mum and Dad since Martin died. They said they were going to search the flat and when they found what they were looking for they would be back to charge me formally. I wasn't to go anywhere.'

'But they never came back?'

Lesley shook her head. 'No. I thought maybe that's why you were here.' She looked at Steven pleadingly and said, 'I don't know anything. I didn't do anything.'

'I know Miss Holland and I'm very sorry you've been put through all this. There is no question of you being charged with anything and I apologise for the behaviour of my colleagues. They've left your flat in a bit of a mess I'm afraid but they won't be back. I'm deeply sorry about the loss of your partner. We'll leave you in peace now.'

As Steven and Lawrence walked back to the car Lawrence said, 'So does that make the Gas Board men Special Branch, d'you reckon?'

'You won't believe me but I'm not at all sure,' said Steven. 'I take it you've had no official word of Special Branch being on your patch?'

'Not a whisper. You're still not going to tell me what all this is about?' asked Lawrence.

'Afraid not.'

Steven left Manchester feeling as if his visit had been a waste of time. Martin Hendry's killers had obviously had the same idea about a possible copy of the story being at his flat and had beaten him to it. But at least they hadn't murdered Lesley Holland, presumably because she clearly knew nothing about what Hendry had been working on but she'd been badly scared. It had been his intention to drive on up to Glasgow if nothing came of his trip to

174

Manchester but thoughts of Jane had altered that. He called her and asked if he could come back to her place for the night.

'Why?' asked Jane.

'Because I want to.'

'Sounds like an excellent reason,' said Jane. 'I actually meant why are you coming back to Leicester when you said you'd be going on up to Glasgow?'

'I'll go tomorrow,' said Steven.

CHAPTER ELEVEN

The Chevalier Restaurant
Chelsea
London

Cecil Mowbray handed his coat to the hovering waiter without making eye contact with the man and sat down. 'What's the problem?' he asked.

Donald Crowe waited until the waiter had moved out of earshot before leaning over and saying, 'Sci-Med has started asking questions about Gulf War vaccines. They've requested a meeting with the powers that be at Porton. Dunbar's behind it. He must know something.'

'Relax,' said Mowbray. 'All the old vaccine stocks have been destroyed in response to the outcry from the veterans' associations. You can't investigate what does not exist any more. Can you?'

Crowe's silence conceded the point.

'But you're right about one thing; this is down to Dunbar,' said Mowbray. 'He does know more than we've been giving him credit for. He knows that Sebring was in touch with the journalist, Martin Hendry before he died.'

'How?'

'He went back to talk to Sebring's wife a few days after the funeral. It must have been her who told him.'

'But I spoke to her at length before the funeral,' said Crowe. 'She didn't tell me anything about that.'

'She must have found Dunbar more persuasive. In fact, she seems to have formed . . . an association with Dunbar.'

'Good God, her husband's only been dead a matter of weeks. What's the world coming to? Cheap tart.'

'Not for us to judge,' said Mowbray.

'God Almighty man, this means she could have been lying all along when she told me Sebring never talked about his past! Maybe he told her everything and now Dunbar knows too!' said Crowe.

'Possible but I think not,' replied Mowbray calmly. 'Dunbar turned up at Hendry's flat in Manchester looking for information. He talked to Hendry's girlfriend too but only after my people had made sure nothing

176

incriminating had been left lying around and that she couldn't tell him anything anyway. He wouldn't have done that if he already knew all there was to know, would he?'

'I suppose not,' agreed Crowe. 'But I worry about what he's going to do next.'

'He's going to Glasgow to talk to a Gulf War veteran named Angus Maclean,' said Mowbray.

'How on earth do you know that?'

'We still have the tap on Sebring's phone.'

'Well, thank God for that,' said Crowe. 'At least it gives us a slight edge. What can this man Maclean tell him?'

Mowbray shrugged and said, 'Absolutely nothing. He's a well-known Gulf War activist, a trouble-maker; full of wild theories but with nothing of any substance to back it up. Think Don Quixote and you won't be far wrong.'

'The name's vaguely familiar,' said Crowe.

'Maclean was trained at Porton. He was one of our Secret Team in the Gulf War,' said Mowbray. 'Maybe you came across him at the time.'

'I don't remember him but if that's the case maybe he knows more than you think?' said Crowe.

Mowbray shook his head. 'We've been keeping tabs on him for years. He's suffered the traditional fate of all long-term anti-government rebels; he's become part of the establishment. He'll probably end up with a gong in some New Year's honours list in the near future.'

'If you're sure,' said Crowe.

'Don't lose any sleep over it,' said Mowbray. 'Everything's fine. Just you concentrate on what you have to do. Any news?'

'Ready for final briefing in two weeks,' said Crowe.

'If you're sure keeping everything a secret until the last minute is still the best idea . . .?' said Mowbray.

'It is,' said Crowe. 'There's very little for your people to take on board. It's all very simple. What about Everley?'

'He's already up there, making friends and influencing people,' said Mowbray. 'Keeps him out the way.'

'Good.'

Leicester

It was after eleven before Steven got back to Jane's house. He was tired after a long day but any suggestion of fatigue disappeared when he saw her standing at the door.

'I'm glad you came back,' she said.

Steven took her in his arms and kissed her hungrily. 'You look wonderful,' he said.

'I thought we might have a late supper,' said Jane. She made a little movement with her head over her left shoulder.

Steven looked and saw the table set with a

bottle of wine sitting in an ice bucket and candles lit. 'Great idea,' he murmured, giving Jane's neck some serious attention. 'But first things first.'

'Would I be right in thinking you are considering an alternative order of priorities, Doctor?' murmured Jane.

'Clairvoyant too,' said Steven, leading her towards the stairs. Jane made to go up first but Steven, catching sight of her bottom, pulled her back into him and cupped his hands over her breasts. Jane responded by gyrating her bottom against him, giggling as she felt his hardness. 'At this rate,' she murmured, 'I fear we're not going to make it to the bedroom.'

'That . . . is a very real possibility,' said Steven as he hitched up Jane's dress over her hips and slipped his hand into her panties to find her already wet. 'God, I want you.'

'I'd never have guessed,' said Jane, reaching behind her to free Steven. 'The only question now, I suppose is geographical?'

'Right here, right now,' said Steven.

Jane bent forward to rest her hands on the stairs as Steven slipped her panties off and entered her from behind.

'You weren't kidding, were you?' she gasped.

When Steven finally withdrew he eased himself sideways to lie down beside her on the stairs, his face beaded with sweat. 'Bloody hell,' he gasped.

179

Jane smiled. 'Not quite the starter I was planning on,' she murmured. 'But nevertheless . . . very nice.'

Steven kissed her lightly on the forehead and said, 'I adore you.'

Jane put a finger on his lips and said, 'You hardly know me. Go shower while I go do things in the kitchen.'

Later as they sat talking and sipping coffee, Jane looked up at the clock and said, 'Look at the time. It's gone one o'clock. If you are planning on an early start in the morning . . .'

'Let's sit in the garden,' said Steven.

'What?'

'It's a warm night. Let's sit outside for a little while.'

Jane looked as if she had tried but failed to come up with an objection. 'All right,' she said. 'I don't think anyone's ever invited me into the garden in the middle of the night before.'

'You should never take summer nights for granted in England,' said Steven.

They sat together on the swing they'd sat on last time, Jane with her head resting on Steven's shoulder, the air heavy with the scent of honeysuckle and the sky above them studded with twinkling stars. 'Look, you can see the dagger in Orion's belt as clear as anything,' murmured Jane.

'A perfect night,' said Steven. 'Now, if only we could make time stand still.'

'But summer's lease hath all too short a

date,' said Jane.

'But thy eternal summer shall not fade,' said Steven squeezing her hand.

'If only,' said Jane.

Steven was about to set off for Glasgow in the morning when his phone rang. After a brief conversation he turned to Jane and said, 'Change of plan. That was Sci-Med. Porton have agreed to talk about vaccines. They've accepted an invitation to a meeting at the Home Office this afternoon. I'll have to go back to London.'

The Home Office
London

Steven was late in getting to the meeting, which was held in Macmillan's office. He apologised, citing a lorry shedding its load on the motorway as the reason, and Macmillan performed the introductions.

'Steven, this is Dr Robert De Fries. Dr De Fries acted as liaison officer between the Porton establishment and the army medical authorities over troop vaccinations before the Gulf War.'

Steven shook hands with a saturnine man who did not bother to smile and appeared to look past him.

'And this is Dr Jonathan Sked, deputy director of the Defence Establishment at Porton Down,' said Macmillan moving on to a

181

tall, angular man with a greying beard who had no problem with eye contact and whose firm handshake seemed reassuring. Steven sat down beside Macmillan to face both Porton men who also sat side by side with their briefcases at their feet.

Macmillan said, 'We're extremely grateful to you gentlemen for agreeing to meet us at such short notice.'

'Yes indeed,' echoed Steven. Flattery was always a good opening gambit.

'How can we help exactly?' asked Sked.

Macmillan nodded to Steven who began by saying, 'You may know, Doctors, that we've been looking into the death of Dr George Sebring, a former employee of yours. Although the police initially thought his death to be suicide, he was in fact, murdered and our investigation has thrown up the possibility that his killing was connected in some way with his time at the defence establishment and what he was working on there. You have told us that he was a member of a team working on the development of an AIDS vaccine but we suspect there is a link between his work and rumoured problems with the vaccinations given to the troops. We'd appreciate any help you can give us in understanding what that connection might be.'

'You are mistaken, Doctor,' said Sked. 'As a researcher, Dr Sebring would not have had anything to do with routine troop vaccinations.

182

He was employed as a viral protein specialist. This is something I checked out thoroughly with Dr Crowe, who was his team leader at the time. I did this when you people first asked about his work.'

'With respect, Doctor, I don't think the troop vaccinations were quite the routine matter you suggest,' said Steven. 'History records that it was extremely difficult to get any information at all out of Porton about what exactly the troops were given.'

Sked spread his hands in a gesture of concession. 'I admit there were problems in that certain components on the vaccination schedule were classified. This fact gave rise to rumour and counter rumour. You know how these things can get out of hand.'

'Perhaps Sebring worked on some classified aspect of the schedule that you don't feel at liberty to divulge?' suggested Steven.

'No,' said Sked firmly. 'It's not a case of hiding anything. As I said, I checked all this out with Dr Crowe.'

'Are these vaccine components still classified?' asked Steven.

Sked shook his head, 'No, all the vaccines were declassified by MOD at the end of 1996.'

'Can I ask what the classified vaccines were?'

'There were three: anthrax, pertussis and plague.'

'The Ministry said at the time that there

183

were five or six,' said Steven, referring to his notes.

'There was a misunderstanding,' said De Fries, speaking for the first time and interrupting what was shaping up to be an awkward pause. 'But I think I can cast some light on this. Our records show that cytokines were being incorporated into the vaccines given to the troops. This was actually the first time such technology had been used. It was believed that this would boost immune response, giving more effective protection to the troops. At one point, when the manufacturers reported that cytokines were running low, a request was put to Dr Crowe's team for a supply of HIV gene envelopes to be used as a substitute—it was thought that they would be just as good in stimulating a heightened immune response.'

'Dr Crowe didn't tell me that,' said Sked, sounding annoyed.

'It probably slipped his mind,' said De Fries. 'It was no big thing.'

'At least we have established a connection,' said Steven.

'Hardly that,' countered De Fries.

'I'm no expert,' said Steven, 'but wouldn't using HIV envelopes also suggest an attempt at providing some level of protection against the HIV virus itself?'

'At first glance, possibly,' said De Fries, 'but there was no such intent. As I say, their use in this case was to boost a general immune response.'

'There has never been any suggestion of anyone ever having contemplated the use of HIV as a weapon,' added Sked.

'Of course not,' said Steven dryly.

Macmillan shot him a warning glance and said pleasantly, 'I must admit I'm a little puzzled too about the use of these gene envelopes. If, as we know, Dr Crowe and his team were trying to develop a vaccine against AIDS then surely they might have been said to have had a vested interest in the outcome of the use of these gene envelopes on the troops?'

Sked bristled visibly and said, 'There is absolutely no question of anyone at Porton having experimented on the troops. Let's be absolutely clear about that.'

'Of course not,' said Macmillan. 'Well, it sounds as if we'll have to look elsewhere for the reason that George Sebring suffered a nervous breakdown and spent the remainder of his life suffering from chronic guilt and periodic nightmares.'

'I'm afraid you will,' said Dr Sked. 'There was nothing at all in his work at Porton to account for anything like that.'

'How about the other members of Dr Crowe's team?' asked Steven.

'What about them?'

'Their state of mind.'

185

'Dr Crowe himself has certainly never struck me as a man who had difficulty sleeping,' said Sked. 'Nor should he have any reason to.'

'Lowry and Rawlings are absolutely fine too,' said De Fries.

Steven remembered from the information supplied earlier by Porton, that there had actually been five people in the team led by Crowe. Mention had been made of four, Crowe, Lowry and Rawlings and Sebring who was, of course, dead. He was about to ask about the member who hadn't rated a mention when he thought better of it. It might have been an innocent omission but it just might have been deliberate, in which case he would try to mine the information from another source.

'Would you object if we had the vaccines that Crowe's team contributed to analysed independently?' asked Steven.

'Not possible, I'm afraid,' replied Sked coldly. 'We've just had to destroy all remaining stocks of it in response to press hysteria and recent objections.'

'From the Gulf War veterans' associations,' said De Fries.

'Her Majesty's Government were, naturally, sensitive to their concerns,' said Sked. 'Although this in no way implies that there was ever anything wrong with the vaccines.'

'Of course not,' said Macmillan.

'Surely there must still be a vial or two lying around?' said Steven.

'Everything was destroyed,' said De Fries. 'With respect, Doctor, I really must point out that these vaccines underwent several independent analyses over the past ten years. Nothing was ever shown to be wrong with them.'

'It was just a thought,' said Steven.

'What do you think?' Macmillan asked Steven when the others had gone.

'We've learned one thing,' said Steven. 'Crowe's team must really have been working with the HIV virus; otherwise they wouldn't have been able to supply HIV gene envelopes when asked.'

'So you were wrong to doubt that?'

'What I doubted was whether they were trying to design a vaccine against the virus,' said Steven.

'You're not suggesting that they were trying to design a weapon based on it?' said Macmillan. 'You heard what Sked said.'

'I heard,' said Steven looking doubtful. 'It may not have been official policy to think about HIV as a putative weapon but it wouldn't be the first time that a scientific team has been given its head to see where a particular road might lead—unofficially, of course.'

'And you think Porton might have harboured such a team?'

'Don't you?'

'Maybe I should ask a few quiet questions in the corridors of power,' said Macmillan.

Steven kicked off his shoes when he got in. He poured himself a cold Stella Artois and plumped himself down in his favourite seat by the window. He put his feet up on the sill and looked up at the clouds as he tugged his tie loose. He had made progress but there was still something he was missing. Even if, in what the press would no doubt call a nightmare scenario, Sebring had been engaged in developing the AIDS virus for use as a weapon, his plan to confess all to the papers would have been no reason to kill him. To a cynical public it would just have been a case of yet one more disaffected government employee blowing the whistle about something or other. With an ex MI5 officer currently spilling the beans to the papers about the incompetence of the intelligence service, one more horror story about the development of biological weapons wasn't going to make much of a ripple. It would just be one more virus to worry about along with smallpox and plague but at least it would be our side developing it this time—*and now for the sports results and the weather* . . . There had to be more to it. If Sebring had been seen as such a threat he must have known something more than what he was seeing but as to what it was . . .

Steven found that he was thinking his way

round in circles, a sure sign that he should stop. He looked at his watch and decided his daughter should be home from school. He dialled the number and his sister-in-law answered.

'Hello Sue, how are things?'

'Wonderful!'

'Really?' asked Steven, slightly taken aback at the enthusiasm of her reply.

'First week back at school for the three monsters after six weeks?' said Sue. 'School holidays are all very well but gosh it's so nice to have them off my hands again,' she laughed. 'I've got my life back. I went shopping, had my hair done, had coffee with the girls. Marvellous. I feel like a new woman.'

'Now I feel guilty,' said Steven.

'You know I didn't mean that,' said Sue. 'I take it you'd like to speak to your particular monster. I'll just get her.'

'Hello Daddy,' said Jenny's voice after a short wait. 'I've got a new teacher.'

'Have you, Nutkin? That sounds exciting.'

'Her name's Miss Campbell and she's got big teeth.'

'That's not very kind, Jenny.'

'Well, she has. She says that we might be going to war soon.'

'Really?'

'She says a bad man has been gathering lots and lots of weapons and plans to use them against the West—that's us. Will you have to

189

fight, Daddy?'

'No, Jenny.'

'Good,' said Jenny. 'Aunt Sue says Uncle Richard won't have to either. She says he's too old and fat.'

'So that's where you get your unkindness from,' laughed Steven. 'Let's hope no one has to go and fight anyone and we can all do something more sensible with our time.'

'Are you coming up to see me this weekend, Daddy?'

'That may not be possible, Nutkin,' said Steven, closing his eyes as he said it. 'Daddy's very busy. Maybe next weekend?'

'All right, Daddy. Bye.'

'Shit,' murmured Steven as he heard the line go dead. What was Jenny thinking now, he wondered. That he didn't care? That he didn't love her? That she wasn't important? 'Shit, shit, shit.'

*   *   *

Steven looked up his notes for the phone number of the hospital lab in Glasgow where Gus Maclean worked, called it, but only to be told that Maclean was not on duty. He had called in sick that morning. Steven asked for a home number but was told that wasn't possible. He asked to speak to the lab manager. When George Drummond came on the line, Steven explained who he was and asked for his help in contacting Maclean.

'Gulf War business?' asked Drummond.

'You could say,' agreed Steven.

'Best I can do is call Gus and ask him if it's all right to give you his number,' said Drummond.

'I'd be grateful,' said Steven.

Drummond called back within five minutes to give Steven the number. He dialled it.

'Gus, I'd like to come up there and talk to you again.'

'What about?' asked Maclean sounding hoarse.

'Same as last time. I don't know if you've heard but the journalist that George Sebring talked to is dead.'

'Jesus, what happened?'

'Suicide.'

'And the story?'

'No trace.'

'Shit.'

'Agreed. Can I come?'

'21, Brandon Street, off Dumbarton Road. Top flat, first.'

'Tomorrow morning?' said Steven.

'I'll be here.'

*   *   *

Before going to bed, Steven called Jane in Leicester to say that he would be going to Glasgow in the morning.

191

'How did you get on with the people from Porton?' asked Jane.

'They're sticking to the official line that George and his colleagues were working on a vaccine against AIDS,' said Steven. 'But it emerged that they did supply a component of a vaccine the troops were given. I guess we can call that progress.'

'It's something,' said Jane.

'Trouble is, they've recently destroyed all the old vaccine stocks so we can't subject them to any new analysis.'

'One step forward, two steps back,' said Jane.

'Was it ever different?'

CHAPTER TWELVE

Steven took a taxi from Glasgow Airport to Brandon Street. It was raining and the cab smelt of dampness and stale tobacco. What was worse; the driver believed himself to be the most sensible person in the world.

'I see Saddam says he's no' gonnae let in they weapons inspectors,' he said.

'I hadn't heard,' said Steven.

'It's no' exactly a surprise,' said the driver. 'Would you want the polis in yer hoose wi' a back room full o' dodgy videos? Stands tae reason.'

'I suppose.'

'They shouldae marked his card last time while they had the chance but no, that wid hae been too easy. The bleedin' herts hud their way and noo we're gonna hiv to dae it all o'er again. Makes me sick, an' see a' they asylum seekers . . .'

Steven grunted at appropriate intervals until the journey was over and he stepped out into the wet at the corner of Brandon Street and Dumbarton Road to walk along the row of red sandstone tenement until he found number 21. He mounted the well-worn stone steps to the top flat where Maclean opened the door in his dressing gown.

'They told me at the hospital you weren't well,' said Steven as he followed Maclean through to a sitting room where he indicated that Steven should sit and then collapsed into an armchair, holding his chest as if he'd just run a marathon. 'A left-over from the Gulf War?' asked Steven.

Maclean nodded and said, 'It comes; it goes. What can I do for you?'

'I remember you told me that you went to see George Sebring to try and get him to tell you what he had been working on at Porton.'

'That's right.'

'The police told me you'd tried contacting other people who had worked there. Did you actually talk to any of them?'

'It was bloody difficult. I only ever managed

193

to get addresses for three of them, Sebring, a bloke named Lowry and another guy, called Michael D'Arcy.'

Steven was pleased to hear an unfamiliar name. 'Did you speak to either of them?'

'Both,' said Maclean. 'Lowry told me to sling my hook or he'd call the police. He still worked at our noble defence establishment at that time. I don't know if he still does. He was none too chuffed that I'd man-aged to track him down but I managed to have a talk with D'Arcy. He seemed a decent enough bloke in an English middle class sort of a way but shit scared of saying anything out of line. He just kept repeating that he was subject to the Official Secrets Act until he sounded like a worn-out record.'

'Who was D'Arcy exactly?'

'He was a pal of Sebring's. They worked together in a section headed by a snooty bastard named Crowe. Never was a bloke more aptly named, cold bastard, would have your right eye out and come back for your left. Didn't have much to do with us squaddies though. I suppose he thought it was beneath him.'

'I think I'd like to go see this D'Arcy. Do you have an address for him?'

'It's been a while,' said Maclean. 'A couple of years at least. He lived down in Kent at that time; worked for a pharmaceutical company, Pfizer, I think. Poacher turned gamekeeper you might say.'

Maclean eased himself slowly out of the chair and shuffled over to a bureau where he supported himself with one hand while he foraged through a small mountain of notebooks and papers with the other.

Steven was appalled at how ill the man looked. He seemed to have aged ten years since the last time he saw him. His cheeks had developed cavernous hollows and the veins on his neck were standing out like cords. 'Just let me know if I can help with anything,' he said.

'Here we are,' said Maclean, holding up a small notebook and keeping the place with his thumb in it until he had sat down again. 'Dr Michael D'Arcy, Flat 12, Beach Mansions, Ramsgate. I remember now; he worked in Sandwich at the Pfizer plant but preferred to live in Ramsgate because he had fond childhood memories of the place. Apparently his folks used to take him and his sister there on holiday. I kind of warmed to him when he told me that. I used to feel the same way about a place called Rothesay. I was taken there on an annual basis when I was young. We used to get the steamer at Gourock and sail down the Clyde to Rothesay Bay. We went with the Grant family who stayed next door to us in Govan. My mother and Effy Grant were great pals. You'd have thought it was a Caribbean cruise we were going on if you'd seen what my mother packed for the trip.'

Steven smiled at Maclean's obvious fondness for the memory.

'I took my own lassie there when she was a bairn, watched her play in the same sand I'd done thirty years before. But that's where it's all ended. She'll not be taking any kids of her own there. She never got the chance.'

'I'm sorry,' murmured Steven. He looked away while Maclean wiped a tear from his cheek with an embarrassed flick of the back of his hand.

Maclean cleared his throat and continued. 'Like I say, D'Arcy was okay. He had a bit of heart about him. Mind you, that probably marked him out as a loser.'

Steven looked at him quizzically.

'Nice people don't make it to the top,' said Maclean. 'Niceness gets in the way. Assholes make it to the top. They trample over everyone in sight and then, when they've made it, they pretend they're nice people.'

'I'd call that cynicism if I didn't know it was true,' said Steven. He got up to go. 'Thanks for your help.'

'Fancy a pint?' said Maclean.

'Are you serious?' said Steven. It was the last thing he expected to hear from a man who appeared so ill.

'Sure I am. I don't believe in letting this thing get me down. If you can just hang on till I get some clothes on, we'll be off. The pub's just on the corner.'

'If you're sure,' said Steven.

Maclean reappeared wearing a white t-shirt and black Levi jeans, a black leather jacket and tan loafers. He still looked like death but managed to affect a smile at the way Steven was looking at him. 'You're buying,' he said. 'Let's go.'

There were about a dozen people in The Rifleman and Maclean appeared to know all of them. Steven assigned them mentally into two classes, the retired and the unemployed. Several of the older men inquired after Maclean's health, including the barman who anticipated what he would be drinking and started filling a glass. 'Same for me,' said Steven.

They took their drinks to a small table equidistant between a dartboard and a pool table although neither was in use. Steven noted that the pool table had a rip in its green baize.

'So what makes you think you'll have any more success with D'Arcy than I did?' asked Maclean, starting to search in his jacket pockets. Steven thought for one incredible moment that he might be about to bring out cigarettes but instead he brought out an inhaler, tilted his head back and squirted it twice into his mouth.

'I don't think that at all,' said Steven. 'But I can't think of anything else to do right now. I've managed to establish a connection between the team that Sebring worked for and the vaccines the troops were given but now I'm dependent on one of that team talking, particularly about anything that went wrong.'

'What sort of connection?' asked Maclean.

'Crowe's team was officially working on a vaccine against AIDS. At some point they were asked to supply something called gene envelopes from the HIV virus to help out with the troop vaccine programme.'

'What the hell for?' rasped Maclean.

'Apparently the vaccine makers had been using cytokines to elicit an improved immune response in the troops—cutting edge stuff at the time—but they'd run low on supplies. The brains reckoned that HIV gene envelopes would have much the same effect.'

Gus Maclean looked thoughtfully at his beer for a long time. 'You know,' he said. 'There was a time when I thought the bastards had actually used the HIV virus against us.'

'What makes you say that?'

'The sheer range of illnesses and symptoms affecting the guys,' said Maclean. 'Although the government seized on that very fact to scotch any idea of a Gulf War Syndrome and Fatty Soames used it to suggest we were all a bunch of sickly wankers on the make, it seemed to me as if our immune system had been buggered.'

'Something that would make you highly susceptible to infection.'

198

'You got it,' said Maclean. 'Once the immune system goes you're a theme park for the entire microbial world.'

'Did you ever float that idea in public?' asked Steven.

'A couple of times,' said Maclean with a wry smile. 'A lot of the guys thought I was going too far. Apart from that they didn't take too kindly to the suggestion they might have AIDS. Let's say, no one was exactly comfortable with the idea, and it's only fair to say that any HIV tests that were done were negative.'

'I wanted to have the vaccines that Crowe's team contributed to analysed by an independent lab,' said Steven. 'But it turns out they were all destroyed after the stink you guys created over plans to use them again.'

'It was a funny business,' said Maclean. 'We got an anonymous tip-off that they were planning to use up the old stuff on the boys getting ready for the Gulf at the moment and no one denied it at the MOD when we asked—most unlike them. They usually deny that Tuesday follows Monday until the evidence becomes overwhelming. Then, when we got in touch with the papers about it, we found that they'd had the tip-off too. It was almost as if someone in government wanted the story to get out and wanted there to be a backlash. I remember feeling at the time that they were using us like lab rats to do some kind of a job for them.'

'Like giving them an excuse to destroy the old stocks,' said Steven, thinking out loud.

'Because they had something to hide?' said Maclean. 'Devious bastards.'

'Well, it looks like they got away with it,' said Steven.

'They always fucking do,' said Maclean with feeling.

'Unless . . .' said Steven, as an idea came to him.

Maclean looked at him expectantly.

'You told me you had carried out microbiological tests on yourself. What exactly did you do?'

'I carried out every standard test any hospital lab would do to determine cause of illness,' said Maclean. 'I took swabs and samples from everywhere. No orifice was left unprobed, you might say.'

'And you drew a blank?'

'No pathogens,' said Maclean.

'What about non-pathogens?'

'Well, of course,' replied Maclean. 'I found all the usual harmless bugs you find in the human body. I identified each and every one, sub-cultured them, cross-referenced them and stored them, cos that's the kind of sad bugger I am.'

Steven smiled but he had just heard what he wanted to hear. He leant across the table and said, 'Correct me if I'm wrong but you have just told me that you have sub-cultures of all the bugs you isolated from yourself over the course of your illness?'

'That's right,' replied Maclean, looking puzzled. 'But in the end it was just an academic exercise; they're everyday, harmless beasties that we all carry inside us. I didn't find any problem bugs.'

'When judged by any standard microbiological or serological tests,' said Steven.

Maclean looked at him questioningly. 'I don't understand. What are you getting at?' he asked.

'I suppose I'm suggesting that all may not be as it seems,' said Steven. 'One of the lambs could be a wolf in sheep's clothing.'

'Jesus, you're talking about genetic engineering, aren't you,' said Maclean. 'The introduction of foreign genes.'

'It's an idea,' said Steven. 'It's well known that the Russians altered smallpox genetically to make it even more virulent so it's a fair bet that they weren't the only kids playing with matches over the past few years.'

'But you are talking about something more than souping up a bug that's already a pathogen,' said Maclean.

'I am,' agreed Steven. 'We'd have to be looking at an everyday sort of bug that had been given new properties. A new personality, you might say.'

'A pathogen that looked harmless and wouldn't actually be spotted as a CB weapon? How very British,' said Maclean sourly. 'It has that wee trademark touch of hypocrisy the world has come to know and love so well. Well, you're right about one thing: routine lab tests wouldn't pick up on anything like that. So, what do you suggest?'

'I suppose it would have to be DNA testing,' said Steven.

'I'm no expert but I do know we're talking molecular biology here and sequencing the entire genome of a single bug can take years,' said Maclean. 'And I've got a collection of around three dozen cultures.'

'You're right,' said Steven. 'I think we're both out of our depth here. I'd have to get expert advice. Our best bet would be to get Michael D'Arcy to tell us what he and his pals were up to at Porton. That would save us all a whole lot of time and trouble.'

'What about the bug collection?'

'What form is it in?' asked Steven.

'There are about three-dozen cultures, each in a glass vial containing soft agar. Each vial is about an inch long by a quarter inch in diameter. They all fit into a partitioned box about the size of an A4 notebook and weigh probably less.'

'Do you keep them at the hospital?' asked Steven.

'In a lab fridge,' replied Maclean.

'Let's leave them where they are for the moment,' said Steven. 'At least until I've talked to some people. I take it you have an inventory of what they all are?'

'All numbered and catalogued and identified according to Bergey's *Manual of Determinative Bacteriology*, complete with details of when and from where they were isolated. I've got a copy in the flat if you want one.'

Steven agreed that might be useful. He accompanied Maclean back to his flat where it took some time for him to climb the stairs. He paused at every landing, holding on to the banister with one hand while resting the other on his knee, looking down at the steps unseeingly until he got his breath back. Steven's offer of an arm was dismissed out of hand. 'It's my problem. I'll deal with it.'

Maclean sat down for a few minutes when he got in before returning to the bureau and the pile of papers. This time however, he opened a small drawer and removed a floppy disk from a manila envelope. He handed it to Steven saying, 'There you go, a complete list of the flora and fauna of Angus Maclean. David Attenborough eat your heart out.'

Steven smiled and slipped the disk into his pocket. 'I hope you feel better soon,' he said.

'I will,' said Maclean. 'A couple of days and I'll be back at work and that'll be it until the next time. That's the way it goes. It's the way it's been for the past twelve years.'

*   *   *

Steven took a taxi back to the airport and called Jane while he waited for a shuttle flight. 'What are you up to?' he asked.

'Preparing classwork for next week,' replied Jane. 'It's start of term. Where are you?'

'Glasgow Airport. I talked to Gus Maclean this morning.'

'Useful?'

'He gave me a name, Michael D'Arcy; mean anything?'

'As a matter of fact it does,' said Jane. 'He was an old friend of George's. He always sent us a Christmas card although I don't think I ever met him.'

'He and George worked together at Porton,' said Steven. 'From what Gus told me, I think they worked on the same team.'

'No need to ask where you'll be going next,' said Jane.

'Give that lady a prize. I'll stop off at the flat when I get back to London and pick up the car. With a bit of luck I should manage to see D'Arcy this evening, assuming he's still at the same address.'

'You're just going to turn up on his doorstep?'

'Best that way,' replied Steven. 'Doesn't give him any time to start phoning anyone to ask if

204

seeing me is a good idea.'

'Well, I learn something new every day,' said Jane. 'When will I see you again?'

'I have to go in to the Home Office tomorrow morning. After that, I could drive up to Leicester or maybe you could come to London? Whatever suits?'

'You come up,' said Jane. 'I've got a pile of stuff to get through for school on Monday so I could use the time.'

Steven said that he would come up late in the afternoon and suggested that they go out to dinner.

'That'd be nice,' said Jane.

'See you tomorrow,' said Steven. His flight was called for boarding as he switched off the phone.

*   *   *

The evening sun was bathing Canterbury Cathedral in pale orange light as Steven drove across Kent and down to the seaside town of Ramsgate. The Glasgow flight had been on time and he'd had no problems in getting in to the city. He'd showered and changed at the flat and been on his way again in seemingly no time—but getting round the M25 orbital had been a nightmare. Roadwork had reduced the speed of travel to a snail's pace and caused him to give up all hope of missing the evening rush hour traffic on the roads leading to the south coast. It was nearly eight o'clock when he entered the outskirts of Ramsgate and stopped to ask for directions to Beach Mansions. The first two people turned out to be holiday makers who had no idea; the third, a local, gave him directions which turned out to be wrong but brought him close enough to find someone who actually did know where the building was.

Steven liked the look of Beach Mansions. He guessed that the building itself had been built around the end of the nineteenth century because of the styling and the fact that it was stone-built, but it had obviously been well looked after and exuded an air of solidity and middle class respectability. The long low building, interrupted in the middle by an arch giving access to an inner courtyard, occupied an elevated position where front-facing flats had uninterrupted views from their bay-windowed rooms out to sea. He noted that at least two of them had telescopes that would allow the residents to watch the comings and goings of cross channel ferries.

Steven parked in one of the white-lined parking bays marked 'visitors' and got out to approach the half of the building to the right of the arch, having been directed by a signboard pointing to numbers 18 to 36. The uniformed man behind the desk looked up from his paper and said, 'Yes?'

'I'm calling on Dr Michael D'Arcy,' said

206

Steven. 'Number 21.'

The man carefully folded his paper before lifting a handset and pressing a button on a board on his desk. Several moments passed before he said, 'Dr D'Arcy's not in.'

'Any idea when he might be back?' asked Steven.

'He often works late.'

'Maybe I'll hang around for a while,' said Steven. 'See if he comes home. What kind of car does he drive?'

'Green Toyota like my son, Gordon. It's got a dent in the back. Some old dear along in Sandwich went right into him last Monday at traffic lights.'

'Gordon or Dr D'Arcy?'

'Dr D'Arcy,' replied the man, looking as if it were a stupid question. 'Gordon works in Newcastle.'

The daylight had all but gone as Steven paused to look down at the lights of the town before getting back into his car and turning on the radio. Half a dozen cars were to come and go in the next hour before Steven saw a green Toyota enter the car park. As it turned to park in a bay opposite he saw the damage to its rear end. He got out but had to delay crossing because another vehicle was coming into the car park. The car, a dark blue Range Rover, slowed to a crawl and Steven could see that its driver was watching the Toyota. His first assumption was that the driver must be a neighbour of D'Arcy's waiting to say something to him when he got out—a view reinforced when Steven saw the driver's window of the Range Rover slide down—but then he saw the gun appear in the driver's hand.

Everything seemed to happen at once. D'Arcy who was now out of his car and locking his door, turned to face the Range Rover just as its driver raised his weapon to fire. Steven yelled out, 'D'Arcy, get down!'

The silenced gun fired and D'Arcy was thrown over backwards from the impact of the bullet and lay spreadeagled on the ground as the Range Rover driver turned his attention to Steven whom he obviously hadn't realised was there. Steven, now in a desperately vulnerable position, sprinted across the car park to throw himself into the shrubbery: it was the only cover available. He was conscious of another two dull plops coming from the gun. One resulted in wood splintering from a nearby branch while the other sent up shards of tarmac in front of him. A piece hit him on the left cheek and opened up a cut.

Steven rolled over and over until he came to a halt under a holly bush and turned to look back just as the Range Rover driver turned his headlights on to full beam and revved his engine. Steven felt like he was on some hellish floodlit stage as the Range Rover's tyres squealed and its rear end twitched as the

208

driver sent it hurtling across the car park directly at him. As he struggled to his feet there was only one decision to be made, whether to jump left or right. It was six of one, half a dozen of the other, he decided. Timing was going to be everything. He had to wait until the very last moment so that the driver would not have time to alter course. The blinding lights raced towards him as he stood there like a capeless matador until the moment of truth came and he threw himself to the left.

The Range Rover careered past him into the shrubbery and the pain of a thousand berberis thorns raked Steven's face and hands as he landed in a dense clump of it. The right rear wheel of the Range Rover just caught the sleeve of his jacket as it hurtled past, ripping it away from his shoulder and reminding him how close he'd come to death. Now fuelled by panic, Steven struggled to free himself from the bush before the driver, who was now reversing the vehicle, could take another pot at him. The commotion, however, had caused lights to go on all over the building and people were coming outside to see what all the fuss was about. It was this that made the driver decide not to try again. Steven sank to his knees in exhaustion as he saw the Range Rover squeal round in a circle on the tarmac and head for the exit to disappear into the night.

CHAPTER THIRTEEN

Steven wiped away the blood coming from the scratches on his face with one hand and brought out his mobile phone with the other. He punched in the emergency number before hurrying over to where D'Arcy lay.

'Ambulance,' he snapped. 'Beach Mansions, Ramsgate, man with serious gunshot wound.'

D'Arcy was unconscious and Steven could see from the puddle on the ground that he had lost a lot of blood but he still had a pulse so, under the gaze of the small huddle of people gathering in the car park, he set about stabilising him as best he could. D'Arcy had failed to drop to the ground in response to his warning shout—most people wouldn't—but in turning to see where the call had come from, he had moved his body just enough to ensure that the bullet had not hit him full front in the chest. It had entered at a slight angle and travelled upwards to smash his left clavicle before making a large jagged exit wound.

'I think you might need these,' said a voice beside him. Steven turned to see an elderly woman, her face framed by a mass of grey hair, crouching down to proffer three rolls of clean white bandaging.

'Yes, thank you,' he replied.

'I was a nurse,' said the woman. 'Perhaps I

can help?'

'Maybe you could organise some blankets to keep him warm and get me some light,' said Steven. 'I've got to stem the blood flow somehow or he's going to bleed to death.'

'Of course,' said the woman. She went back to the small group of onlookers and Steven heard her say, 'It's Dr D'Arcy: he's badly injured. We need blankets and a torch.' She stemmed a chorus of, 'What happened?' by saying, 'Quickly now!'

Blankets appeared and the nurse covered D'Arcy before directing a powerful torch beam on to the wound. Steven secured the pressure pad he'd fashioned from one of the bandage rolls over the gaping, jagged hole in D'Arcy's shoulder but the thick white wadding turned red in a matter of seconds.

'Won't do,' said Steven. 'Pressure alone's just not working.'

'How about a tourniquet?' asked the nurse.

'Nothing to tie it round,' said Steven. 'The blood's not coming from his arm. Quick! I need paperclips and forceps . . . or tweezers,' he said. 'Tweezers would do.'

'Quickly someone,' said the nurse to the onlookers. 'You heard the doctor.'

One of the ground floor residents brought out a box of paperclips and two more appeared with tweezers in their hands. Most of the group turned away in horror as Steven started fishing around inside D'Arcy's wound

211

with his bare hand. He glanced at the nurse's face and read the criticism there. 'If I don't do this, he's going to die,' he muttered.

'I was actually thinking of you,' said the nurse quietly. She looked at Steven's bare hands covered in blood.

Steven found the severed artery. It still spurted blood as he brought it to the surface between thumb and forefinger bringing gasps from the few onlookers who still dared to watch through fingers over their faces.

'Paperclip,' said Steven, holding out his palm. The nurse dropped one into it and after several abortive attempts punctuated by muffled curses, he managed to clip the end of the exposed artery. It was a slippery, messy business but the blood stopped spurting and Steven allowed himself a moment to recover before replacing the wadding over the wound and fixing it in place with yet more bandage which the nurse unrolled for him. 'Thanks, you're doing a great job,' he said as a wail of sirens in the distance heralded the imminent and welcome arrival of the emergency services.

Steven knew the police would attend because of the mention of a gunshot wound he'd made. It was inevitable, as was the appearance of an armed response unit, which arrived just after the ambulance and two ordinary patrol cars. Two paramedics took over care of D'Arcy after Steven had briefed them on what he'd done already.

Steven stood up and rubbed the stiffness out of his knees before turning round to see a number of squad officers in full Kevlar armour and carrying automatic weapons clatter out of their van and start deploying round the car park.

'No point,' said Steven approaching the officer in charge. 'The gunman's gone.' He held out his ID and said, 'If you come to the hospital, I'll tell you as much as I can.'

'Now wait a minute,' said the officer, a portly but erect man in his late forties with a small moustache—which only seemed to emphasise the roundness of his face—and an aura of self-importance about him. 'You're going nowhere. I don't care who or what you are. You can't just swan off from the scene of a serious crime.'

'I'm going with the patient,' said Steven. 'I need to talk to him as soon as he comes round. For your information, three shots were fired, one at the victim two at me then the gunman made off in a blue Range Rover. You'll find the shell cases in the car park. That's all you're going to come up with here.'

'There are still procedures to be followed,' said the policeman.

'Then you follow them,' said Steven, thinking that the policeman looked like a man who had dedicated his whole life to following procedures at the expense of imagination.

'How is he?' asked Steven, turning his

213

attention back to D'Arcy as the two ambulance men loaded him carefully into the back of their vehicle.

'Very weak,' replied the black paramedic who climbed in to continue treating him. 'By God, you did a good job for a GP.'

Steven smiled as he climbed in and the back doors were closed. 'I'm not a GP,' he said. He knew very well that trained paramedics were a lot more use at the scene of an accident than the average doctor although this was not a view the BMA—that most conservative of bodies—liked to encourage.

'A&E?' asked the man.

'Army field medicine,' said Steven.

'Bloody hell,' said the man. 'This guy's guardian angel was sure on the ball. What are the chances of a field medic being around when you stop a bullet in the street?'

* * *

A nurse set to work on cleaning up Steven's scratches and abrasions while an A&E team worked on D'Arcy, with the angry inspector who had followed the ambulance to the hospital hovering beside Steven. Steven could appreciate the man's frustration. Not only had he been unable to provide any description of the gunman, he had not managed to get the registration number of the Range Rover either.

'You're a professional. What were you thinking of, man?' complained the policeman.

'I was trying to keep my arse in one piece,' replied Steven through gritted teeth. 'It was dark and a man with a gun was trying to kill me.'

'Even though . . .' said the policeman.

'He didn't finish the job he set out to do,' interrupted Steven. 'I'll need a guard on D'Arcy until we can move him.'

'What's this all about?' growled the policeman. 'If you think you can turn my patch into the OK corral and ride roughshod over . . .'

'Stop right there!' snapped Steven. 'I appreciate that you're pissed off but I know exactly what I can and can't do and it might be in your interests if you were to find out too. I suggest you check with the Home Office if you're in any doubt. In the meantime, just arrange an armed guard for D'Arcy and stop belly-aching.'

'What a bloody circus,' mumbled the policeman as he withdrew.

'How's D'Arcy?' asked Steven as he saw the doctor in charge step back from the table and strip off his gloves.

'Stable but not out of the woods by a long way. They're prepping a theatre for him. He needs quite a bit of surgery,' replied the A&E consultant. 'Are you a friend? A relative?'

'Neither,' replied Steven.

'Then what?'

Steven showed the man his ID.

'You're a doctor. So it was you who applied the paperclip?'

Steven nodded.

'Well, if he lives, that'll be the reason. I don't suppose you're going to tell me what this is all about?'

'I'm not really sure myself,' said Steven. 'I was on my way to interview the man when a gunman decided to end the conversation before it had begun. I think it only fair to warn you that there might be another attempt. I've asked for a police guard to be mounted.'

'What is he? Some big-time criminal?'

'Far from it,' replied Steven. 'He's a gifted scientist who, from what I hear, wouldn't say boo to a goose.'

'Why would anyone want to kill him?'

'I'd like to ask him that when he comes round,' said Steven. 'I need to stay with him.'

'You're a doctor,' said the consultant, 'so I won't give you the standard spiel about my only interest being the patient's welfare and then tell you to fuck off out my department like they do on TV but you'll appreciate just how fragile he is. Go easy.'

'Thanks,' said Steven. He left the emergency room and called Sci-Med on his mobile to inform the duty officer what had happened. He kept an eye on what was going on inside through one of the windows in the

216

swing doors while he spoke.

'Do you want me to wake Mr Macmillan?' asked the duty man.

'Yes,' replied Steven flatly.

Macmillan called back within five minutes. 'Is he still alive?'

'Touch and go,' replied Steven. 'I'm going to stay with him but I'd like him moved as soon as it becomes possible.'

'You think they may try again?'

'Common sense says so.'

'They may think he's dead of course,' said Macmillan.

'Too many people at the flats knew he was still alive when the ambulance took him away.'

'Right, I'll arrange it. We have to speak. I have some news.'

'As soon as D'Arcy's safe,' said Steven.

*   *   *

It was three in the morning before D'Arcy was brought from the operating theatre to the Intensive Care Unit. Steven spoke to the surgeon while D'Arcy was being connected to the monitoring equipment. 'What d'you think?'

'He was in a right mess—I'd take a guess at a soft-nosed bullet judging by the state of the exit wound—but, providing there are no complications, he should get back to something approaching normality unless he

217

happened to be a left-arm spin bowler, in which case he's just retired.'

'He wasn't,' Steven assured him with a smile.

'A&E sent up the paperclip. He may want it to show his grandchildren one day,' said the surgeon turning to look up at the clock. 'The charge nurse has it.'

'Any idea when he might come round?' asked Steven.

'He'll be out for at least three hours,' said the surgeon. 'Maybe longer. You look as if you could do with some rest yourself.'

Steven satisfied himself that the two, armed officers outside the entrance to ICU understood that no one was to be allowed in without his say so before settling down in a chair beside D'Arcy's bed and allowing himself to cat nap. The stifling warmth of the unit and the soft muted lighting from the consoles made it easy.

Steven was lazing on a sunny beach. Jane was trickling a handful of sand on to his back while Jenny played happily among nearby rocks when something touched his arm and the dream vanished in an instant. The speed of his recovery to full wakefulness alarmed the nurse who'd touched him and she took a startled step backwards and put her hand to her mouth. 'Sorry, I didn't mean to alarm you,' she said. 'I just thought you should know Dr D'Arcy is showing signs of coming round.'

Steven was equally apologetic. There had been occasions in the past when such a response to any strange sound or touch when asleep might have saved his life and old habits died hard.

D'Arcy was asking all the usual questions of a nurse who was used to answering them. Her soft gentle voice assured him that he was warm and safe in hospital and there was no cause for him to worry about anything.

'Want to know . . .' murmured D'Arcy.

'All in good time,' soothed the nurse. 'You must rest.'

'You were shot, old son,' said Steven, attracting a critical look from the nurse. 'You've undergone surgery but you're going to be all right.'

'Shot? But who . . . ?'

Steven gave the nurse what he hoped was a reassuring look to signify that he would not overtax D'Arcy and she withdrew with a less than convinced expression on her face.

Steven told D'Arcy who he was and waited for a response.

'Sci-Med . . . I know Sci-Med.'

'Good. I know that you are going to find this all a bit much to take in, old son, but I have to make you understand what's been going on.'

D'Arcy grunted his understanding.

'A few weeks ago an old colleague of yours, George Sebring was murdered by the same people who tried to kill you last night. They wanted to stop you talking about something that happened many years ago when you were both working at Porton Down.'

'That's . . . crazy . . .'

'Something happened,' said Steven. 'Something that was kept secret, something that not even the government were told about.'

'Dr Crowe . . . told them.'

'No, he didn't,' said Steven. 'They were never informed. It was a problem with a vaccine, wasn't it?'

D'Arcy gave an almost imperceptible nod. 'They wanted HIV gene envelopes . . . George made . . . a . . . mistake.'

Steven felt a sense of excitement well up inside him. He had to concentrate on keeping his voice calm as his throat tightened. 'What kind of mistake, Michael?'

'He gave them an early version of the agent we were working on,' said D'Arcy.

'What agent was that?'

There was a long pause, which strained Steven's nerves to the limit, before D'Arcy said, 'Special project; we were to design a new biological agent . . .'

'Not a vaccine against AIDS,' said Steven.

'No . . . that was just the team's cover story . . . The Government wanted an agent that wouldn't kill . . . but weaken and demoralise . . . infectious but not detectable . . . also had to be curable.'

'And that's what went into the vaccine?' said

220

Steven, trying to sound matter-of-fact but feeling shocked.

'Yes . . .' said D'Arcy. 'But Crowe thought it wouldn't be . . . a problem.'

'Not a problem,' Steven repeated, unable to stop himself as he thought about the war veterans. He wanted to ask D'Arcy where the hell he thought Gulf War Syndrome had come from, but from what Maclean had said about D'Arcy he suspected that the man would have accepted the official view of things without question.

'Did you continue working on this agent after the accident?' he asked quietly.

D'Arcy gave a little shake of the head. 'No, all work on it was stopped. I left Porton after that.'

'The agent you were working on, it involved genetic engineering, didn't it?'

A nod. 'Yes.'

'What did you do exactly?'

'Tired . . .' said D'Arcy. 'Very tired . . .'

'I know, Michael,' said Steven. 'Just tell me which genes were involved and then you can sleep.'

'M . . .'

The nurse appeared as if by magic at Steven's shoulder and said, 'That's enough. He has to rest and I think you know that.'

Steven accepted the rebuke. The nurse was right. He was a doctor and he knew very well. But by God, he had come so close to getting

221

out of D'Arcy what he needed to know. He couldn't resist the single expletive that whispered across his lips as he left the room to call Sci-Med to ask about the arrangements for D'Arcy's transfer.

'We've been restricted by intensive care requirements,' said the duty man. 'The safe houses have been ruled out so Mr Macmillan's arranged for private facilities in St Thomas's Hospital without anyone being told who he is. When do you want him moved?'

'Not my call,' said Steven. 'But I should think we'll be given the okay around lunch time.'

'We'll send an ambulance and an escort?'

'I'd like to keep things as low key as possible,' said Steven. 'Plain clothes armed escort, unmarked police cars.'

The surgeon who had operated on D'Arcy finished his examination and gave the all clear for the move just after eleven o'clock. He'd been assured by Steven that IC facilities would be available at the new location without his actually telling him where that would be. The man handed over D'Arcy's case notes. 'Can't say I'm that sorry to be seeing the back of you all,' he said, glancing at the armed policemen by the door.

'Can't say I blame you,' said Steven. 'Thanks for all you did for him.'

'I still came second to a paperclip,' smiled the surgeon. 'Good luck.'

*   *   *

D'Arcy was transferred to St Thomas's Hospital in London without incident. Steven thought he would take the opportunity to go to the Home Office and speak with Macmillan while D'Arcy was settled in to his new environment and was still under sedation. First, he called Jane in Leicester to say that he wouldn't be coming up after all. He told her what had happened.

'Oh my God,' she said. 'This is a nightmare. Are you still down in Kent?'

'No, we didn't think it was safe to leave him there. We've moved him as Mr Jones to a private room in St Thomas's Hospital in London.'

'Has he come round at all?' asked Jane.

'He was able to tell me quite a lot last night but not quite everything. I'm hoping to talk to him again after I've seen Macmillan.'

'But you managed to get an idea of what they were working on at Porton?' said Jane.

'The AIDS vaccine story was a cover,' said Steven. 'They were designing a new biological agent that would disable and demoralise rather than kill.'

'Why?'

'Social control I suppose,' said Steven. 'But that's only half the story. A prototype version of it found its way into the troop vaccines by mistake. I gather George was to blame.'

'God almighty,' said Jane. 'No wonder he was so alarmed about plans to use the old vaccines again.'

'Quite,' said Steven. 'It seems that neither the government of the day nor the present one has any record of this ever happening. If they did they couldn't possibly have considered using it again.'

'But now you can tell them?' said Jane.

'I need D'Arcy to tell me more about the agent and how it was constructed. Part of their brief was to make it undetectable.'

'What a world,' said Jane. 'No wonder George kept having nightmares. He deserved to!'

'Don't be too hard on him,' said Steven. 'People tend to accept anything that has official approval without question. George probably believed that he was just doing his job at the time. If every soldier was to stop and consider the implications of his actions every time an officer yelled, "Fire!" we wouldn't have an army. Most just pull the trigger and get on with their lives.'

'I suppose,' agreed Jane reluctantly. 'Call me when you can.'

*   *   *

Macmillan was sitting at his desk, his head slightly to one side, fingers steepled under his chin and looking very worried when Steven entered. 'How's D'Arcy?' he asked.

'The medics think he'll pull through. He suffered no ill effects from the transfer, which was my big worry. He should surface from the sedation in a couple of hours and I'll be able to talk to him again.'

'What a mess,' sighed Macmillan. 'What a bloody mess.'

'You said you had some news?' said Steven.

Macmillan looked at him thoughtfully and Steven saw in his eyes that he was in need of sleep.

'After our last conversation I asked a friend in high places about special project teams at Porton,' said Macmillan.

'And now you wish you hadn't?'

'Something like that,' said Macmillan. 'You were right. It goes back a long way—to the days of the Second World War, in fact—when a group of scientists was asked to investigate the possibility of infecting cattle feed with anthrax. The idea was to drop it on German fields. They were called the Beta team and a special budget that by-passed the normal reporting and accounting procedures was assigned to it. In the end the stuff wasn't used but the infrastructure supporting the team was never completely dismantled ...'

Steven could see that there was more to come. 'Go on,' he said quietly.

'My informant tells me that at some point in

the eighties the Beta team appears to have been reactivated. Accounts were rendered for its support using the old procedures and paid without question.'

'You mean Porton fancied a bit of extra money?' said Steven.

'Not quite that simple,' said Macmillan. 'Porton—in terms of its director and administrators—appears to have known nothing at all about it.'

'Bloody hell,' said Steven.

'My informant is continuing to pick away at it but it looks as if someone who knew about the existence of the Beta Team budget decided to recruit for it at Porton and have the team work on something the others knew nothing at all about.'

'The agent D'Arcy told me about last night,' said Steven. 'Crowe's team was the Beta Team of its day.'

Macmillan nodded. 'Which raises several awkward questions . . .'

'Not least, did the government know anything about this project at the time?' said Steven. 'Maybe they even instigated it?'

'A can of worms on its own,' said Macmillan.

'But it looks as if the accident at Porton was kept secret from them otherwise they wouldn't have contemplated using up the old vaccine stocks,' said Steven.

'On the other hand there have been several changes of government in the last twelve

226

years,' said Macmillan. 'We can't overlook simple cock-ups.'

'I suppose not,' said Steven.

'Happily we are not alone in this. My man in high places—who must remain nameless—is equally worried. He'll get back to me when he's established whether or not he thinks it was a government-of-the-day initiative or whether it was some kind of . . . private enterprise.'

'I'm not sure which of these would be the more comforting,' said Steven with a rueful shrug. 'In the meantime I'll try and get as much as I can out of D'Arcy.'

Macmillan's phone rang and he snapped into it that he had asked not to be disturbed.

Steven heard the faint, soothing tones of explanation being given by Rose Roberts.

'Put him on,' said Macmillan.

Steven watched Macmillan's face turn ashen as he listened. He appeared to age before his eyes before he said, 'Thank you for letting me know.'

'It's D'Arcy,' said Macmillan. 'He's dead.'

Steven felt a hollow open up in his stomach. 'But how?' he asked. 'He was quite stable and in an IC unit, for God's sake.'

'A "doctor" whom the hospital's people believed to be one of ours and whom our people believed to be one of theirs gained access to D'Arcy and administered a lethal injection. He was dead within seconds.'

Steven felt a mixture of anger and shock.

227

'How could they possibly have known where he was?'

'What a good question,' said Macmillan.

CHAPTER FOURTEEN

'I told Jane Sebring,' said Steven.

'I see,' said Macmillan. The question, *why*, was hanging in the air but wasn't asked. Instead Macmillan said quietly, 'Am I right in thinking that this woman means something to you?'

Steven nodded. 'A great deal.'

'Show me a man who's never made a fool of himself over a woman and I'll show you a man without a heart,' said Macmillan.

Steven acknowledged the kindness and smiled but it faded almost immediately and he said, 'But Michael D'Arcy's dead.'

Steven faced another question he had been trying to avoid. Why had an attempt been made on D'Arcy's life on the very day he had intended to confront him? The man had been in possession of whatever secret information he'd held for nearly twelve years so why had he suddenly been seen as a danger on that very day? Coincidence? Or had someone been tipped off about his impending visit? Only one person had known about it and that was Jane.

Steven closed his eyes to hide whatever was

228

showing there from Macmillan's gaze as he felt the acid drip of suspicion burn inside his head.

'Of course we could be jumping to conclusions here,' said Macmillan. 'Are you absolutely sure about this?'

Steven told him that Jane was the only person who knew of his plans yesterday.

'Maybe someone overheard you telling her?'

'I told her over the phone.'

Macmillan's eyes hardened. 'Mobile?'

'My mobile . . . but her house phone,' said Steven, suddenly seeing what Macmillan was thinking. 'Same as when I told her about D'Arcy's transfer!'

'They've probably had a tap on George Sebring's house phone for years,' said Macmillan.

Steven felt a flood of relief surge through him but almost immediately he started to feel guilty over what he'd imagined. 'Oh my God,' he sighed.

'Now, we don't know for sure that's what's been happening,' cautioned Macmillan. 'But I think my money's on it.'

Steven nodded.

'But if that's the case,' said Macmillan, 'they must know everything that's passed between you two over the phone. Where does that leave us?'

'I'll have to think back.'

'Did you pass on what D'Arcy told you

about the agent before he died?'

Steven admitted he had.

'In which case,' said Macmillan slowly measuring his words, 'They may conclude that Mrs Sebring knows too much . . .'

'But we know about it too,' said Steven. 'There would be no point in harming Jane.'

'Unless they saw her as a loose cannon who might go to the newspapers and stir up a hornet's nest about the contaminated vaccine and her husband's death?'

'God, I have to get up there.'

'Does she have a mobile phone?'

Steven shook his head. 'We joked about it. She won't have one. She got so fed up with her pupils' phones ringing in class that she took a real dislike to them. She refuses to have one herself. I've got to warn her.'

'You can't risk the house phone,' said Macmillan.

'I know, I know,' murmured Steven, drumming his fingers lightly and rapidly on the desktop as he sought inspiration. 'Look, maybe you could ask the Leicester police to go round there on some pretext,' he said. 'Get them to take her down to headquarters and hold on to her until I get there?'

'I'll get on to them right away,' said Macmillan.

'And maybe Rose could set up safe-house accommodation? I'll call later to get the details,' said Steven, anxious to be on his way.

230

Macmillan picked up the phone but indicated that Steven should not leave just yet. He opened the bottom drawer of his desk with his free hand and withdrew an automatic pistol and a shoulder holster. 'You know how I feel about these things,' he said. 'But after what happened last night to D'Arcy I got Rose to order up this for you. It's your preferred weapon. Sign for it before you leave.'

Steven took off his jacket, slipped on the Burns Martin holster and checked the magazine of the gun before putting it away and re-donning his jacket. He pocketed three boxes of shells and all without comment. He had no greater liking for guns on the streets than Macmillan but on occasions it made sense and this was one of them.

Steven went out to Rose Roberts' office and signed for the weapon.

'If you lose it you pay for it,' smiled Rose but there was little humour in her eyes when she said it, nor was there much in Steven's answering grin. When he returned to Macmillan's office he asked, 'All right?'

'They're on their way,' said Macmillan. 'I'll call you as soon as I hear she's safe. Perhaps on the drive up to Leicester you can give some thought to how we go about getting more information about this damned agent now that D'Arcy's dead. We have to know more than we do before we can start to make waves.'

'I already have,' said Steven. 'But I need to

talk to a molecular biologist.' He told Macmillan about Maclean's bacterial culture collection. 'I'm convinced the agent is lurking in that lot somewhere but it's been so well disguised that it's going to be a bit like looking for a needle in a haystack,' he said. 'I'm hoping there may be some quick way of checking for DNA changes in bacterial strains other than sequencing the entire genome of every bug.'

'I'll see what I can set up,' said Macmillan.

Steven had been driving for some forty minutes when his mobile rang. He slowed so that he could hear it above the engine noise. It was Macmillan to say that Jane was now safe at police headquarters and was none too pleased because no one could or would tell her what was going on.

'Sounds like her,' said Steven. 'How about accommodation?'

'That's been arranged too,' said Macmillan. 'Rose will text you the details.'

*   *   *

'Steven, just what the hell is going on?' demanded Jane when she saw Steven enter the interview room where she was seated at a table, an untouched cup of tea in front of her. 'Why am I being held here? No one will tell me anything.'

Steven raised both his palms in a placatory gesture. 'I'm sorry,' he said. 'You're not being held. I asked them to bring you here for your own safety.'

'My safety,' said Jane, her anger giving way to something more circumspect. 'What does that mean?'

Steven sat down and took both her hands in his. 'Michael D'Arcy was murdered earlier today in St Thomas's Hospital,' he said.

Jane's eyes searched Steven's, trying to make some connection between the news and her own predicament. 'How awful,' she said.

'I take it you didn't tell anyone he was there?'

'Of course not,' said Jane. 'Who would I tell?'

'You were the only person outside of Sci-Med who knew where he was,' said Steven.

Jane looked at him as if she couldn't believe what she was hearing. 'I don't think I understand,' she said. 'What are you suggesting?'

'That your home phone has been tapped,' said Steven, having seen all he wanted in Jane's reactions. 'Someone has been listening in to all our conversations.'

'Oh my God,' said Jane, letting her head fall down on to her chest.

'You made me promise to tell you everything,' said Steven.

Jane nodded slowly but more in trepidation than conviction.

'I told you over the phone about going to

233

see D'Arcy unannounced. They beat me to it. I told you over the phone where we were going to squirrel him away and they got to him and finished the job. I told you over the phone about the agent George had been working on,' said Steven.

'And?' asked Jane.

'There's a chance that they may see you as a potential problem . . .'

Jane looked as if she were about to go on to overload. 'Are you saying that someone may try to kill me?' she asked in a very small voice.

'It's a possibility,' said Steven. 'Maybe a remote one but we didn't want to take any chances.'

'But I only know what you and your organisation know,' Jane protested weakly.

'I thought that too,' said Steven. 'But John Macmillan pointed out that they might be afraid of you going to the papers with what you know. He has a point.'

'Who'd believe me?' said Jane.

'You're the wife of a former Porton Down scientist who was recently found murdered,' said Steven. 'They might very well run it just to see what happens.'

'So what happens now?' asked Jane, now visibly angry.

'I think you should move out of your home for the time being,' said Steven. 'Just until we get to the bottom of this.'

'Move out,' repeated Jane as if it were a

death sentence. 'Leave my home, my friends, my job . . . and go hide somewhere?'

Steven came round to Jane's side of the table and put his arms on her shoulders. 'I know,' he whispered. 'I'm so sorry I got you into this. I'd do anything to turn back the clock and give you your life back but there's nothing anyone can do now. Hang in there and we'll come through this together.'

'A brighter tomorrow,' said Jane, her voice tinged with sarcasm. 'If I live that long.'

'I won't let anything happen to you; I promise,' said Steven. He brought Jane to her feet and held her tight. Jane felt the weapon under his left arm as she reciprocated. 'Oh my God,' she murmured. 'If I were a braver person I'd make some kind of Mae West joke but I'm not. Right now I'm a very scared person.'

Steven kissed the top of her head. 'Let's get started,' he said.

'I take it you're going to let me pick up some things from my house?' asked Jane as they got into Steven's car.

'Of course,' said Steven. This had not been his intention but he saw that denying her might be a step too far after what Jane had been through. In the current situation some clothes and a few personal possessions might well assume an importance beyond their actual substance.

Steven turned the car round and parked it

235

in the street as they wouldn't be staying long. He waited downstairs while Jane got some things together, looking out of the window while he waited.

From upstairs he heard Jane call out, 'This is crazy. What will all my friends think if I just disappear? What about the school? My classes? Look, I really don't think I can do this.'

'Everything will be fine,' Steven replied. 'I'll get you a mobile phone and you can call your friends. Just don't tell them where you really are. Invent a sick relative in Yorkshire.'

'It sounds like you're used to this,' Jane called out.

'Not really,' said Steven distantly. His attention had been caught by a car going past the end of the drive. Unless it was identical to one that had passed a few minutes earlier it was on its second circuit of the area. The thing that chilled him was the fact that it was a blue Range Rover.

'Jane,' he called out.

'What?'

'Come down, will you?'

'I'm not quite fini—'

'Just come down.'

Jane heard something in Steven's voice that made her comply without any more comment. 'What is it?' she asked as she came into the room behind him.

'I think we may be about to have company,'

236

replied Steven without turning away from the window.

'You mean we're too late?'

'A blue Range Rover has passed the house twice in the past five minutes. I think it may have been the same one that turned up in the car park in Ramsgate.'

'Just tell me what to do,' said Jane. She sounded calm and collected and it drew a nod of approval from Steven. 'Make sure all the doors and windows are closed and locked,' he said. He had barely got the words out before the Range Rover passed the house again, slower this time. Steven saw from behind the curtain that it held two male occupants.

'All secure,' said Jane as she returned.

'I think they'll go for a knock on the door,' said Steven. 'With a bit of luck they may not know that I'm here with you. I left the car outside.'

'What do you want me to do?' asked Jane.

'When they knock try to delay them. Call out that you're just coming and then wait for my signal.'

Jane nodded. They were both watching the end of the driveway. After what seemed like an eternity one man appeared at the entrance to the drive. He was wearing a smart suit and carried a briefcase in his right hand. He had a clipboard under his left arm. He put down the briefcase and examined the clipboard as if checking address details.

'Damn,' said Steven. 'Where's the other one? There were two of them in the car.' He told Jane that he was going to check the back. 'Keep an eye on him,' he said. 'Let me know what's happening.'

Steven hurried through to the kitchen, keeping his body below window level until he'd reached the far wall where he could straighten up to sneak a sideways look outside. A shadow moved somewhere in the garden and he dropped down again. He thought he understood the plan. The man at the front would divert Jane's attention while the other gained admission through the back.

Steven pressed himself up against the wall and watched as the figure outside etched a circle in the glass next to the back door with what he guessed was a diamond-tipped marker because of the scratching sound it made. It was done expertly and in one continuous movement, something that gave Steven a clue as to the quality of the opposition he was facing. The man outside stretched sticky tape across the etched circle before tapping it lightly and removing it to leave a hole six inches across.

The doorbell rang and Jane called out, 'Just a minute.'

Steven watched a man's arm come in through the hole in the glass and reach up to unlock the Yale. He let him unlock it, and then allowed him to open the door slowly and take

238

his first step inside before catching him hard on the left temple with the butt of his gun. He reached out quickly to grab the man and stop him falling noisily. He lowered the unconscious figure to the ground.

Although he suspected the man would be out for some time, he still searched him quickly for arms and removed an automatic pistol, which he slipped into his jacket pocket. The doorbell rang again and he heard Jane call out, 'Just a minute will you, I'm coming.'

Steven dropped down beside her behind the couch and gave her shoulder an encouraging squeeze. 'When I signal, answer the door,' he whispered. 'Listen to what he says and then invite him in.'

Steven took up station behind the door, his pistol checked and held at the ready, barrel creating a furrow in his right cheek. He nodded to Jane and she walked over to open the door.

'Sorry about that,' she improvised. 'I was on the phone.'

'Mrs Sebring? Allow me to introduce myself. My name is John Deveron. I represent . . . Paveright Driveways.'

Steven thought that Jane wasn't the only one improvising. Deveron would be wondering just where the hell his partner was.

'I couldn't help but notice that you have stone chippings in the drive,' said Deveron. 'Have you ever considered a more modern

239

brick-paved one?'

'As a matter of fact, I have been thinking about that, Mr Deveron,' said Jane pleasantly. 'Why don't you come in and tell me all about it.'

Deveron took his first step inside and Steven put the barrel of his gun up against his temple. He frisked the man and removed the pistol he was carrying before ordering him to lie down on the floor with his hands behind his head.

'Who are you?' demanded Steven.

'You're making a big mistake, my friend,' gasped the man on the ground as Steven kept the gun to his head and went through his pockets.

'ID, inside pocket on the left,' said the man.

Steven flipped open the ID and gave a long sigh.

'Just stepped out of your league, huh?' said the man on the floor.

'What is it, Steven?' Jane asked.

'I need something to tie these two up,' he replied, deliberately ignoring the question.

'Would plastic clothes-line do?'

'Perfect.'

Jane went to fetch the line and Steven brought out his own ID and showed it to the man on the floor, just allowing him enough leeway to read it.

'Sci-Med? What the hell are you doing here?'

240

'The difference between us,' murmured Steven, 'is that I know why you are here. Now, who sent you?'

'You know I can't tell you that,' grunted the man as Steven once more forced his head down on the floor.

'Of course not,' cooed Steven sarcastically. 'It'll be a secret.'

'For Christ's sake man,' said the man on the floor. 'There's obviously been some kind of screw-up here. Why don't you just let me up and we can sort this whole mess out?'

Jane came back into the room and handed the line and a small vegetable knife to Steven who set about tying up the man. He then moved on to his unconscious colleague in the kitchen and did the same to him.

'So what now?' asked the man on the floor when he returned. 'What's the point of all this? Why don't we just get it all sorted out like civilised people?'

'Your friend sleeping through there broke into this house,' said Steven. 'I'm handing you both over to the police.'

'Jesus,' snorted the man on the floor. 'What do you think plod's going to do when he sees our ID?'

'He's not going to see it,' replied Steven. 'I'm taking it with me along with your firearms and if one of these guns should happen to be the weapon that put a bullet in Michael D'Arcy you'll be seeing the Kent Police as well.'

'Whose side are you on, Dunbar?'

'You know, I sometimes wonder,' said Steven thoughtfully, looking down at the man as if he were a zoo exhibit. He picked up the house phone and then thought better of it. 'Maybe not,' he murmured, changing to his mobile and calling the police.

'Ready?' Steven asked Jane. She replied with a nod of the head.

'For Christ's sake, Dunbar, this is ridiculous,' complained the man on the floor.

'Absolutely,' said Steven, ushering Jane through the door and closing it behind them.

Jane did not say anything until they were inside the car then she slammed her hand down on Steven's as he made to put the car into gear. 'Just what the hell is going on?' she demanded. 'You seemed to know these people or they knew you. I want some answers before I go anywhere with you.'

'Unless they're carrying fake ID, they're MI5,' said Steven.

Jane looked long and hard at him before saying, 'Well, pardon me, but aren't they supposed to be on our side?'

'I thought so too,' said Steven.

'Are you seriously saying that it was MI5 trying to kill me?' asked Jane, her voice betraying the incredulity she felt.

'That's what it looks like.'

'Not a Mr "E"?'

242

'There has to be an explanation,' sighed Steven.

'Will I live to hear it?' said Jane.

'I'll sort it out. I promise.'

CHAPTER FIFTEEN

At eight in the evening the car park at the Service area on the M1 was relatively quiet, as Donald Crowe had hoped it might be. He had no trouble in parking his Mercedes estate car well away from other vehicles and tested the doors to make sure they were locked after using the remote. Satisfied, he walked over to the Travel Lodge and told the receptionist that he had booked small conference facilities for 8.15pm.

'Yes sir, you're in the Salisbury Room, through there and to the left.'

Crowe followed her directions and found the Salisbury Room where a lectern placed outside frosted glass doors held a peg-board sign announcing the room as being reserved for Mercury Graphics, the name Crowe had booked under. He entered and put his briefcase down on the table before walking slowly around the room. It was designed to seat twelve around a central table and had a slide projector at one end along with several computer points. 'Courtesy' notepads had been placed at each position along with complimentary pens carrying the logo of the hotel. It was ideal, thought Crowe. There were only going to be six of them, just another bunch of anonymous reps discussing sales and marketing.

Crowe moved over to the window and opened the vertical blinds slightly. He was in time to see a Toyota Land Cruiser pull up beside his car and Cecil Mowbray get out. He was accompanied by four other men. They all wore dark suits and carried briefcases as requested. Crowe checked his watch. They were right on time.

'So this is what it feels like to be a pedlar on the road,' said Cecil Mowbray as he entered ahead of the others.

'As long as that's what it looks like,' said Crowe.

'You worry too much,' said Mowbray. He introduced the four others to Crowe as, Mr Brown, Mr Black, Mr Grey and Mr Green. 'All ex-Special Forces and veterans of the Dark Continent.'

Crowe took this to mean mercenaries. He nodded to the men and opened his briefcase to take out four envelopes and hand one to each. 'Half your fee, as agreed, gentlemen,' he said. Next he brought out a map and spread it on the table while the men checked the contents of the envelopes. When they'd finished, Crowe said, 'Next Tuesday you are going to take part in a military exercise. You will play the part of terrorists; you'll be up against soldiers of the Territorial Army who will do their best to stop you achieving your objective.'

'A toughie then,' said one of the men to the amusement of the others. Mowbray permitted himself a small smile too. Crowe remained impassive. 'This is the area of operations,' he continued. 'Your target is here, deep in this forest. It's an aqueduct. The soldiers will be aware that three dangerous terrorists are at large in the area and will be charged with hunting you down while others guard the aqueduct.

'The three terrorists will allow themselves to be captured at times throughout the day which I will specify.'

The men looked at each other in puzzlement.

'Normal security at the site has been suspended for the duration of the exercise,' said Crowe. 'When you leave here I will give you four containers. The terrorists will carry with them on the day of the exercise—the ones with the blue marking. There will however, be one other container with red markings.'

'What do we do with that?' asked Mr Green.

'I'm coming to that,' said Crowe.

When he'd finished, one of the men said, 'Clever.'

'What happens to us after we get captured?'

'The exercise will end when the third man has been captured. You will then be released.'

'And no one will ever know,' said Mr Brown.

'Nothing ever happened,' said another. 'A triumph for the Territorials.'

'Quite,' said Crowe. He turned back to the map and said, 'I suggest you leave your vehicle here and proceed on foot. The rest I leave up to you. I'm told you are the best.' He picked up an internal phone and said, 'I think we'll have our coffee now if you please.'

Fifteen minutes later all six men left the room and meandered out past Reception talking loudly about key accounts and computer graphics. They walked slowly over the car park to the cars where an insulated plastic container of the sort used for keeping beer cool on fishing trips was transferred from Crowe's car to the back of the Land Cruiser. Crowe and Mowbray said goodbye to the men before driving off together in Crowe's car.

'Well, that all went very smoothly,' said Mowbray as they exited the car park to join the motorway. 'I take it you used Everley's money to pay them?'

Crowe agreed that he had.

'Everley called me today,' said Mowbray. 'He's getting suspicious.'

'What about?'

'He was complaining that the local Tories are not taking him seriously enough when he tells them that there's going to be a radical

246

change in public opinion coming soon. He thinks they're not doing enough to benefit from it.'

'Well spotted, Rupert,' said Crowe under his breath.

'What are the arrangements for pay day?' asked Mowbray.

'Half the money will be paid into our Zurich accounts when the papers start carrying stories of a strange illness, the other half when it reaches epidemic proportions and general disaffection breaks out.'

'What happens when Rupert finds out he can't capitalise on it?'

'He'll have to come to terms with it,' said Mowbray. 'He's no stranger to failure and he can hardly go and complain to the authorities.'

'Suppose not,' agreed Crowe.

Mowbray's mobile phone rang and he answered it. Crowe heard immediately that something was wrong from the stream of anxious questions that Mowbray started asking. 'What's up?' he asked as Mowbray ended the call.

'Pull the car over,' said Mowbray.

'We're on a motorway.'

'Just stop the car.'

Crowe pulled off on to the hard shoulder and turned off the engine. 'What is it, for God's sake?'

'Two of my agents are being held by the Leicester police. I sent them to deal with

247

Sebring's wife. I didn't want her shooting her mouth off to the papers. Apparently Dunbar was with her when they arrived. He outwitted them and called the police.'

'Bloody hell,' said Crowe. 'What the hell do we do now?'

'Keep our nerve,' said Mowbray. 'I think we can still brass this out but we must keep our nerve. Is there anything left in your lab to link you with the agent?'

'No, I went to great pains to clear everything out.'

'So they can't prove anything,' said Mowbray. 'Work on the agent still stopped back in '91. The accident with the vaccine had to be kept a secret for the sake of the government and national security. If we stick to that line they can't touch us. Agreed?'

'Agreed,' said Crowe.

'But be warned . . . they're going to try.'

Crowe glanced in his rear view mirror and said, 'Shit! It's the police.'

The traffic patrol car pulled off the carriageway and stopped in front of Crowe's car at an angle. Two officers got out and Crowe wound down his window.

'Problems, gentlemen? asked the police driver.

'Not really, Officer,' replied Crowe as pleasantly as his nerves would permit. 'I took a spot of cramp in my right leg. I thought it safest to stop and stretch for a couple of minutes. I was just about to drive off again when you chaps appeared.'

'Then we won't detain you any longer, sir,' said the officer with a smile.

* * *

Steven stayed the night with Jane in the Kensington flat that Rose Roberts had arranged as safe accommodation. Neither of them slept much—Jane because she was struggling to come to terms with all that had happened and Steven because he wasn't at all sure who he could trust any more. Every sound in the night had his eyes moving to the gun that hung in its holster on the end of the bed. Never had the dawn of a new day been more welcome.

Breakfast was a silent affair punctuated with smiles of encouragement, with both of them opting for just juice and coffee although the cupboards in the kitchen and the fridge had been well stocked with just about anything they might have fancied.

'I'll be back as soon as I can,' said Steven as he prepared to leave for the Home Office, holding Jane close and hugging her.

'Take as long as you like,' said Jane with a brave attempt at a smile. 'Just sort this mess out.'

'Don't ans—'

Jane held up her hands and said, 'I think

I've got the picture. Believe me, I have got the picture.'

*　　*　　*

Macmillan grimaced as Steven pushed the two IDs across his desk. 'God, this is hard to believe,' he said.

Steven followed up with the two automatic pistols he'd taken from the men at Jane's house. He'd put them in plastic bags. 'I'd put money on one of them having been used on Michael D'Arcy,' he said.

'I'm going to have to take this right to the top,' said Macmillan. 'I can't believe any of this had government sanction. These two must have been pursuing their own agenda.'

'The one I spoke to behaved as though he were doing his job,' said Steven. 'He had the confidence that comes with the ID.'

'Which could mean that the problem might well be further up the chain,' said Macmillan. 'Not a happy thought.'

'It's all beginning to sound a bit like the situation at Porton,' said Steven. 'Everyone's assuming that everything has official backing.'

'I've been making some progress there,' said Macmillan. 'My source has come up with a name behind the Beta Team budget. He's Sir James Gardiner.'

Steven shook his head and said, 'Doesn't mean much I'm afraid.'

'Right-wing Tory, had his day in the Eighties, very influential. It turns out it was he who resurrected the budget for the experimental team at Porton Down and also instituted the accounting measures necessary to keep it out of the way of prying eyes.'

'And recruited for it?' asked Steven.

'My man didn't know that but presumably Gardiner had some purpose in mind when he set about putting the funds in place. Whether he had official sanction for it or not is a bit more problematical. It seems that Gardiner was involved in setting up a right-wing think-tank at the time—something he did with a man named Warner, Colonel Peter Warner, and a few others we don't know too much about although rumour had it that Rupert Everley, the property magnate, was supplying the financial wherewithal for the group.'

'Then they weren't short of a bob or two,' said Steven. 'What did they get up to exactly?'

'Apart from feeding rumour and innuendo about Labour politicians to the media and generally underpinning right-wing causes, we don't know too much about them,' said Macmillan. 'There were suggestions about links with the National Front but then there always are about groups like that. There was nothing ever concrete. It could even have been the other side's rumour machine having a go at them.'

'If Donald Crowe was the leader of the Beta

251

team at Porton maybe he was one of them?' said Steven.

'You may well be right,' said Macmillan.

'George Sebring and Michael D'Arcy were definitely under the impression that they were working for the government during their time there,' said Steven. 'Maybe these two . . .' Steven reached over for the two ID cards to examine the names, 'are under a similar sort of delusion?'

Macmillan thought for a moment before saying, 'I'm going to the Home Secretary with this. We can't risk aiming any lower.'

'Let's hope he's not a pal of Gardiner's too,' said Steven.

'Wrong party,' said Macmillan.

'Bit hard to tell them apart these days,' said Steven.

'But as a priority, I'm going to have him ask the Leicester police to hold on to these two until we at least know where their instructions came from.'

'Good,' said Steven.

Macmillan clicked on the intercom and asked Rose Roberts to set up an urgent call to the Home Secretary 'What will you do in the meantime?' he asked Steven.

'Did Rose have any success coming up with a molecular biologist?'

Macmillan opened his desk drawer and took out a small card, which he slid across to Steven, saying, 'Professor William Rees of the

Medical Research Council's Laboratory of Molecular Biology at Cambridge is expecting your call. He'll actually be in London today and tomorrow at the MRC's head office in Park Crescent. He said that it would be all right if you wanted to speak to him there.'

'That might save some time,' said Steven. 'I'll call him and see if I can fix something up for this afternoon.'

'Why don't we meet back here later and exchange notes?' asked Macmillan.

Steven agreed. They settled on 6pm.

Steven set up a meeting with Rees for 2pm that afternoon and then went back to the safe house to check on Jane, using a bus and two taxis in a roundabout route just in case he was being followed. He didn't think he would be but where Jane's safety was concerned he didn't intend taking any chances. He told her about Macmillan going to the Home Secretary.

'I still can't believe this is happening,' said Jane. 'It's as if everything I've ever believed in has been swept away and I'm floating around in a sea of suspicion.'

'I'm sorry,' whispered Steven, gathering her in his arms. 'I know what you're going through.'

'Do you?' challenged Jane. 'Do you really?'

'Yes,' said Steven. 'I felt exactly the same way the first time I crossed swords with the establishment and realised what they were

253

capable of. The world suddenly stopped being black and white. The clear distinctions I'd imagined existed between right and wrong, good and evil became blurred and everything was etched in shades of grey.'

'So how do you cope?'

'I support the lighter shades,' smiled Steven. 'I try to do what I believe to be right—that's a much more difficult thing to do than you might imagine. The right thing to do is not always the wise thing, the safe thing or even the legal thing. It can be a hard road to travel.'

'If you say so,' said Jane. 'What happens now?'

'I'm going to talk to a scientist this afternoon about how we can identify the agent your husband and Michael D'Arcy were working on and then I'm seeing Macmillan again at the Home Office to find out what's happening.'

'In the meantime I will thrill to the magic of daytime television,' said Jane.

'It won't be for long,' said Steven.

'Better not be,' said Jane. 'If it comes to a choice between a bullet in the head and watching *Countdown*, it's going to be a pretty close-run thing.'

Steven smiled and kissed her on the cheek. 'I'd best be off.'

*   *   *

Steven was shown into one of the committee rooms at the headquarters of the Medical Research Council and offered coffee while he waited. He declined and took a seat at the long, polished wooden table, surrounded by portraits of past secretaries of the council looking down at him from the walls. Not the happiest looking bunch of people, he concluded in the silence before turning his attention to an assortment of periodicals lined up on a shelf next to the period fireplace. Predictably, they were either scientific or medical. He flicked through the pages of *Nature* and *Molecular Microbiology* before the door opened and a short, stocky man with wiry dark hair and wearing a tweed jacket entered. His first utterance betrayed the fact he was Welsh.

'I'm Rees, sorry I'm late.'

'Not at all, I'm grateful to you for seeing me at such short notice,' said Steven.

'I never put off till tomorrow what I can do today,' said Rees. 'Unlike some of them round here who make a career out of "asking for clarification" and "deferring decisions" in the hope that the question will go away if they sit on the bloody fence for long enough.'

'Sounds like you've been asking for funds,' said Steven with a smile.

'For a new unit,' said Rees.

'A lot then,' said Steven.

'The Americans will be conducting field

trials by the time we lay the foundation stone,' said Rees. 'Some things never change.' He shook his head and looked down at the floor for a moment before appearing to remember why he was there and breaking into a smile, saying, 'I'm sorry; excuse my rudeness. What can I do for you?'

Steven explained the problem.

'Well, we certainly don't need to sequence the entire genomes of these things,' said Rees.

'That's a relief,' said Steven.

'The fact that you suspect that the foreign genes might come from the HIV virus means that we can construct probes and check for any homology in the host DNA.'

'Is that a big job?' asked Steven.

'It's no walk in the park,' replied Rees, 'but nothing like sequencing the entire chromosome would be: that's a non-starter. You say you have three dozen of these cultures?'

'All normal body commensals according to the man who isolated them,' said Steven. 'No pathogens.'

'This man's a doctor?' asked Rees.

'A medical technician,' said Steven.

'Maybe I could have a look at the list?' said Rees. 'It would be nice to narrow the field down if it is at all possible.'

'I thought you might want to see it,' said Steven. 'I've brought it with me on disk.'

'Excellent,' said Rees. 'I have my laptop

here. Let's have a look, shall we?'

Rees set up his computer and Steven handed him the disk that Gus Maclean had given him.

Rees brought out a pair of half-moon spectacles from his jacket pocket and perched them on the end of his nose but still had to tilt his head back slightly to be able to read down the list of bacteria that Maclean had isolated from himself.

'Certainly no pathogens,' he murmured. 'But . . .'

'You've found something?' asked Steven, feeling excited at the prospect.

'I'm not sure,' said Rees. 'It's certainly a bit unusual . . . to find three different isolates in any one individual . . .'

'Sorry, I'm not with you,' said Steven, looking over Rees's shoulder.

'These *Mycoplasmas*,' said Rees, pointing to the list with his finger. 'Funny buggers . . . They inhabit the no-man's land between bacteria and viruses. They don't have a proper bacterial cell wall so they're fragile little beasties—hard to grow in the lab—but you can still treat them with antibiotics if need be, unlike viruses.'

'Then they can cause disease?' asked Steven.

'Lots of strains cause problems in animals but only one variant causes disease in man, *Mycoplasma pneumoniae*. It can give you a

257

pretty nasty pneumonia but it's not one of the ones listed here,' said Rees. 'There's been a suggestion around for some time that they contribute in some way to rheumatoid arthritis but that's controversial: the jury's still out on that. For the main part, they're regarded as pretty harmless—just bugs you find in the upper respiratory track of normal healthy human beings. The thing that caught my eye though is that we've got three different strains here in the one patient. That's something I wouldn't have expected.'

'A starting point?' suggested Steven.

'Could well be,' said Rees. 'If you can get these cultures to me I think we'll take a closer look at these three beasties before we do anything else. We'll do some standard tests and then extract DNA from them and check them out with a series of HIV probes.'

'I'll get on to that right away,' said Steven.

'I'll be back in Cambridge the day after tomorrow,' said Rees.

* * *

The first thing Steven did when he left the offices of the MRC was walk up to nearby Regents Park and phone Gus Maclean. After initial enquiries about his health when he learned that Maclean was back at work, he said, 'Glad to hear it. I need your culture collection.'

258

'Needles in haystacks time?' said Maclean.

'Might not be as bad as we thought,' said Steven. 'MRC Cambridge are going to take a look at things.'

'Well they don't come any more high-powered than that,' said Maclean. 'How should we do this?'

'I'll have a courier pick up the collection at the hospital if that's okay with you?' said Steven.

'I'll be waiting,' said Maclean. 'You will let me know if they find anything, won't you?'

'Of course,' said Steven, realising almost immediately as he put the phone back in his pocket that he had replied too glibly. Telling Maclean might not be an option if Rees should come up trumps. In fact, it was difficult to see how much of the truth could ever be allowed to come out and how much would be covered up 'in the public interest' as the much-abused phrase went. Even he—a confirmed advocate of openness in Government—could see that telling the nation that their soldiers in the Gulf War had been given a vaccine contaminated with a biological weapon might not be the brightest thing to do on the eve of sending them off again. Apart from the effect on morale that this kind of revelation would have, lawyers all over the country would be bound to go into a feeding frenzy, intent on bankrupting the public purse—*pro bono publico*—and doing themselves no harm at all while they

259

were at it.

The other side of the coin was that he did not want to see the people who had genuinely suffered because of the mistake—men like Gus Maclean—continue to be ignored in their rightful claims for a fair deal. As he continued to walk in the park, wondering just how the many who had suffered could be compensated in any realistic way, Steven remembered what Michael D'Arcy had said about the agent he and the others had been commissioned to design. It had to be non-lethal but debilitating, undetectable and . . . curable. This third and last criterion was something he hadn't given much thought to but now it was interesting.

If Rees were to succeed in finding the agent in Gus Maclean's collection then Gus's recurrent health problems bore testament to D'Arcy's first condition having been met. He hadn't been killed, he had been debilitated. The fact that the bug hadn't shown up in any conventional microbiological screen satisfied the second criterion of being undetectable, but what about the third? He wondered. Curable? This intriguing thought stayed with him as he checked his watch and set out for the Home Office. Was it possible that so-called Gulf War Syndrome was curable?

CHAPTER SIXTEEN

John Macmillan was looking grim when Steven entered his office just after six.

'It's been a busy afternoon in the corridors of power,' he said. 'I don't think I can ever remember anything quite like it.'

Steven remained silent but he listened in trepidation.

'When I told the Home Secretary about our two friends in Leicester, he got in touch immediately with the head of MI5 and demanded an explanation. He in turn, investigated and it would appear—as you suggested—that the men did believe they were carrying out orders—Government orders.'

'Issued by whom?' asked Steven.

'Their section head, a man named Mowbray, Cecil Mowbray. He's now been suspended and is currently being held by Special Branch. Mowbray still maintains that—'

'Don't tell me,' said Steven. 'He was only obeying orders from above?'

'Something like that,' said Macmillan. 'He's taking the line that in his senior position he does not have to be given direct orders but is expected to use his initiative in protecting government interests. He maintains that the development of the agent at Porton *was*

261

Government sanctioned and top secret and it was his job to keep it that way in view of what happened. He has cited Sir James Gardiner as the initiator of the project.'

'Gardiner again,' said Steven.

'Quite so,' said Macmillan. 'Apparently he's on holiday with his wife, staying at Reid's Hotel in Madeira; he's due back tomorrow. Special Branch will pick him up at the airport. In the meantime, they've also been speaking to Donald Crowe—like I say, it's been a busy afternoon. Not surprisingly Crowe's singing from the same hymn sheet as Mowbray. He insists the Beta Team and their work had Government approval.'

'What about the agent itself? Do we know any more?'

'Although all work on it stopped after the accident at Porton, Crowe says that the team wanted to come clean about what had happened but couldn't because of the effect it would have had on the troops about to go to the Gulf.'

'Very public-spirited of them,' said Steven. 'Did he give any details about its construction?'

'Only that it was a very early attempt at designing an agent commissioned by the government of the day,' said Macmillan.

'No technical details? Nothing about what it was based on?'

'He was very vague,' said Macmillan. 'He

said they were just trying out a few ideas.'

Steven gave a long sigh and said, 'I've got an awful feeling they're going to walk away from this.'

'I wouldn't bet against it,' agreed Macmillan.

'What about the two MI5 men the Leicester police are holding?'

'They clearly believed they were acting under orders so officially they've done nothing wrong,' said Macmillan.

'On the other hand they murdered George Sebring and Michael D'Arcy,' said Steven.

Macmillan nodded and said, 'It's difficult; a moral minefield, you might say. From another perspective it could be argued that Sebring and D'Arcy were responsible for the incapacity and death of many who served in the Gulf War after what happened at Porton with the vaccine.'

'And everyone was only obeying orders,' said Steven. 'Now, where have I heard that before?'

'Maybe Gardiner wasn't,' said Macmillan.

'I think I'd like to be there when Special Branch pick him up,' said Steven.

'No problem,' said Macmillan. 'The Home Secretary has agreed that we be kept in the picture at all times. I'll have Rose inform them of your interest. She'll text you the details of his arrival time. How did you get on with Professor Rees?'

'Nice man,' said Steven. 'He thinks it might well be possible to identify the agent in Gus Maclean's culture collection if it's there. I've arranged for it to be delivered to him in Cambridge.'

'There doesn't seem to be much point now,' said Macmillan. 'We know what they were doing at Porton and what happened with the vaccine.'

'I think I'd still like to have him go ahead,' said Steven.

'Why?' asked Macmillan.

'I think I'd be happier if we had an independent assessment of what they were making, just in case they left anything out.'

'Like what?'

'Just anything.'

'All right,' conceded Macmillan. 'Let's just hope it doesn't put too big a hole in our budget.'

'Can I take it it's now safe for Jane Sebring to get on with her life without any more attention from MI5?' asked Steven.

'Mowbray has been suspended from duty pending further inquiries and the two agents concerned have been made aware of what's happened.'

'That must have been a magic moment for the pair of them,' said Steven. 'Sorry chaps, you weren't licensed to kill after all.'

'Let me know what happens with Gardiner tomorrow,' said Macmillan.

Steven took Jane out to dinner to Alfredo's, his favourite Italian restaurant, located in a side street off the Strand. He was known there and the staff always took trouble to make his guests feel especially welcome. Alfredo, a short, stocky man with a bushy moustache and twinkling eyes—who looked more Turkish than Italian despite his proud Neapolitan heritage—took personal charge of ensuring Jane's comfort, all the while insisting that a woman so good looking must have Italian blood in her.

Steven was pleased to see Jane smiling and relaxed after the trauma of the past couple of days. 'He's right, you are beautiful,' he said as the candles on their table were lit with a flourish.

'What is this?' laughed Jane. 'What are you softening me up for?'

'How could you?' said Steven, feigning hurt.

'Now tell me,' said Jane.

Steven paused to thank Alfredo who had brought them an aperitif on the house then he said, 'We agreed from the outset that I would tell you everything that was going on. Well, that has a downside to it.'

'Go on,' said Jane cautiously.

'There are some things that have to remain a secret,' said Steven.

'I never supposed anything else,' Jane replied.

'Good, but that includes things that you might actually want brought out in the open.'

'Like what?'

'There's a real chance that it might not be possible to bring George's killers to justice.'

Jane's eyes narrowed. 'Why not?' she asked.

'They believed that they were acting under Government orders,' said Steven.

'The same men who came after me?' said Jane.

Steven nodded.

'But surely they *weren't*?'

'But they thought they were,' said Steven. 'Somewhere in the chain of command above them was a rogue element.'

'So you can charge the rogue element,' said Jane.

'I'd like to think we could,' said Steven. 'But if you think it through it would be impossible to charge him or her without charging the two men who actually carried out the killing—and that's where the problem lies.'

'You mean, they will maintain that they were only doing their job,' said Jane.

'Yes.'

Jane appeared to think for a moment before saying, 'Well, I suppose it serves George right for getting into such a messy business in the first place. And nothing's going to bring him back now, is it?'

'I hoped you might see it that way,' said Steven.

*   *   *

Steven remained in the background as the Special Branch officers moved in to intercept James Gardiner at Heathrow airport. They did so just after he and his wife had reached passport control. Gardiner reacted in just the manner Steven had supposed he might, given what he'd learned about him from John Macmillan. He initially adopted an air of detached amusement as if some mistake had been made and he had been confused with some ordinary mortal but this quickly changed to outrage when the officers persisted and culminated in demands to know if the officers realised who he was. When he was eventually persuaded to calm down by the two experienced officers who had seen and heard it all before, he was given a few moments to speak to his wife before finally being separated and led off to an interview room where Steven joined them.

The door closed and for a few moments there was silence in the room as no one spoke while the seating arrangements were worked out. General airport noise was largely cut out by the soundproofing although an intermittent vibration every few minutes served to remind them where they were as yet another aircraft took to the skies.

'Who's he?' said Gardiner, becoming aware of Steven's presence.

Steven showed him his ID without saying anything and Gardiner examined it with the same disdain that he'd shown towards the Special Branch men. He waved it away with an imperious hand gesture. 'Just what the hell is this all about?' he demanded.

'We'd like you to answer some questions, Sir James.'

'What about? My holiday in Madeira?'

'We are looking into the circumstances surrounding the deaths of two ex-government scientists, Dr George Sebring and Dr Michael D'Arcy. We think you may be able to help us.'

Gardiner swallowed hard but maintained his equilibrium. 'Never heard of them,' he said.

'Tell us about the Beta Team at Porton Down,' said Steven.

Gardiner looked long and hard at him before saying, 'I don't know what you're talking about.'

'We already know that you were responsible for reactivating it back in 1989,' continued Steven. 'So maybe we can bypass the blank denials?'

'1989?' snickered Gardiner. 'I was responsible for a lot of things back then,' he said, leaning back in his chair and looking off to the middle distance as if enjoying a stroll down memory lane. 'Presumably I signed some piece of paper or other. I don't remember.'

'Dr Sebring and Dr D'Arcy were members of that team,' said one of the Special Branch men.

'I still have no idea what you're talking about,' said Gardiner.

'Donald Crowe is in custody,' said Steven. 'We know about the accident.'

'What accident?'

'The one that led to the contamination of vaccines given to the troops before the Gulf War in 1990,' said Steven sharply.

Gardiner seemed to diminish in stature over the next few moments. All traces of arrogance and pomposity left him; he let out his breath in a long sigh and allowed his shoulders to slump forwards. 'You do, do you?' he said.

'Cecil Mowbray is also being held,' said Steven. 'He, of course, was not a member of the Beta Team.'

Gardiner's eyes betrayed a darting unease as he looked up at Steven.

'But he was a member of another sort of team, led by you,' said Steven. 'Set up around the same time as the Beta Team . . . along with Colonel Peter Warner, Mr Rupert Everley and maybe a few others.'

'My, we have been doing our homework,' murmured Gardiner. He affected an amused smile but Steven could see that he was considering his position, weighing his options.

'But then, it wouldn't be difficult for you,' he continued. 'We had nothing to hide. As far as I know there is still no law that prevents like-minded people from banding together to act on behalf of and for the good of their country—unless New Labour brought one in while I was away—and I wouldn't put it past them.'

'It depends what these "like-minded" people get up to,' said one of the Special Branch officers. 'We tend to draw the line at murder.'

'I know nothing about any murder,' said Gardiner, giving the officer a withering look.

'Sebring and D'Arcy were subject to direct action by the intelligence services,' said Steven. He deliberately employed the euphemism as a sop to Gardiner's sensibilities.

'Then you must speak to them,' said Gardiner.

'Mowbray has decided that he was only acting in the best interests of the country,' said Steven.

'So has Crowe,' added one of the Special Branch men.

'We all have to do that,' said Gardiner, although a note of caution had entered his voice.

'Did you order the deaths of these men in order to keep the accident at Porton a secret?' asked the Special Branch man.

Gardiner looked askance and then said,

'Don't be ridiculous. I have had no executive power for many years. To suggest that I could issue orders these days to members of the intelligence services or even the scientific civil service is a notion that would be laughed out of court should it ever come to that.'

'Not if it were shown that you took it upon yourself to re-activate the Beta Team for your own reasons back in 1989 and let it be known that it had Government approval . . . when it hadn't.'

'Of course it had,' said Gardiner.

'At least you now remember it,' said Steven.

'Can you prove that you had Government sanction?' asked a Special Branch man.

Gardiner looked at the man as if he were mildly amused by the question. 'Considering the number of people who have passed in and out of the ever-revolving door of ministerial power during the last decade, can you prove that I hadn't?' he asked.

'We'll give it our best shot,' said the officer but Steven saw that Gardiner had latched on to the one thing that would save him. He suspected that it would prove well nigh impossible to show that Gardiner had never at any stage received even a tacit nod of approval for the setting up of Beta Team. Everyone involved in the affair was going to end up claiming that he or she had only been obeying orders and the murderers of George Sebring, Michael D'Arcy and the journalist Martin

271

Hendry, were going to walk free. The thought encouraged him to make a last ditch attempt at rattling the man.

'Come off it, Gardiner,' he snapped. 'It was you and your fascist chums who set up the Beta Team, wasn't it?'

He saw a flash of anger appear in Gardiner's eyes but it faded almost as quickly as better judgement prevailed and he recovered his composure before saying, 'I suppose in your book a fascist is anyone who can read and write and string two words together without them being, "Yes Tony."'

'No, it's anyone who decides to impose his will on others by using any means available to him without compunction, including murder,' said Steven.

'How many times must I repeat that I know nothing at all about any murder?' said Gardiner through gritted teeth.

'But the involvement of your group . . .' began one of the policemen.

'We have always acted within the confines of the law!' interrupted Gardiner. 'The rule of law is fundamental to us. It was the very basis on which we wanted to rebuild our country—to reclaim it from the tide of mongrel trash and deviant flotsam and jetsam that has washed over us during the past decade.'

'Adolf was a big believer in law and order,' said one of the Special Branch men after a silent pause.

'Saddam is too, I believe,' said his colleague.

'How dare you!' said Gardiner.

'Tell us about the accident,' said Steven.

'I'm no scientist,' said Gardiner. 'All I know is what I was told at the time. Someone on the Beta Team gave the wrong thing out in response to a request from colleagues.'

'The wrong thing being the agent that the Beta Team had been commissioned to design,' said Steven.

'Yes.'

'Tell us about that.'

'I say again, I'm no scientist,' said Gardiner.

'But you knew the basic characteristics,' insisted Steven.

'We—the government of the day, that is,' said Gardiner with a nuance of self-satisfaction in his voice, 'thought it politic to look into the possibility of designing a biological agent that was not just an outright killer but a vector for achieving population control in a hostile environment.'

'Why?' asked Steven.

'I understood that science had progressed to a point where it could do more than simply design killing agents. The potential was right for investigation.'

'Go on.'

'The team was commissioned to design an agent that was to be disabling but not lethal, undetectable by conventional means and, in the long run, curable.'

There it was again, thought Steven, the third criterion, curable. 'What was this agent based on?' he asked.

'What do you mean?'

'Presumably they weren't being asked to create a new life form out of fresh air. Which bacterium or virus was used as a starting point?'

'I've no idea,' said Gardiner. 'Not my field I'm afraid.'

'If they were to be curable, wouldn't that defeat the whole purpose?' Steven asked.

'I think there was more to it than that,' said Gardiner. 'But I've no idea what. I have to keep telling you, I'm not a scientist. What does it matter now anyway? The whole venture was abandoned after the accident.'

Steven nodded to indicate to the Special Branch men that he had finished questioning Gardiner.

'Can I go now?' asked Gardiner.

'I'm afraid not, Sir James,' said one of the Special Branch men. 'We're going to have to hold you for further questioning. If you'll come with us, please . . .'

Steven watched as the two officers led away the protesting Gardiner and he was left alone and feeling dejected in the empty interview room. The words, 'Population control in a hostile environment' were uppermost in his mind. Was this a plausible aim for a Government sanctioned initiative? And would

274

a court of law believe that it was?

The answer seemed to be affirmative in both cases. It could be argued that such technology might also be attractive to subversive or terrorist groups but Gardiner's insistence that the government had been behind the project would probably win the benefit of the doubt—not that it was going to come to that, he was convinced. The smart money was on the whole thing being dropped.

As he drove back into the city Steven found himself wondering if Gus Maclean's cultures had arrived safely at Rees's lab in Cambridge and if Rees had begun work on them. Thinking this made him suddenly wonder why it should still be necessary to start from scratch. Despite admissions all round about the purpose of the Beta Team back in 1990 and what they'd been trying to create, not one technical detail had emerged about the agent's construction. D'Arcy had died—no, he had been murdered—before he could supply the information, Crowe had been vague when asked by John Macmillan, and Gardiner had just pleaded complete ignorance of science.

He supposed it was just possible that John Macmillan, not being a medic, had not asked the right questions. But if Crowe could be persuaded to provide some simple technical answers it would undoubtedly save Rees a lot of time and trouble. By the time he had reached the safe house where Jane was, he had decided to go see Crowe himself next morning. He called Sci-Med to ask that they arrange it.

'Good day?' asked Jane.

'I've known worse,' smiled Steven. 'Good news and bad news.' He told her of Gardiner's response to the charges put to him.

'So he's going to get away with it too?' said Jane.

'It would be impossible to prove beyond doubt that he did not have Government approval,' said Steven.

'And the good news?' said Jane.

'You can go home tomorrow and get on with your life,' said Steven.

Jane smiled ruefully and said, 'Good. I'm not sure it's ever going to be the same again.'

'It's in our nature to get over things,' said Steven.

'Sounds like a variant of, "Time's a great healer",' said Jane.

'I suppose,' agreed Steven. 'Let's go out to dinner.'

*   *   *

'Shouldn't you be feeling pleased with yourself, or is there something you have to tell me?' asked Jane, very much aware of Steven's preoccupation throughout dinner.

Steven smiled and said, 'I'm sorry, no, it's nothing like that and the only thing I have to tell you is that I am so glad I met you.'

276

Doubt remained on Jane's face. 'Then what?'

'There's something about the whole thing that's bugging me and it's not just the fact that your husband's murderer is not going to be brought to justice. There's something I just can't put my finger on.'

'Maybe you are one of those people who just can't let go?' said Jane.

'You missed out "those annoying bloody",' said Steven with a smile.

Jane smiled and said, 'Are you going to come up to Leicester with me tomorrow?'

Steven said not. He was going to question Donald Crowe. He confessed that one of the things still puzzling him was the fact that there had still been no mention of any construction details about the agent the Beta Team had been making.

'Well, Crowe must certainly know,' said Jane. 'After all, he was in charge of the whole damned thing. Dreadful man.'

'He must,' agreed Steven. 'But he managed to avoid saying anything about that when he was interviewed. Strange.'

'Well, it was all a long time ago, I suppose,' said Jane.

'Mm,' said Steven.

'You see something sinister in it?'

Steven shrugged and said, 'Maybe, maybe not. It's hard to see why he would want to keep that a secret when we know exactly what

277

happened.'

'It's hard to see why they would want to kill my husband and the others in order to keep a twelve-year-old accident a secret too,' countered Jane.

Steven looked at her unseeingly as the hairs on the back of his neck started to rise. He had been about to point out that the financial repercussions of having to admit liability to the Gulf War veterans would have been an obvious reason when he saw an alternative explanation. 'Sweet Jesus,' he murmured under his breath.

'What's the matter?' asked Jane, sounding concerned at the change that had come over Steven. 'You look as if you've seen a ghost.'

'They didn't abandon it,' he said.

Jane appeared bemused. 'Didn't abandon what?' she asked.

'The construction of the agent,' said Steven as his mind raced ahead of him. 'I'd been assuming it was the accident itself that they wanted to keep secret because of the financial fall out but that's not it at all. It's the agent they want to keep secret. They didn't abandon it! They went on working on it.'

'Tell me this is just an academic exercise you're going through in your head,' said Jane.

'The more I think about it,' said Steven, the bit now between his teeth, 'the more it begins to make sense. Disabling, undetectable and curable. They succeeded! That's why they

278

want to keep it a secret.'

'But you can't be sure about this,' said Jane. 'It could just be your imagination. Please God, it's just your imagination!'

'Somehow I don't think so,' said Steven. 'If Crowe doesn't come clean about everything tomorrow when I ask him outright that'll be proof enough.'

'More Government intrigue?' said Jane.

'Quite the reverse I think,' said Steven. 'I think we could be looking at private enterprise here.'

'Gardiner and his gang?'

'Gardiner made a big thing about his group always acting within the law,' said Steven. 'He said at one point that he was contemplating disbanding the group because he felt they weren't getting anywhere.'

'What exactly were their objectives?'

'Oh, a misty-eyed return to England for the English, warm beer, cricket on the village green, bobbies on the beat, kids behaving themselves and everyone leaving their doors unlocked.'

'Sounds good to me,' said Jane. 'If he can combine that with Santa Claus being real and the tooth fairy dealing with next month's Visa Card bill I just might join up.'

Steven was still deep in thought.

'You're serious about this, aren't you?' said Jane.

The look on Steven's face answered her

279

question. 'Maybe some other members of the group have rather different ideas about how they should go about achieving their aims.'

Jane's eyes opened wide. 'You're suggesting that they might actually use the agent?' she gasped. 'But how? How would you use something like that?'

'You'd have to come up with a way of infecting a sizeable proportion of your target population before you could begin to exert any control over them,' said Steven. 'Designing delivery systems for biological weapons is a hi-tech-science in itself. It's as difficult as designing the weapons themselves. You can't just infect one person and depend on them passing on the disease. You have to contaminate a large number of people at the same time. Saddam used missiles with non-explosive heads to create air bursts over his intended targets. Crop duster aircraft can be used in much the same way but each organism throws up different problems when it comes to turning them into aerosol mists or even powder form. Some of the most lethal organisms on earth are actually fragile little creatures in their own right. They don't like being exposed to hostile environments and they die very quickly. Then there are the limitations imposed by the vagaries of wind and weather. A sudden change in the wind and you can end up infecting your own troops.'

'It makes me ill to think of this,' said Jane.

'Throwing up our hands in horror is no defence.'

'What is?' asked Jane.

'Intelligence is all-important,' said Steven. 'Knowing what agent is being used is paramount. If you know that you can vaccinate against viruses or give antibiotic umbrellas against bacteria.'

'But if you don't know what's coming . . .' said Jane.

'You're in real trouble,' said Steven. 'Vaccination is not much use after the event and antibiotics will be fighting a losing battle— always assuming you can come up with a suitable one or combination in the first place. Bio-weapons are nearly always designed to be resistant to antibiotics.'

'If you are right about the existence of this new agent and it being in private hands . . .' said Jane.

'We need to know exactly what it is and how to detect it—not easy if it has been designed to be undetectable—and finally how to treat it,' said Steven. 'But it was designed to be treatable . . .' he added as a puzzling afterthought.

'I can understand how something like smallpox or plague can be used as a weapon,' said Jane. 'They will obviously create fear and terror and will kill a lot of people but I'm not so sure about this new thing?'

'The idea was first mooted at an

international conference on biotechnology about fifteen years ago,' said Steven. 'If you can create conditions where the majority of the target population are ill most of the time and feel generally run down and under the weather they will start to turn against the social structure that they're living in. They will blame their government for their miserable state and embrace any promise of radical change on offer. It's a modern day variation on brain-washing. In that state it's possible to change people's whole political philosophy.'

'Don't they just pretend?' said Jane. 'In order to get away from their captors, I mean.'

Steven shook his head and said, 'No, they really believe it. You can still see this happening from time to time at big religious rallies. People get swept up in the contrived emotion of it all. Some—the most vulnerable—become so disorientated that they become hyperreceptive to the ideas on offer and experience "miraculous" conversion.'

'They see the light,' said Jane.

'Yes, but they've been brainwashed,' said Steven. 'They just don't realise it.'

CHAPTER SEVENTEEN

'The word is we're not going to be able to hold them much longer,' said the Special Branch officer to Steven when he arrived next morning to which he replied that he had already come to that conclusion himself but he wanted the chance to have a last word with Crowe and then maybe Mowbray?

'No problem.'

Crowe was escorted into the room and as expected Steven found it impossible to discern anything about the man from his demeanour. The yellow, parchment-like skin, the tight thin lips and the eyes hidden by tinted lenses shielded any emotion that might be there. Crowe carefully angled his chair, sat down and crossed his legs languidly.

'I understand that you will be released later today,' said Steven.

'About time too,' said Crowe. 'This has all been hugely embarrassing and totally unnecessary. It should never have got this far.'

'You were only doing your job,' said Steven. He said it in such a way that Crowe detected sarcasm and reacted accordingly. 'Do you have a problem with that?' he asked.

'Not at all,' said Steven. 'The government of the day asked you to design a biological agent and you went to work. That was your job. You can't be held responsible for any accident that happened or for any of the repercussions.'

'Quite,' said Crowe.

'What was the agent based on?'

'What does it matter? It was all a very long time ago,' said Crowe.

'I'd just like to know,' said Steven.

'I'm not sure I can even remember after all this time,' said Crowe. 'There were a number of possibilities under consideration at the time . . .'

'The early form of the agent, the one that got into the vaccine, what was that based on?' asked Steven, leaning closer and enunciating each word clearly.

'I really can't say,' said Crowe.

'Can't or won't?'

Crowe made an unsuccessful attempt at a smile. 'Can't,' he said. 'Call it the effects of advancing years but I really can't remember . . .'

'And I really can't believe you,' said Steven.

Crowe held Steven in his dark gaze for a few moments before saying, 'So, where do we go from here?'

Steven sat back in his chair and said, 'You set out to create an agent in which three criteria were to be satisfied. It was to be disabling rather than lethal, undetectable through conventional means and lastly it was to be curable. Tell me about that; how were you going to make a biological agent curable without making it useless as a weapon?'

'You know, that escapes me too, I'm afraid,' said Crowe.

Steven noted the suggestion of challenge in Crowe's voice. He could see that he was going to get nowhere although the man's determination to say nothing at least seemed

284

to confirm his fears that the agent must actually exist. 'Very well, Doctor,' he said. 'I am now going to request that Porton take your lab apart.'

'How very inconvenient,' said Crowe. 'Might one ask why?'

'I think you know why,' said Steven.

'I'm afraid you've lost me,' said Crowe.

I wish, thought Steven. The bottom of a swamp would have been his place of choice. 'I'm not convinced that work on the agent was discontinued after the accident,' he said. 'I think perhaps development was continued and the agent now exists.'

Crowe regarded Steven through his tinted lenses for nearly thirty seconds before saying, 'An interesting but altogether fanciful notion, I'm afraid. That would have been quite illegal. All work stopped after Sebring's blunder. End of story.'

Steven nodded to the officer by the door and Crowe was led away while he sat considering whether or not it would even be worthwhile talking to Mowbray. He concluded that it would. If Mowbray proved to be as evasive as Crowe it would at least confirm that he was in cahoots with Crowe and he would have identified two of the breakaway faction.

It was immediately evident from Mowbray's attitude when he was brought in that he was less than amused at being called for interview again. Steven presented his ID but Mowbray

285

waved it away saying, 'I know perfectly well who and what you are.'

'I'm just clearing up some loose ends, Mr Mowbray,' said Steven.

'Still enjoying your moment in the sun, eh Dunbar? You and that Mickey Mouse operation you work for.'

'We do our best,' replied Steven pleasantly. 'Even though we're heterosexual and none of us went to Cambridge—a big disadvantage in the intelligence services I believe.'

'Highly amusing.'

'Tell me about the biological agent you thought worth killing for,' said Steven.

Mowbray seemed unfazed. 'We can't all wear the white hats and play the Lone Ranger, Dunbar,' he said. 'Unlike Johnny Macmillan and his science police some of us—the professionals—have to operate in the real world and do the dirty jobs. Even you must appreciate that there are some things that must remain secret—whatever the cost.'

'And the Beta Team's agent was one of them?'

'The accident with it was one of them,' corrected Mowbray.

'Not the agent itself?' said Steven, watching for Mowbray's reaction but not learning much.

'It was an early prototype,' said Mowbray. 'Work on it was abandoned.'

Steven looked at Mowbray long and hard before saying, 'Was it?'

'Of course.'

'What bug was the agent based on?'

'I'm not a scientist.'

'Are you telling me that this never came up at any of the meetings you had in the aftermath of what happened?' said Steven. 'It was never mentioned in assessing the potential risk to the troops?'

'It may have been,' said Mowbray. 'But it wouldn't have meant anything to me.'

'How did they plan to make it undetectable?'

'I've no idea. Probably take it up to the turret room of a castle and pass a current through it at the height of an electrical storm I should think. I'm not a scientist.'

'How were they planning to make it curable and still have it remain viable as a weapon?'

'Sorry, can't help you there either,' said Mowbray. 'It was very clever, I'm sure but it was all just scientific gobbledegook to me.'

Steven nodded and smiled. 'Thank you, Mr Mowbray,' he said. 'You've been very helpful.'

'Is that it?'

'Yup.'

*   *   *

Steven went directly to the Home Office to voice his new fears to John Macmillan.

'But you've no proof of this,' said

287

Macmillan.

'Everything points to it,' said Steven. 'I'm convinced that was why Sebring, D'Arcy and Hendry were killed. It was to keep the origins of the agent a secret—not the accident. That's why they've all been so reticent when it came to questions about its construction. Work continued on it after the accident. They actually made it.'

'But why?' said Macmillan. 'What are they going to do with it?'

'God knows,' sighed Steven.

'What do you want me to do?' asked Macmillan.

'Have the director at Porton Down close Crowe's lab and conduct an audit of all materials. Analyse the contents of every test tube. Go through his lab records with a fine-tooth comb looking for anything to prove that work continued on the Beta Team agent after the accident.'

'And if they find it?' asked Macmillan.

'If we can show that work did continue there's no way they can claim to have had Government sanction for that after telling us that all work on it was ordered to cease after the accident. They could be charged under the Prevention of Terrorism Act.'

'There would be a certain poetic justice in that,' said Macmillan.

'I don't suppose we could continue to hold them a bit longer?' said Steven. 'Just until the search of Crowe's lab and records is complete?'

'I could put it to the Home Secretary,' said Macmillan. 'But I have my doubts. I don't know what the collective noun for a bunch of high-powered lawyers is but whatever it is, these two have got one. How confident are you that a search of Crowe's lab will produce anything?'

'Actually he didn't flinch when I brought up the subject,' confessed Steven. 'On the other hand it would be difficult to conceal absolutely every last detail about any project that has been carried out in a lab.'

Macmillan looked uncertain. 'Unless of course it never happened,' he said.

Steven shrugged, unable to offer anything else in support of his case.

'I'll press hard for the official search but I might have to pass on trying for an extended hold on Crowe and Mowbray,' he said.

'Your call,' said Steven, appreciating the difficulty Macmillan was in. If he was wrong about all this, Sci-Med could be wiping egg off its face for some time to come.

'I'll call you when I know something,' said Macmillan.

*   *   *

Steven went back to his apartment and took a long hot shower before wrapping himself in his white towelling bath robe and plumping himself down in his favourite chair by the window to phone Jane and ask about her day.

She sounded a little distant. 'It's so good to be home,' she said. 'I've contacted the school to say I'll be in tomorrow—God, I hated having to lie when they asked about my sick relative in Yorkshire. Now I'll have to go through the same thing with all my friends.'

'It will all soon be in the past,' said Steven. 'Apart from me, I hope.'

Steven said it lightly but the pause that followed spoke volumes. He felt as if he'd just read the first line of a Dear John letter and his heart sank.

'Steven,' began Jane hesitantly. 'Coming home like this has made me realise just how much I liked my old life—the school, the outings, colleagues, friends, all the things I've been taking for granted. I think I need some space, some time. This has all been a bit much for me. I think it might be better if we didn't see each other for a bit—just until I get back into my old routine and feel a bit more secure in myself.'

'If that's what you really want,' said Steven.

'I know what I said at the beginning about wanting to be kept informed about everything but I've changed my mind about that too. I don't think I want to know any more about the things you're involved in. It's not for me. Maybe you could call me when it's all over?'

The line went dead and Steven murmured, 'And when the valley's hushed and white with snow.' He got up and padded over to where he kept his drinks bottles, having just decided how he was going to spend what remained of his evening. Gordon's gin was going to play a starring role.

*   *   *

Steven woke at 4am feeling cold and uncomfortable. He had fallen asleep in the chair and now had a painful crick in the neck to show for it. He was cold because the heating had gone off at eleven and the temperature had dropped considerably in the flat. It was raining heavily outside and a cold east wind had allowed some of it to permeate indoors through the window he'd opened earlier to air the place. The left side of his shirt was wet. He let out an involuntary grunt of discomfort as he reached up to close the window and pain surged up his neck. He rubbed it with the flat of his hand and moved his head slowly from side to side as he went through to the kitchen to turn on the electric kettle to make coffee. He also turned the heating back on.

Fortified by coffee and more aspirin than was recommended on the label he went through to bed to try to get some proper sleep. Whether he fell asleep or passed out was a moot point but he remained unconscious until the phone woke him at nine-thirty. It sounded louder than it ever had done in the past.

'Dunbar,' he croaked.

'Sounds like you have a cold,' said William Rees's voice.

'A bit of a sore throat,' lied Steven, clearing it with a cough. 'What can I do for you?'

'Any chance of you coming up to Cambridge?' asked Rees. 'I think I may have something here that will interest you.'

'Every chance,' said Steven. 'Give me half an hour and I'm on my way.'

*   *   *

Steven thought about Jane on the drive up to Cambridge and wrestled with mixed emotions. He wanted to feel bitter because she'd hurt him but he found he couldn't. Jane had had a perfectly ordered life before he'd appeared on the scene. She had probably never known anything other than the safety and security of middle class life—maybe without even realising that—and in a few short weeks he had swept all that away, exposing her to fear, uncertainty and even an attempt on her life. He really couldn't blame her for wanting her old life back. She was just behaving like any normal woman. The bottom line to all this was, he concluded, that he might have to find himself an extraordinary woman.

Lisa, his wife, had been one, he

292

remembered with a smile. Before he had even met her, she had gone to war with the might of the hospital establishment in Glasgow where she'd worked in order to expose what she saw as an injustice. She had suffered the consequences in terms of victimization and subsequent unemployment when she could least afford it with an ailing mother to look after. That had taken enormous courage—the courage of an extraordinary woman. 'I still miss you, love,' he murmured, raising his eyes momentarily to the sky.

Steven ignored the 'Permit Holders Only' sign and parked in the one empty space he found outside the Medical Research Council lab. He presented his ID to the man at the Reception desk and a phone call later he was shown up to Rees's office on the second floor. It was a bright, airy room with plenty of light coming in from three large windows along one wall. Rees sat behind a light pine desk at right angles to the windows. He was in shirt sleeves with his jacket hanging over the back of his swivel chair. The wall behind him was comprised entirely of book shelves, all of them full of either text books or scientific journals.

'How's the throat?' asked Rees.

'Oh, fine,' said Steven, affecting a slight cough and hoping he didn't look as rough as he felt. 'But I could do with some good news.'

'I think I can help you out there,' said Rees. 'You remember I was a bit puzzled about there being more than one strain of *Mycoplasma* present in Maclean's collection?'

Steven nodded. 'There were three.'

'The first thing I did was to grow up the different strains and run routine microbiological tests on them. They all appeared to be the perfectly harmless bacteria one would assume them to be . . . just as your man, Maclean, concluded.'

'But?' said Steven.

'I tested them for their susceptibility to antibiotics. One of them turned out to have a very unusual sensitivity pattern. It proved resistant to every antibiotic in the book.'

'How could that happen?' asked Steven.

Rees leaned across his desk and said, 'It could be a freak of nature but the simplest explanation is that someone engineered it that way. They altered it so it could not be treated with antibiotics.'

'They genetically altered a harmless bacterium?' said Steven. 'Sounds like you've found the needle!'

'Modesty prevents comment,' said Rees with a mischievous grin that made Steven warm to the man even further.

'Would that have been difficult?' asked Steven.

'Easiest thing in the world to make bugs resistant to drugs,' replied Rees. 'You just select for the natural mutants that are always present in bacterial populations. You simply spread large numbers of them on a growth medium containing the antibiotic and let nature do the rest. Only a mutant resistant to the antibiotic can survive and grow. You then grow the survivor up and go through the same procedure with another antibiotic and so on until you finish up with a strain that is resistant to every drug in the book.'

'But ostensibly this is still a harmless bug, right?' asked Steven.

'Right,' said Rees. 'What's inside it in terms of DNA is another matter but I think we have found our candidate for genetic alteration. I'm going to test it with the HIV virus gene probe.'

Steven tapped his thumbnail against his front teeth.

'You're looking thoughtful,' said Rees.

'I was just thinking,' said Steven. 'If you're right and this *Mycoplasma* thing should turn out to be the agent it would mean that it could not be treated by drugs?'

'That's the usual way of things with biological weapons,' said Rees. 'What's the problem?'

'The people who designed this thing were asked to make it treatable. It was a specific requirement.'

'Wouldn't that defeat the purpose?' asked Rees.

'You'd think so,' agreed Steven. 'But, as I say, it was a definite criterion.'

Rees took off his glasses and leaned back in

his chair. 'Strange,' he said. 'But interesting. Do you play chess, Doctor?'

'Badly,' said Steven. 'My main tactic is to engineer an exchange of every powerful piece on the board I can on the grounds that they are liable to be of much more use to my opponent than me.'

'That in itself is a clever tactic,' said Rees. 'You accept your shortcomings and level the playing field so that things become more equal. You bring a superior opponent down to your level.'

'That's one way of putting it,' said Steven with a smile at Rees's bluntness.

'But when that is not an option we have no alternative but to consider what our opponent might do with the powerful pieces that are still on the board.'

'Like the agent,' said Steven.

'Here we have a strain of *Mycoplasma* which has been genetically altered,' said Rees. 'If, as we suspect, genes from the HIV virus have been introduced to it then we have a perfectly harmless looking organism that has the capacity to seriously damage the human immune system, rendering its victims vulnerable to a wide range of conditions and diseases—not to the extent of the HIV virus itself but still pretty debilitating. On top of that, it is immune to antibiotics so there is no way of treating it. All in all, a powerful biological agent for population control and manipulation, wouldn't you say?'

'You'd think so,' agreed Steven.

'So why would they want to introduce a weakness?' said Rees.

Steven shrugged.

'It doesn't make sense,' said Rees. 'But there's a danger we are taking our eye off the game. It's always a mistake to look back when we should be thinking about what might happen next. The real question is what they intend doing with such a powerful piece on the board, not what they might have done with it in the past.'

CHAPTER EIGHTEEN

The sun had moved round so that it was now shining directly into the room. Rees half closed the Venetian blinds causing horizontal bands of light to stripe the left side of his face.

'Well, chess master,' said Steven. 'What would you do?'

Rees smiled. 'I'm hardly the one to ask,' he said. 'There's no one I would want to control apart from my grandchildren when they run amok in my garden on a Sunday. Using biological weapons might be going a little far.'

'As I see it, they're either going to sell it or use it,' said Steven. 'These are the two possibilities.'

'Do you really think that someone might consider using such a weapon in this country?'

'You know as well as I how much this country is hated in some quarters,' said Steven. 'Our current love affair with the Americans isn't exactly improving things.'

Rees conceded the point with a nod. 'You're referring to Islamic terrorist organisations, but frankly this agent would not be an attractive proposition for them. They have neither the time nor the infrastructure to benefit from it. Terrorism is by definition a case of kill and run, bomb and disrupt. Its perpetrators create an atmosphere of fear and uncertainty in order to promote the demand for change. Making people ill would not fit the bill unless the people affected knew that they'd been attacked and why they were ill. The very nature of this agent militates against that. It was designed to be a secret.'

'So we can eliminate sale to a third party?' said Steven.

'We can eliminate sale to terrorist groups,' said Rees. 'That's different.'

'At least it narrows down the field,' said Steven.

'But to what, I must leave up to you,' said Rees. 'The time has come for me to retire to the confines of my comfortable little ivory tower and get back to the rigours of academe.'

*   *   *

298

Steven drove back to London feeling less than optimistic. He knew he was pre-empting Rees's findings but the suggestion of genetic alteration to one of the apparently harmless bugs Maclean had found in his body made this seem reasonable and he had to think ahead. Crowe had been responsible for its construction and Mowbray had made sure it had remained a secret, but who was going to use it? Both of them had been members of Gardiner's group—something he had been inclined to dismiss as a small collection of right-wing dreamers although on the other hand it had been in existence for twelve years; plenty of time to build up a significant infrastructure. There was no easy way of knowing how widespread or how deeply it had penetrated into British life in that time—who was a member and who was not. The natural home of the political right was out there in suburbia among the roses and forsythia of bungalow-land where the silent majority never voiced their opinions openly but got on with their shopping and gardening and went about their business while secretly harbouring resentment against the more vociferous left.

He reckoned that he believed Gardiner's stated regard for the rule of law but Crowe and Mowbray were a different kettle of fish. Maybe these two and God knows who else had simply moved in and taken over. He had reconciled himself to getting nothing out of either so that only left the other two group members he knew of to approach, Colonel Peter Warner—the ex soldier now retired— and the would-be politician, Rupert Everley. Sci-Med would have set up an investigation into the background of both of them as soon as their involvement had become known so he would take a look at what they had come up with before deciding whom to approach first. He needed to find an Achilles heel to make progress.

Steven waited until he had got home before calling Macmillan and telling him about Rees's discovery. 'It's going to take a few more days to be absolutely sure but it looks as if he's on the right track.'

'Well done, Professor Rees,' said Macmillan. 'So the last part of the secret is about to be no longer a secret. I'll pass the news on to the Home Secretary.'

'What's happening to Crowe and Mowbray?' asked Steven.

'I'm sorry but they're being released,' said Macmillan. 'The Home Secretary did however, agree to your request for a search of Crowe's lab. It's already begun.'

'Good,' said Steven.

'I need hardly add that if nothing is found it will probably be an end to the matter,' said Macmillan. 'There's absolutely no other evidence that any work continued on the agent

300

after the accident in 1990.'

'But I know that it did,' insisted Steven. 'And if they were prepared to kill to keep it secret after twelve years it must mean that they have plans for it, plans that mean a lot to them.'

'I hope you're wrong,' said Macmillan.

'I do too,' said Steven. 'But I fear I'm not.'

*   *   *

Newsnight finished on BBC2 and Steven drained the last of a gin and tonic before clicking the remote. He found the silence welcome but with it came thoughts of the day and his conversation with Rees. Although he and Rees had agreed that it wouldn't make any sense to design such a weapon with an inherent weakness—treatability—and indeed, Rees had found that it had no such weakness; D'Arcy had insisted that one of the main design criteria had been that the organism be treatable. This worried him because he couldn't see the logic behind it and a lack of understanding meant vulnerability in any situation. Logic said clearly that you would not deliberately introduce a weakness . . . therefore . . . it had to be a strength . . . What they were seeing as a weakness must actually be some kind of advantage. But if an enemy could cure the condition how could that possibly be? . . . Steven suddenly thought he

301

saw the answer. They couldn't! Only the designers of the agent could cure it! That was why the bug had been made resistant to all the other antibiotics. It was so the other side couldn't cure the condition. Like the bug itself, the cure was a secret too.

Feeling so pleased with himself he couldn't stop a smile on his lips, he looked at the time. It was just after midnight but this couldn't wait until morning. He called Rees at home and woke him up.

'Give me a moment,' said Rees when he heard Steven's voice. 'No need to disturb my wife as well.'

Steven waited until Rees had left the bedroom and gone downstairs to his study.

'Right,' said Rees. 'You are now free to tell me while you've got me out of bed at this ungodly hour.'

'I've been thinking,' said Steven, immediately imagining something disparaging in the silence that followed. 'About the agent, I mean. I think they did make it treatable but not by any conventional means. I think the treatment is a secret too.'

'A secret,' repeated Rees, but not unkindly.

'It makes perfect sense,' said Steven, enthusiasm welling up in his voice. 'It's actually a very clever addition to the bug's properties. It would give you the power to selectively cure who you wanted to of the condition. You can even take the logic one stage further. You could use the agent to debilitate the population and exert control and then you cure the ones among them who come round to your way of thinking. They regain their health and there's an implicit suggestion that their new political philosophy is the way back to health and happiness so more people come round to your way of thinking and they in turn are cured and so on.'

'Isn't science wonderful,' murmured Rees, but he sounded intrigued.

'You're now going to tell me that all this is fantasy?' said Steven.

'No,' said Rees thoughtfully. 'No, I'm not.'

'Then you think it possible?'

'To come up with a new antibiotic that no one else knows about? Absolutely, it's a search carried out every day by drug companies. Mind you, the vast majority of new antibiotics are no good at all and there's a school of thought that says we've already come up with all the useful ones but . . .'

'But what?'

'They are looking for antibiotics that work against bugs that cause disease. No one looks for drugs that act against harmless beasties.'

'How would you go about it?' asked Steven.

'Antibiotics occur widely in nature,' said Rees. 'Many bacteria and fungi produce them for their own defence. Genus *Streptomyces* and *Bacillus* are the most prolific.'

'So it wouldn't be that difficult?'

303

'No.'

'Would they do that before or after they had made all the other changes to the bug?' asked Steven.

'Definitely before,' said Rees. 'Otherwise there would be no guarantee they would be able to come up with a cure after they had carried out all the other work. It could be wasted.'

'That is a very important point,' said Steven. 'Let me see if I've got it right. The sequence of events would be that they take a harmless strain of *Mycoplasma* and search for a new antibiotic that kills it, then they make it resistant to all *known* antibiotics, and finally they introduce genes from the HIV virus in order to make it harmful?'

'Correct,' said Rees.

'Bastards,' said Steven. 'They could have cured it all along but they said nothing.'

'Sorry, I'm not with you,' said Rees.

'If coming up with the new antibiotic was the first thing they did, they could have cured Gulf War Syndrome all along,' said Steven.

'Still not with you,' said Rees.

'The treatable property would have been present even in the very earliest forms of the agent so it would have been there in the prototype that found its way into the vaccine. They could have cured all these people by making their new antibiotic available but they kept quiet and said nothing.'

304

'Because if that should become public knowledge their agent becomes useless as a weapon,' completed Rees.

'They've been keeping it a secret now for twelve years.'

'Ye gods,' said Rees. 'People.'

'What are the chances of finding another antibiotic that would kill this thing?' asked Steven.

'We could certainly start looking,' said Rees. 'But the people who came up with this thing are no fools. It's odds on that they would have selected a starting strain that was naturally resistant to many antibacterial agents, perhaps through some aberration in its outer membrane or the like. There are thousands and thousands of antibacterial compounds out there so it would be a question of going through them all until we found the one that worked. That could take time. It would also have to be tested for toxicity before it could be used. Many antibiotics are so toxic that they can't be used for fear of killing the patient. How much time have we got?'

'I don't know,' said Steven.

*   *   *

In the morning Steven got to the Home Office shortly before Rose Roberts arrived. 'You're an early bird,' she said.

'Looking for information on a couple of

worms,' said Steven. 'Peter Warner and Rupert Everley.'

'You're in luck,' replied Rose. 'I just finished collating the files on these two last night. Mr Macmillan hasn't seen them yet.'

'I don't think he'd mind,' said Steven, responding to her questioning look. 'Anything interesting?'

'Nothing we didn't know already,' said Rose, handing them over. 'What's your interest all of a sudden?'

'I want to talk to them,' said Steven.

'Everley is away in Scotland where he's been for the last month,' said Rose. 'But Warner should be at his home in Kent.'

'Then Warner first,' said Steven, flicking open the first folder. He had just finished working his way through the second when John Macmillan arrived in the office.

'I've just had a word with the Home Secretary,' he said. 'A team of searchers have been going through Crowe's lab at Porton all night. So far they haven't found anything at all suspicious.'

'Pity,' said Steven, following Macmillan through into his office where he told him about his late night conversation with Rees. 'Not only have these bastards known all along about the cause of Gulf War Syndrome,' he said. 'But they could have cured it if they'd chosen to.' Steven told him about the first step in construction being the isolation of the new antibiotic. 'Even the very early versions of the agent would have been treatable,' he said. 'The fact that they didn't say anything about that . . .'

'Must mean that they have a pretty serious reason for keeping it secret,' completed Macmillan. His gaze moved to the files that Steven was still holding.

'I thought I'd see if I could get something useful out of Warner or Everley,' said Steven.

'Did you ask Rees about the possibility of coming up with another drug to tackle the agent?'

Steven nodded. 'Could take a month, could take a year,' he said. 'There's no way of knowing.'

'The Home Secretary is meeting with the PM this morning to keep him appraised of developments. How would you rate the threat?'

'Unknown,' said Steven.

'He'll love that,' said Macmillan with a sigh. 'Who are you going to see first?'

'Warner,' said Steven. 'Everley's in Scotland.'

'Doing what?'

'Kissing Tory arse according to this,' said Steven, holding up the file. 'He's been unable to get himself adopted as a candidate in any English constituency where he had even the remotest chance of being returned so it looks as if he's turned his attention north of the

307

border. He's been doing the rounds.'

'I didn't think there were any Tories left up there after the debacle with the poll tax,' said Macmillan. 'You'd think he had even less chance.'

'No doubt he'll find that out for himself, him being a bright sort of a chap . . .' said Steven.

'Or there's something we don't know about,' said Macmillan.

*   *   *

Steven was walking up the steps at Channing House in Kent when he heard singing coming from the garden at the side of the house and stopped to listen.

'Early one morning, just as the sun was rising . . .'

Although singing tends to disguise accent, Steven didn't think that the voice belonged to a gardener. He retraced his steps and walked along to the wicker gate at the right hand side of the house where he could see a man of military bearing, dressed in tweeds, pruning a large berberis shrub with secateurs.

'Colonel Warner?' he asked.

'Who the devil wants to know?' spluttered Warner, having to use bluster to disguise the fact he'd been taken by surprise.

Steven walked in through the gate and showed Warner his ID.

Warner grunted and said, 'James Gardiner warned me you might come calling. I can't tell you any more than he did. What happened all those years ago was an accident; nothing more nothing less. There wasn't anything that any of us could have done about it and that's an end to it.'

'Not quite,' said Steven as Warner resumed his pruning. 'A great many men were left incapacitated because of that so-called accident.'

'I think that's a moot point, if you don't mind my saying so,' said Warner.

'Oh, I know there were a whole lot of other contributing factors which served to muddy the water and gave you all something to hide behind,' said Steven. 'But the Porton agent still played a leading role. I think you know that.'

'As I say, that's a moot point and to be regretted if it should be true,' said Warner.

'Of course, these men needn't have suffered at all if the whole truth had come out at the time,' said Steven.

'I don't think I know what you mean,' said Warner, pretending that the piece of berberis he was cutting at the time had suddenly become extremely interesting. He examined it closely.

'From the very outset there was a known cure for the agent,' said Steven. 'If it had been made available as soon as it became clear there was a health problem, Gulf War

309

Syndrome would never have become an issue.'

Warner stopped pruning and looked slightly stunned. 'What the devil are you talking about?' he said. 'How could there be a cure? It was just a prototype of something they had just started work on.'

'The first thing Crowe and his team did once they had decided on the bug they were going to base their agent on was to come up with an antibiotic to cure it,' said Steven. 'Even the earliest prototypes would have been treatable with it.'

'Look here, science is all a bloody mystery to me,' said Warner. 'If what you say is true and they had a way of undoing the effects of the accident wouldn't they have done so? You're not making any sense.'

'Because they intended continuing development of the agent,' said Steven, watching Warner closely. 'The cure had to remain a secret otherwise it would have rendered the agent useless as a weapon.'

'But all development work was stopped after the accident,' said Warner.

'I think not,' said Steven.

'You mean, Crowe?'

'I've good reason to believe that he continued development work on it and succeeded in constructing a biological weapon that satisfied the original design criteria.'

'Good Lord,' said Warner, clearly taken aback. 'Looking back, I never did like the fella,

310

always something about him. So what's he going to do with it now that he's got it?'

'I was rather hoping you were going to tell me that,' said Steven.

Warner looked astonished. 'You thought that I . . .'

'And James Gardiner and the other members of your group . . .'

'Now hold on! James warned me about this nonsense. Just because we love our country and hate seeing it fall into the hands of the kind of below-stairs trash that seem to be into everything these days doesn't make us a bunch of terrorists. Everything we did, we did within the law.'

'How about developing the agent in the first place?' said Steven.

'That had Government sanction,' said Warner.

'Did it?' said Steven.

'James assures me that it did,' said Warner.

'Crowe was a member of your group.'

Warner gave a deep sigh. After a pause he said, 'James insisted that our group should include like minded people from all walks of life. He thought that Crowe fitted the bill at the time.'

'And Mowbray?'

'And Mowbray,' said Warner, looking down at the ground.

'You needed someone like him?'

Warner nodded. 'An insider in Intelligence?

311

Of course we did. Cold fish but . . . horses for courses, as they say.'

'What about Everley?'

Warner gave a snort of derision. 'Man's a buffoon,' he said. 'A self-opinionated clown.'

'But a rich one,' said Steven.

'We needed his cash,' agreed Warner.

'How big is the organisation?' asked Steven, hoping that this key question would just slip into the run of things but Warner saw it immediately. 'Just the four of us,' he said, returning to his pruning.

'It's not the group I'm asking about,' said Steven. 'I need to know about the organisation it was fronting. I think that Crowe and Mowbray may have been using it for their own ends.'

'I really don't know what you're talking about,' said Warner.

'You said you loved your country?' said Steven. 'Do you really want to see it influenced by the likes of Crowe and Mowbray?'

Warner stopped pruning again and turned to face Steven. 'You're serious, aren't you?' he said.

'Never more so,' said Steven.

'I'll have to talk to James.'

CHAPTER NINETEEN

Steven drove back to London having been assured by Warner that he would call him after he had spoken to James Gardiner later in the day. In the event it was Gardiner himself who called just after six in the evening.

'I think we should meet.'

'Just tell me where and when,' said Steven.

'My wife and I are in the process of moving house but I'm keeping on the small flat I have in town. Come there at eight?'

Steven wrote down the address and said he'd be there.

Gardiner's small flat turned out to be twice the size of his own, furnished minimally but expensively and with a location that afforded fine views of the river from a terrace that bordered both south and west aspects. On a balmy evening the doors leading to the terrace were wide open.

'Drink?' asked Gardiner.

'Thanks. Gin and tonic,' said Steven, moving outside to admire the view while Gardiner fixed the drinks. Gardiner joined him on the terrace and handed him his drink.

'So you're tired of London?' said Steven.

'And therefore, by implication, tired of life,' said Gardiner. 'No, I don't think so. Alice and I are moving up to our place in Scotland to begin a new one away from . . . other people.'

'Sartre was right?'

'With the greatest of respect to M. Sartre, Hell is not other people; it's other people being in charge.'

'I think that's called democracy,' said Steven.

'A much overrated concept,' said Gardiner.

'You don't believe in the will of the people?' said Steven.

'The so-called will of the people is all too often a celebration of ignorance and mediocrity,' said Gardiner. 'If we were to decide democratically on one single newspaper for the entire country we'd end up with the *Sun*, simply because it sells more copies than any other so therefore would get more votes and be elected our national paper. Need I say more?'

'Democracy may have its shortcomings but it's still better than any other system,' said Steven.

'I know,' said Gardiner, looking out over the river. 'Maybe that's what I find so bloody depressing. Warner tells me you think Crowe and Mowbray have been pursuing their own agenda?'

Steven told Gardiner what he knew.

'So why don't you arrest them?'

'We did but they've been released. There's no proof,' said Steven.

'You could be wrong, of course?'

314

'Everything points to Crowe having continued work on the agent,' said Steven. 'The fact that they've killed three people in the last few months to keep it a secret says that they intend using it.'

'What exactly is it you want from me?' asked Gardiner.

'I need details of the infrastructure of your organisation,' said Steven. 'I think Crowe and Mowbray may be using it.'

'You want names and addresses?' said Gardiner doubtfully.

'If they intend using the agent I have to understand the size and nature of the organisation they have available to them,' said Steven.

'Perhaps I could just tell you without having to divulge personal details?' said Gardiner.

Steven gave him a look that Gardiner had no trouble in interpreting. 'I suppose not,' he said. 'But before I even considered such a thing I would need certain assurances from you.'

'These people have nothing to fear if they have done nothing wrong,' said Steven. 'You have my word.'

'The rule of law is fundamental to all of us,' said Gardiner.

'Things might be different now,' said Steven.

'These people are not just mindless automatons,' said Gardiner. 'They're people

315

who care what happens to Britain. They can think for themselves.'

'You'd be amazed at what some otherwise intelligent people are capable of doing when asked if they believe the request has official backing,' said Steven.

'I need some kind of firm assurance,' said Gardiner.

'That's not within my power,' said Steven.

'Then no deal,' said Gardiner.

Steven looked towards the setting sun and took a moment to consider his position. He could simply refuse to compromise and issue a series of official threats to Gardiner but he knew well enough that that would get him precisely nowhere. On the other hand he could take a chance and get what he wanted but at some risk to himself in career terms.

'All right,' he said. 'You have my word that I will destroy any information given to me immediately after I've taken what I need from it.'

Gardiner turned on his heel and went indoors. He returned with a computer disk, which he handed to Steven. 'The database,' he said.

Steven slipped the disk into his laptop as soon as he got home before pouring himself a drink and settling down to analyse it. The list comprised some four thousand names entered in database form. It contained details of names, addresses, ages and occupations. It only took Steven a few moments to realise that he had no real idea of what he was looking for. If he had been hoping to see clear evidence of an organised conspiracy he was sadly disappointed. These people were scattered all over the country and in just about every occupation under the sun—well, maybe every middle class occupation under the sun, he corrected. He took a sip of his drink and pondered his next move. The database came with useful analytical tools so he requested average age and came up with the figure 45.

'Shit,' he whispered under his breath. These people weren't revolutionaries. They were representative of the middle class, middle-aged, middle income voters of bungalow-land. How could such people be organised to promote social change after an attack using Crowe's agent? There was just no cohesive factor.

Steven felt a mixture of disappointment and embarrassment. He couldn't imagine Crowe and Mowbray having formed some other secret organisation capable of supporting such a big venture so that must mean he was wrong about their intention to use the agent. They must have made it to sell.

Despite the fact that it was Sunday and it had gone ten o' clock he called the duty officer at Sci-Med and asked him to arrange for a full financial scrutiny of both Crowe and Mowbray's personal accounts. 'I don't care who you have to wake,' he added.

'What period?' asked the duty man.

'Let's begin with the last two years.'

Steven returned to the names on the database. Just out of interest he asked the search engine for 'Civil Servants'. A list of almost three hundred names appeared on the screen. Next he asked for 'Doctors' and was rewarded with thirty-three names but this gave him an idea. He narrowed the search and asked for 'Pathologists': this reduced the list to three. One of them was Dr Melvyn Street, a forensic pathologist attached to Perthshire police.

'Well, well, well,' murmured Steven. 'Now I understand why you didn't see the marks on Martin Hendry's wrists, Doctor.'

It was 1am and Steven tired of searching for patterns in the database. He turned off the computer and switched on the television, flicking through the cable channels for 24-hour news programmes. His attention was taken by the mention of Rupert Everley's name in an item presented as 'Tory squabble in Scotland'. The leader of the Scottish Conservatives, David McLetchie, had been engaged in a furious row with property developer and prominent Tory supporter in England, Rupert Everley. McLetchie had been annoyed at Everley's recent tour of Scottish Conservative Party organisations, and had accused Everley of talking 'puerile rubbish' and of attempting

318

to undermine his authority and ingratiate himself with the party faithful through large cash donations. Everley had retaliated by accusing McLetchie of being short-sighted and resistant to change. There was a short film clip of Everley looking earnestly sincere, saying that the time was right for Scottish Conservatives to make a comeback but only if they brought in 'fresh minds with fresh ideas to turn things around'.

'Like yours, Rupert?' murmured Steven. 'Clown.'

Steven reached for the remote but stopped himself as a thought chilled him. Everley had been in Scotland for the past month according to Rose Roberts. Surely he hadn't been paving the way for political success on the back of a change to be induced by Crowe's agent? No, the idea was preposterous, Steven told himself. The Scottish electorate would have to be wired to the mains before they'd vote for anyone like Rupert Everley. They'd be as well putting up Jeffrey Archer or Neil Hamilton. But that did leave the question, why was Everley there in the first place?

Maybe Everley didn't realise the futility of his mission? Pompous fools never saw themselves as others saw them. That's why they kept accepting invitations on to game shows on television. They didn't realise they were there to be made fun of.

But Everley wouldn't have come up with

319

this notion in the first place, someone must have conned him into thinking it was a good idea—someone like Crowe or Mowbray or both . . . because . . . they . . . needed Everley's money? . . . To do what? . . . To finance a hit on Scotland was the only thing Steven could come up with. They were going to use the agent on a target somewhere in Scotland. But where in Scotland and why?

'Sweet Jesus,' murmured Steven, suspecting his imagination was running away with him. 'Let's just slow down a bit.' What would be the point of such a hit if there was no infrastructure in place to take advantage of the situation? It wouldn't make any sense. Steven felt a sense of relief arrive with this thought. He used it as a brake. Such an attack wouldn't achieve anything at all, he reasoned . . . except that you'd find out if it worked.

The brakes were off again. Crowe and Mowbray could be considering some kind of trial run of their agent on a target in Scotland. But why? . . . To impress a prospective buyer, that was why! He was there. It was a terrifying prospect but it all made sense . . . at three in the morning.

Steven wondered if he should sleep on it but then decided that he couldn't take the chance. He called the duty man at Sci-Med and called a code, double red.

'You got it,' said the man. 'First time I've ever had one of these.'

320

Steven knew that emergency calls would now be made to a team of expert advisors whose expertise was available to Sci-Med in times of emergency. They would be brought in to the Home Office from their homes all over the city and beyond just as fast as they could dress and a police car could get them there.

Steven himself was there within fifteen minutes. John Macmillan joined him five minutes later. Steven had never seen him unshaven before. He briefed him while they waited for the others.

'It's either brilliant or ridiculous,' said Macmillan when he'd finished.

'And no way of picking the favourite,' said Steven. 'I just felt I couldn't take the chance.'

'You were right,' said Macmillan. 'Where does Rose keep the coffee round here?'

Steven looked in a couple of cupboards and found a plastic bag of ground coffee sealed with a metal clip. He handed it to Macmillan and between them they set up the coffee machine so that people arriving over the next forty minutes could at least have coffee to help keep them awake.

John Hamilton, a computer expert, was the last to arrive at twenty past four, having come furthest. He took his seat at the table and Steven was invited by Macmillan to tell the five experts—four men and one woman—why they had been called in. When he'd finished he was met with a shocked silence for a few moments before Hamilton said, 'Can I just summarise to make sure I've got this right—you think that a biological attack is about to be made on a target in Scotland?'

Steven nodded and sipped his coffee.

'But you don't know where and you don't know when?'

'Correct,' said Steven.

'But you do know what the agent being used is?'

'We think we do,' said Steven.

'But you don't know how the attack will be launched?'

' 'fraid not,' agreed Steven.

'Bloody hell,' said Hamilton. 'I think it's a clairvoyant we need here.'

'If the attack is to be carried out by a small group of people, strange to the area—as seems likely here,' said Dorothy Jordan, a specialist in medical microbiology, 'they're probably restricted to using aerosols for a small target or contaminating water supplies for a bigger one.'

'Good,' said Macmillan. 'That's what we need,' he said with a sideways glance at Hamilton. 'Good positive input.'

'If it's to be an aerosol attack we would be probably looking at a confined space like an air conditioned building or a subway station.'

'Why air conditioned?' asked Macmillan.

'The windows would be kept closed,' replied Jordan.

'What's your gut feeling?' asked Macmillan.

'Personally I'd go for water supplies,' said Jordan. 'It would be easier. Reservoirs are generally much more accessible than targets in towns.'

'Drawbacks?'

'Large dilution effects if you're thinking about hitting a reservoir with bacteria or viruses,' said Jordan. 'Strong poisons would be a better bet. You are sure they're going to use bugs?'

'Yes,' said Steven.

'Then they'd need a hell of a lot,' said Jordan, putting down her pen on top of her notepad to indicate that she thought her contribution might be over.

'No clues about people involved?' asked Charles Bristow, a clinical psychologist and profiler.

Steven held up the disk Gardiner had given him. 'Four thousand names,' he said. 'Among them might be a few people called upon to help but probably without knowing the big picture.'

'Let's have a look,' said Hamilton. 'Why don't you and I go through this?' he said to the psychologist.

'Do we know why they are they doing this?' asked Alan Deans, Home Office expert on counter-terrorism.

'It's not political,' said Steven. 'I think they are out to demonstrate the agent's potential to

323

a prospective buyer.'

'Commercial not political,' smiled Deans. 'Now there's a new one.'

There was a knock on the door and the duty officer came in carrying several sheets of paper. 'The financial details on the two you asked for,' he said to Steven. 'Incidentally,' continued the duty man, 'the people who came up with them said that asking for bank statements in the middle of the night was, in their opinion, bureaucracy gone mad.'

'Thank you for that,' said Steven equably.

In reply to Macmillan's questioning look, Steven said, 'Crowe and Mowbray's bank statements. I hoped we might get some idea about who they might be doing business with if they really are selling the agent.'

'A good thought,' murmured Macmillan. 'Maybe I should make some more coffee . . .'

Steven ran through Mowbray's details first. There had been a number of payments in to his accounts over the past two years that did not have a source that meant anything to Steven but they did not seem to have anything in common so he turned to Crowe's statements. As with Mowbray's he started with the most recent and worked his way back. Almost immediately he noticed a quarterly payment coming in to his account that had undergone a currency conversion. The sterling equivalent was just over five thousand pounds. The only source details were given as

W. Corp 5771.

'A retainer,' exclaimed Steven, picking up the internal phone and calling the duty officer. 'Get these bank people back on the phone, will you? Quick as you can.'

'They're going to love this . . .' muttered the man.

'Got something?' asked Macmillan.

'Looks like Crowe was on some sort of retainer,' said Steven. 'Twenty grand a year. Not bad.'

'Could be a consultancy,' said Macmillan.

'Or a lucky break,' said Steven. 'C'mon, c'mon,' he murmured, looking at the silent telephone. It was another ten minutes before the bank rang. Macmillan smiled as he heard Steven say, 'Yes I am sure that this is absolutely necessary, now will you please get me the details of a quarterly payment into the account of Dr Donald Crowe, account number 00449547288. It's listed as coming from W. Corp 5771 and required a currency conversion.'

Macmillan and Dorothy Jordan watched Steven scribble down details before hanging up the phone with a smile on his face.

'The payments came from an American company called the Wallenberg Corporation. The currency conversion was necessary because the payment was made in US dollars.'

'What do we know about the Wallenberg Corporation?' asked Macmillan.

325

'I've heard of them' said Dorothy. 'I think they're a biotech company.'

'Dr Hamilton, I think we need you,' said Macmillan to Hamilton who was still engaged on analysing Gardiner's disk. 'See if you can come up with something on the Wallenberg Corporation in the USA will you?'

'You got it,' said Hamilton. 'Charles will fill you in on what we have.'

Charles Bristow joined the others at the table with his notes. 'Not a lot, I'm afraid,' as he sat down. 'We tried separating out those with Scottish addresses but there are over four hundred and they're scattered all over. We've done various break-down analyses of the four hundred in Scotland, looking for those with potentially useful skills or information to people mounting an attack but no clear favourites have emerged as yet.'

Steven nodded and said, 'As I said, I don't think any of these people will have any direct involvement in any attack. That makes it doubly difficult.'

'Eureka!' exclaimed Hamilton from his seat at the computer. The others went over to join him.

'Dorothy was right. Wallenberg are a biotech company. They're big and have close US government links. Rumours of involvement in US biological weapons programmes abound and best of all, listen to this. Back in 1997 the corporation was fined

326

heavily for carrying out an experiment on the streets of Chicago. Apparently they wanted to assess the potential spread of an agent in a big city. They used a harmless bug but the authorities took a dim view of things and warned of serious repercussions should they ever try anything like that again.'

'Bingo,' said Steven.

'So it's the Americans who want this agent,' said Macmillan. 'Makes sense; the agent would be much more useful to an invading army than a small terrorist group.'

'Have our closest allies any plans to invade anywhere?' asked Hamilton.

'It would have been useful in Afghanistan,' said Steven. 'And Iraq could well be next by all accounts.'

'Well done people,' said Macmillan. 'I think we've found our customer.'

'And why they can't carry out their own field trials,' added Hamilton.

'Good point,' said Steven. 'All we need now is to find out when and where.'

CHAPTER TWENTY

It had been getting light outside for some time. Steven saw that it was nearly seven thirty. All of them had had a go at trying to extract useful information from Gardiner's database but without any real success and it was beginning to look as if they'd hit the wall. He got up from his chair to stretch his legs and walked over to the window to look out at a grey drizzle that was falling gently through early morning mist. A bus passed with an advert for internet access on its side. It gave him an idea.

'There is something we could do,' he said.

All eyes were on him as he turned round.

'If Crowe and Mowbray did use any of these people in the database,' he said. 'They must have been contacted recently—they probably used the group's e-mail server to make it appear official.'

'Seems reasonable,' agreed Dorothy Jordan.

'So?' said Hamilton.

'If Gardiner has been considering disbanding the organisation, it's probably been a while since he had any reason to contact anyone on the list officially. If I could persuade him to send out a message today, asking anyone who has been approached in the last month or so to get in touch with him personally . . . He could say there's been some kind of e-mail delivery problem.'

'Worth a try,' said Macmillan.

'Absolutely,' agreed Dorothy.

'Anything that narrows it down,' said Hamilton.

Macmillan checked his watch and said, 'No one is going to be up and about for another hour or so. I suggest we take a break, have a shower, get some breakfast, whatever, and meet back here at nine?'

Steven stayed behind to speak with Macmillan. 'I only hope Gardiner is in town,' he said. 'He's in the process of retiring to the Highlands of Scotland with his wife.'

'It would be ironic if he happened to end up in the middle of the target area,' said Macmillan. 'Maybe you should try him right now if there's any question he might not be in London?'

Steven used his mobile to call the number of Gardiner's flat in town. He smiled in relief and nodded to Macmillan when he heard Gardiner demanding to know just who the hell was calling him at this time in the morning.

'It's Steven Dunbar, Sir James,' said Steven respectfully. 'I need your help. The country needs your help.'

Macmillan gave an approving nod at Steven's approach.

'I can't talk about it over the phone. Could I possibly come over there and speak to you as soon as possible?'

'You'll have to give me time to get my bloody clothes on, man,' growled Gardiner.

'Would half an hour be all right, sir?'

'Make it forty minutes. This had better be damn important.'

When Steven arrived at the flats he saw an elegant, well dressed young black woman, carrying an overnight bag, leave the building and get into a taxi. She seemed harassed and appeared to be leaving in a hurry. Surely not, thought Steven, but when Gardiner let him in he couldn't resist being on the look-out for any sign of her origins.

Gardiner was alone in the flat. 'Has Lady Gardiner gone up to Scotland already, Sir James?' Steven asked pleasantly.

'She has,' replied Gardiner, who was wearing a plaid dressing gown and sheepskin slippers. 'Left me to fend for myself for a few days while she sorts out carpets and curtains. Coffee?'

Steven accepted and ran his eyes round the room as Gardiner filled two cups, which he placed on the low table by the doors leading to the south terrace. He walked over to pick up his and noticed a lipstick lying on the carpet at the side of the table. He picked it up and said, 'Hope she'll not be missing this.' He placed it slowly down on the table.

'Good Lord, she was looking everywhere for that,' said Gardiner, snatching it up as if it were a long lost friend and slipping it into his pocket of his dressing gown.

'Nice colour,' said Steven. It was purple.

'What is it you want from me?'

Steven explained, now feeling more confident than he had been that Gardiner was going to be helpful.

'What exactly do you want me to say in this message?' asked Gardiner when Steven had finished.

Steven told him and added, 'We'll have to change the group's mailing list to exclude Crowe and Mowbray so that they don't receive it and cotton on to what's happening, and I'd also like to put a divert on for the replies so that they will be automatically forwarded to me at the Home Office.'

Gardiner waved his hands vaguely in the air and said, 'I hope you know how to do all this. Takes me all my time to switch the damn machine on.'

'Leave it to me,' said Steven.

The message went out to the people on the database at 8.45am and Steven returned to the Home Office after thanking Gardiner for his cooperation, adding, 'I hope I won't have to bother you again, Sir James.'

'Always glad to help my country,' said Gardiner with an uneasy smile.

Nerves were beginning to fray when it got to ten o'clock without any sign of a reply but then Steven's computer bleeped to herald an incoming message and he clicked it open. The sender was a man named Eric Pope, which Steven read out aloud so that the others could start checking the name against the database. The message read, 'Worried about having missed mail. Last communication received 2nd September confirming date of exercise. Is there a problem?'

'He works for Scottish Water,' announced

Dorothy Jordan, who was first to come up with the man's details.

For a moment they all looked at each other in silence then Hamilton murmured, 'Bloody hell.'

'I'll have the troops see what they can come up with on Pope,' said Macmillan. He left the room to brief the regular Sci-Med support staff.

It was twenty minutes before the next message came in. 'From a David Innes,' Steven said, reading out the sender's name. The message read, 'Understand exercise going ahead as confirmed on September 2nd. Please advise of any change or update.'

'What exercise?' muttered Steven.

'If we ask, they may get suspicious,' said Alan Deans.

'Innes works for the Nationwide Building Society,' said Charles Bristow.

'A building society?' exclaimed Dorothy Jordan and Alan Deans, almost in unison.

'Search me,' said Steven, returning to his screen as the computer beeped yet again.

This time the e-mail came from a man named John Curtis. Dorothy ran the cursor down the list on her screen. 'Diamond Security,' she said. 'Scottish area supervisor.'

The message read, 'Last message received 2nd September, requesting suspension 8am-6pm, on day of exercise. Please confirm.'

Macmillan came back into the room saying,

'Pope is a middle manager with Scottish Water. He has wide responsibilities for their operations. The Scots haven't privatised water yet so we couldn't narrow it down any further area-wise.'

'Damnation,' murmured Steven. 'Where does that leave us? A water-board manager, a building society employee and an area supervisor with a security firm.'

'Some kind of hit on a building society?' suggested Hamilton without much conviction.

'The water connection worries me,' said Dorothy Jordan.

'Me too,' agreed Steven. 'In spite of what you said about dilution problems with bugs.'

'These people will be waiting for replies,' Deans reminded them.

'Can you deal with that?' Macmillan asked Hamilton. 'Simple confirmation, I think. We can't risk asking questions at this stage.'

*   *   *

Hamilton nodded and took Steven's place at the computer as a young woman came into the room and handed a piece of paper to Macmillan. Her body language suggested that she knew Macmillan was going to be pleased. Macmillan read it and raised his eyes briefly to the ceiling before saying, 'Building Society Man, Innes, is actually *Major* David Innes: he's an officer in the Territorial Army.'

'Now the word "exercise" starts to make sense,' said Steven.

'Curtis mentioned "suspension" in his message,' said Bristow. 'He could be talking about suspension of security measures supplied by his firm . . .'

'While Innes and his men carry out an exercise,' said Steven.

'In an area with some connection to Scottish Water if Pope is involved,' said Macmillan.

'It's my bet that Innes has organised this as a genuine military exercise,' said Steven after a few moments thought. 'And if that's the case, he would have to have filed details with his superiors. It's the army way.'

'That's something we can check,' said Macmillan, leaving the room again.

'Contacts have been reassured,' said Hamilton getting up from the computer.

'You're sure they'll think the message came from the same source as the enquiry?' asked Steven.

'Trust me,' smiled Hamilton. 'God, I'm knackered.' He stretched his arms in the air and let out a big yawn. It set everyone else off.

'I could sleep for a week,' said Dorothy, rubbing the back of her neck.

'You've all done well,' said Steven. 'We're almost there. Why don't you take a break while John tackles the MOD. I'll monitor the screen in case any more messages come in.'

'You must be just as tired,' said Dorothy.

'I'm carrying the can for this if it all goes belly-up,' said Steven. 'That gives me more adrenalin.'

Alone in the room, Steven swivelled round in his seat and put his feet up on the table. It was something he would not normally have done. His tie had long since been discarded and successive buttons on his shirt had been opened to allow the flat of his hand to rest on his chest. The stubble on his chin was beginning to itch and a shower was beginning to seem like the most desirable thing on the planet. For the moment he made do with yet more black coffee while he waited to see if anyone else on the database would make contact. His eyelids were starting to go together when Macmillan came back into the room.

'Most unlike the MOD to be so efficient,' he said. 'Here it is.' He waved a handful of paper in the air. 'A summary of the entire exercise. Where is everyone?'

'I suggested they take a break,' said Steven.

'Get them back, will you.'

Luckily only Dorothy Jordan had left the building. Steven found her outside, arms crossed, looking down at the pavement as she walked slowly up and down, apparently deep in thought. He apologised and told her that Macmillan needed everyone back.

She responded with a nod as if too tired to say anything and followed him back inside.

'The exercise we've been hearing about is to take place in the Loch Ard Forest in Scotland,' announced Macmillan when everyone had reassembled. 'I think maybe we need maps . . .'

Hamilton took his cue and sat himself back down at a computer to start typing in instructions.

'Loch Ard and its forest,' continued Macmillan, 'are part of the Forestry Commission's Queen Elizabeth Forest Park, which comprises some 50,000 acres of mountains, lochs, forests and open rough country. For the purposes of the exercise, Major Innes and his men are charged with hunting down three armed and dangerous terrorists who will be on the loose in the forest, intent on damaging water board installations in the area.'

'Maps for everyone,' announced Hamilton, collecting several sheets of paper from the printer beside the computer and handing them around.

After a few moments study, Deans asked, 'Is Loch Ard used as a reservoir?'

'Looks too small,' said Macmillan, 'but we'll check that out.'

'Maybe that's what would make it attractive for a field trial,' said Dorothy Jordan. 'It would get round the dilution factor.'

'Strange,' said Steven. 'There's an aqueduct marked on the map but its position with regard to the contour lines suggests it isn't

336

carrying water from Loch Ard . . . I'm not sure I understand it. There's no water to the north of it; in fact, the ground rises quite steeply to the hills north of Aberfoyle.'

'Oh my God,' said Dorothy Jordan, turning pale. 'I think I know what that is.'

The ensuing silence was broken by Hamilton coming back from the computer and saying, 'Loch Ard is not used as a reservoir . . . What's wrong? Who's seen a ghost?'

All eyes stayed on Dorothy Jordan as she said, 'I remember reading about this in one of the medical journals. The aqueduct Steven has picked up on is part of a water supply system built in Victorian times by a man named Baleman, if my memory serves me right. It carries water taken from Loch Katrine, which certainly is a reservoir and, as you will see on the map, is well to the north of the area. Underground pipes are used to bring the water south except here where it flows for a short distance across an open aqueduct before going underground again.'

'Where is it going to?' asked Hamilton.

'Glasgow,' replied Dorothy. 'This is the source of Glasgow's water supply!'

'They plan to attack . . . an entire city!' exclaimed Hamilton, aghast at the very idea.

'It's ironic really,' said Dorothy Jordan. 'This water supply system is largely credited with wiping out cholera in Glasgow in the late eighteen hundreds. That was the substance of the article I remembered.'

'That's how they plan on getting round the dilution problem,' said Steven who'd been staring at his map. 'Instead of trying to contaminate the entire reservoir—Loch Katrine must be ten miles long—they're making the hit downstream on water that's already been taken from the loch and is on its way to the taps of the city—a tiny proportion of the volume.'

'Clever.'

'Very.'

'Well done everyone,' said Macmillan. 'It is clever but you have proved equal to the task and beat them to it; I think you can all go home now and get some well-deserved rest. We here will set the wheels in motion to make sure this doesn't happen.'

When the last of the team had left Steven turned to Macmillan and asked, 'When is this scheduled to take place?'

'The 8th of September,' replied Macmillan as if his mind was already working on something else.

'But that's tomorrow!' exclaimed Steven.

'Yes, it is,' said Macmillan. 'I thought we should talk in private. Let's not panic. Let's keep our nerve and establish priorities. First and foremost we must ensure that the agent doesn't get into the water supply. We could do that through sheer weight of numbers but what else do we have to consider?'

'We want to get our hands on the agent,' said Steven. 'I know Rees is working on an early version of it and it looks as if he's going to come up with the goods but it would be better to know just how sophisticated the finished article is. If we draft hundreds of police and troops into the area we'll scare off the opposition and end up back at square one.'

'Right,' said Macmillan, mentally ticking off a list. 'We want the agent.'

'It would also be in our interests to take the three "terrorists" alive so we can question them and establish the connection with Crowe and Mowbray,' said Steven.

'I don't think the Territorials will be planning on shooting them,' said Macmillan.

'You're leaving it up to weekend soldiers?'

'If the hares see us change the hounds to the Marines they're going to smell a rat,' said Macmillan. 'I thought we could mount a professional guard on the aqueduct itself—I'll call on Hereford—and let the Territorials go through the motions of the man-hunt in the forest as planned.'

'Good idea,' agreed Steven. 'Maybe it would be as well to have some kind of a stop put on the water downstream of the aqueduct, just in case things go wrong. I think we have to assume that these three will be good.'

'Probably ex-Hereford themselves,' agreed Macmillan, referring again to the home of the SAS. 'Mind you, that might not be possible if the water goes back into underground pipes again,' said Macmillan. 'But we can certainly make enquiries. Anything else?'

'I'd like to be there,' said Steven.

'I can't say I'm surprised but are you sure that's wise?'

'I'd like to see this through to the end,' said Steven.

'Your decision,' conceded Macmillan. 'But you badly need some rest. Go home now and come back this afternoon. We'll talk further then.'

'You've been up all night too,' said Steven.

'I'll set some wheels in motion then I'll grab a couple of hours too.'

*   *   *

Steven showered and set his alarm for three in the afternoon before drifting off into a fitful sleep. His limbs felt heavy and he wanted to sleep for a week, but there were so many questions going round in his head that he couldn't manage to escape the grey margins dividing true sleep from wakefulness for more than a few minutes at a time before being plagued by thoughts of the exercise to come. He couldn't see why they had organised it in the first place. Surely a straightforward assault on civilian security at the aqueduct would have been simpler. After all, three Special Forces men were not going to have too much trouble

340

evading Territorial troops or overcoming a guard mounted by weekend soldiers so it would come to the same thing in the end. Unless of course . . . they wanted to keep the contamination a secret!

It was so obvious that Steven shook his head slightly on the pillow without opening his eyes and told himself he really should have seen it earlier. Going through the pantomime of the military exercise would allow the opposition to taint the water without anyone realising what had really happened. He must really be tired not to have seen that.

*   *   *

When Steven got back to the Home Office he noticed that Macmillan was wearing the same clothes and deduced that he hadn't left the building.

'You haven't had any sleep at all, have you?'

Macmillan responded by taking out a packet of pills from his desk and showing Steven the label. 'Benzedrine,' he said. 'I couldn't spare the time. They'll see me through.'

Steven nodded. He knew the stimulants would keep Macmillan awake and alert as long as he kept taking them but sleep deficit would build up and the price would have to be paid when he stopped. 'What's new?' he asked.

Macmillan turned the map on his desk towards Steven and said, 'There are a number of breather ducts above the pipeline south of the aqueduct. I've arranged for a team from 45 Commando at Arbroath to gain access at one and interrupt the water supply for the duration of the exercise.'

'Good,' said Steven.

'Six men from the SAS regiment have been detailed to support you in mounting the guard on the aqueduct if you're still intent on being there?'

Steven said that he was.

'In that case I've to let them know. They're going up by helicopter. They've made a special arrangement to pick you up at City Airport at 6pm. Don't be late. They don't want people asking questions.'

'I won't,' said Steven.

'Best be off then,' said Macmillan with a look that wished him well.

CHAPTER TWENTY-ONE

Steven had a not unpleasant feeling of *deja vu* as he sprinted across the tarmac in a crouching run to get into the helicopter.

'Just like old times,' he said as the door was closed behind him and he barely had time to sit down before the whirling blades had plucked them up and away.

'We heard you were regiment,' said one of

342

the six men sitting there in combat gear but with no badges or indications of rank. 'I'm Mick.'

'A long time ago,' said Steven.

Mick turned to the others and pointed as he said, 'Terry, Jonesey, Popeye, Cluedo and Walsh.'

Steven nodded and said, 'You've been briefed?'

'Three hours ago,' said Mick. 'They said you would fill in the missing bits.'

Steven nodded, screwing up his face with the effort of trying to converse above the noise of the engines. 'Where are we headed?'

'We plan to keep well away from the area in question,' said Mick. 'We'll land on the west side of Loch'—he pronounced it, Lock—'Lomond and boat it across south of Inversnaid. We'll tab it cross country from there to the Loch Ard Forest and skirt round the bottom of Loch Chon, staying in the forest all the way along the south shore of Loch Ard before approaching the aqueduct. Think you're up to it?'

'I hadn't anticipated this,' said Steven.

'Just a walk in the park,' smiled Mick.

Steven's answering smile was a bit more fragile.

The engine noise made unnecessary conversation difficult so the remainder of the journey was largely completed without it.

343

Steven felt a slight hollow feeling in his stomach as he watched the helicopter take off into the night sky, leaving them a couple of hundred metres inland from the west bank of Loch Lomond. He busied himself getting into the kit that had been brought along for him while the others prepared the inflatable boat for the crossing. Luckily it was a calm night with stars visible in a clear sky, although it had been raining earlier and the ground was wet and the air full of the smell of pine needles.

'Ready?' asked Mick as Steven secured his Bergen rucksack after having packed away his own clothes in it.

'As I'll ever be.'

The loch crossing was bumpy but not as uncomfortable as Steven had anticipated. By the time they were pulling the boat up on to the east shore and finding a suitable place to hide it away, he had actually started to feel exhilarated. It was certainly a change from what he would normally be doing on a Monday night and he felt very much alive. He felt even better when Mick said, 'There's a forestry track leading inland from here. We'll use that.'

They headed inland and were discussing radio codes and channels to be used when Walsh, who was walking up ahead, held up his hand and signalled that they get down. They dropped to their knees and remained quiet

344

and motionless while Walsh investigated whatever it was that had caught his attention. He reappeared as if by magic a few moments later at Mick's shoulder and whispered, 'Two blokes camping. They sound like bank clerks.'

Mick nodded and said, 'We're crossing the route of the West Highland Way here. We'll skirt round them.'

The six men made a slight detour to the north to bypass the men who would never realise they had been there and rejoined the path to head inland. It was heavily rutted in parts through use by heavy Forestry Commission vehicles but easy-going compared to what Steven had feared. Trying to make good progress through knee-deep bracken on ground that never seemed to be level, as he remembered from Highland walks in the past, could be soul-destroying. He was to become reacquainted with the feeling when, south of Loch Ard, Mick said it was time to leave the track.

At three in the morning they were in position at a point west of the aqueduct which afforded them a good view of it.

'Get your head down for a couple of hours,' said Mick to Steven. 'I'll wake you if anything's going down.'

Steven needed no second invitation. He woke at six, alerted by a burst of static on the radio.

'Marines are in position in the breather duct

one mile south of here,' said Mick.

'Good,' said Steven accepting the glasses which Mick offered him and taking a good look at the aqueduct and the area round about through them. There was a white van parked near the base with 'Diamond Security' on its side.

'We'll move closer as soon as the civvies clock off,' said Mick. 'In the meantime we'll have a brew . . . won't we Terry?'

'Yes boss,' replied Terry who set about making tea.

Mick outlined plans for guarding the aqueduct during the course of the exercise. They would split up to individually cover all possible angles of approach, the exception being Steven who would stay beside Mick in case his advice was needed.

'How dangerous is this stuff?' asked one of the men.

'It won't kill you,' replied Steven. 'But you could end up wishing it had if you get infected. Ideally we want to take it from these three characters before they have a chance to open whatever they're carrying it in—probably something that looks like a thermos flask.'

'So don't go having a fly cuppa, Cluedo,' said Mick. 'You might get more than you bargained for.'

The comment served to release the tension that had been building almost imperceptibly.

When it got to seven thirty the men turned

their radios to the channel being used by the Territorial Army for the duration of the exercise so that they could listen in to what was going on. At a quarter to eight it started to rain and at five to, Walsh, who'd been keeping watch on the aqueduct, reported, 'Civvies moving out, Boss.'

Almost at the same time the radio crackled into life and the men heard Major David Innes ask his deployed units to report their position. Mick marked them down on the map as they radioed in. 'Can't fault that,' he murmured.

'Operation underway gentlemen,' said Innes. 'Good luck everyone.'

'Half a dozen Terries by the aqueduct, Boss,' said Walsh.

Mick took a look at the soldiers who'd been detailed to guard the aqueduct and said, 'Time we moved in. Anyone who gets himself spotted by a Terry gets my foot up his arse.'

The men made last minute adjustments to their camouflage clothing, a couple of them adding yet more bracken to better the match with their surroundings. They wished each other well before moving out at ten second intervals. Steven and Mick moved south east of the aqueduct and fashioned themselves a hide in a small hollow, which they augmented with a makeshift roof made out of dead wood and leaves from the forest floor.

'What happens to the flasks when we get them?' asked Mick.

'A mobile lab will be in position just outside Aberfoyle on the east side,' said Steven. 'They'll take care of them.'

'The very thought of germ warfare makes my flesh creep,' said Mick.

'Can't say I'm a big fan either,' said Steven.

Three hours went past slowly in complete radio silence and the small talk had long since run out when Mick let out his breath in a long sigh and murmured, 'C'mon.' He looked at his watch and frowned but it was another half hour before he suddenly clapped the earphones, which had been hanging round his neck, to his ears. 'They've got one,' he told Steven. He slipped the earphones down again and marked the position on his map. 'Well done the Terries,' he said. 'Captured one man and secured the container he was carrying.'

Stevens facial expression indicated that he was impressed too. He was even more impressed when at one thirty a second terrorist was taken prisoner by the soldiers.

'Did they get the flask?' asked Steven.

'Yup, safe and sound. Who would have thought . . .' said Mick, thoughtfully. 'These guys are good. I take back everything I ever thought about them. They're doing a cracking job.'

By four in the afternoon both Mick and Steve were getting edgy. Steven was even beginning to think that the third man might have abandoned the mission if he had been aware of the capture of the other two. He was about to say this to Mick when the radio crackled into life again and Mick smiled broadly as he relayed news of the capture of the third man.

'Bloody hell,' said Mick. 'We were a waste of space. The Terries got them all.'

Mick switched the radio back on to speaker mode and Steven heard Innes tell his men that the operation was now over. They had taken all three terrorists prisoner and captured the 'biological weapons' they were carrying intact.

'Well done everyone,' said Innes before giving out a map reference for the troops to rendezvous at.

'Time to offer our congratulations, I think,' said Steven getting to his feet. 'I take it you have a cover story?'

'MOD observers,' said Mick with a smile.

The SAS men met up and marched together to the rendezvous point given out by Innes. They arrived there fifteen minutes later, attracting strange looks from the soldiers already there. Steven sought out Innes, showed him his ID and introduced Mick and his men as MOD observers sent in to monitor the exercise without forewarning. Innes beamed as he was congratulated on the performance of his men. 'We do our best,' he said modestly like the captain of the winning team on school sports day.

Steven asked about the containers the

349

terrorists had been carrying.

'They're being brought in with the prisoners,' said Innes. 'They should be here at any minute.'

Steven used his mobile phone and asked to be patched through to the mobile lab waiting at Aberfoyle. He requested that it make its way down to the rendezvous point.

'Roger that.'

As he ended the call, Mick came across and told Steven that the men from 45 Commando were asking if it was all right to restore the water supply.

'Tell them, yes,' said Steven.

'Here they are,' said Innes as a long wheelbase Land Rover appeared through the trees. When three soldiers got out unaccompanied, Innes asked where the prisoners were.

'You said the operation was over, sir,' replied the driver, a corporal. 'They asked to be dropped off about a mile back. They said they'd hidden their vehicle there in the trees. It made more sense than coming in here and then having to get a lift back.'

'I suppose,' said Innes.

The news made Steven's throat constrict to a point where he could hardly speak. He exchanged alarmed glances with Mick. 'And the flasks they were carrying?' he croaked.

'Right here,' replied the corporal, returning briefly to the Land Rover and returning with three metal flasks with apparently unbroken seals.

'You're sure this was all they were carrying?' Steven said.

'Absolutely,' replied the corporal.

'Anything wrong?' asked Innes, aware of Steven's unease but failing to understand it.

'No, nothing,' replied Steven. 'Really.'

'Then I suggest that beer in Aberfoyle might be in order,' announced Innes in a loud voice. This brought a cheer from the troops. 'I'm sure we'd be delighted if you chaps would join us?'

'Thanks, Major,' said Steven. 'We'll be along shortly.'

'Just to make sure that you do, I'll leave you one of the vehicles,' said Innes, now filled with the surge of confidence that success brings.

'Thanks,' said Steven.

'Everything all right, Steve?' asked Mick as the Territorials started to move out.

'I'm not sure,' said Steven. 'Something doesn't feel right . . .'

The mobile lab appeared at the end of the track and the sight of it interrupted his train of thought. As it pulled in to the side and drew up Steven took the three flasks round to the back of the vehicle and waited for the doors to be opened. The two men in the back were wearing white biohazard suits. Only the full hood visors were missing.

'You have something for us,' said one of the

men.

Steven handed the sealed metal containers to them and said after a moment's hesitation, 'I realise that you chaps are only expecting to transport these south—and this may be a very stupid question—but is there any way you could tell me right now if these containers contain living biological material?'

'You have doubts then?'

'Yes,' replied Steven without really knowing why.

'There's no way we could go about identifying any bug or virus,' said the man. 'But if it's a simple yes/no you're after, that's possible—if it's really important?'

Steven took a moment to consider the man's obvious reluctance to open the flasks before saying, 'It is.'

The man shrugged and said, 'Okay, just give us ten minutes.'

Steven watched the men don their hoods and check the sealing on each other's suit before closing the back doors of the vehicle.

Steven felt the need to be on his own. He walked over to the edge of the trees and looked back down the valley at nothing in particular. When he heard the doors of the mobile lab being opened again he turned round and hurried towards it.

'Well?' he asked the first man to take his hood off.

'As far as we can tell,' said the man. 'The

three flasks contain nothing but red dye . . .'

'Fuck,' said Steven as his world suddenly crumbled around him. It had been a perfectly genuine exercise with three mock terrorists attempting to carry out an attack on water supplies with red dye and being thwarted by men of the Territorial Army!

The SAS men seemed to sense Steven's embarrassment and stayed away from him as he walked back over to his vantage point over the valley to look into the middle distance as he fought to come to terms with what he now saw as complete and abject failure.

But why had it been arranged through Gardiner's organisation at all? asked a small voice inside his head. Why use these people at all to arrange details like . . . suspension of civilian security . . . from eight till six on the day of the exercise? From eight till six on the day of the exercise . . . The phrase repeated itself. Steven looked at his watch. It was 5.30. Who was guarding the aqueduct right now? He asked himself. No one, replied the little voice.

Steven spun round on his heel as suddenly it all started to make sense. What was it Mick had said earlier when the Territorials made light work of capturing the second terrorist? Who would have thought . . . Who would have thought?

YOU IDIOT! THEY WERE MEANT TO CAPTURE THEM! screamed the voice inside

353

his head.

'Sweet Jesus fucking Christ in a basket!' Steven yelled at the SAS men. 'There are more of them!' He ran to the Land Rover left behind by Innes and tugged at the starter as the SAS men piled in behind him. Mick swung his legs in the front as Steven took off, sending up a hail of stones from the spinning wheels.

'The aqueduct is unguarded from now until six o'clock,' yelled Steven above the roar of the engine, which he kept in low gear, using high revs to keep up speed. 'The third man made sure he was captured well before that time in order to ensure a gap.'

'And the water supply has been restored,' yelled Mick.

'What an idiot!' Steven berated himself. 'It's perfect, just what they wanted! Officially it's been a completely successful exercise with the squaddies triumphing and the terrorists getting nowhere near the water supply. They planned to slip the agent into the water after the exercise was over so that no one would ever be able to work out where the infection came from. It was to be another bloody secret!'

'There's a security van there,' said Mick as the aqueduct came into view.

'I don't believe it,' yelled Steven. 'Civvies don't start early.'

'Christ, there's a bloke up on the aqueduct!' said one of the others. They all caught sight of a dark clad man moving along the gantry

354

before dropping out of sight again.

'Get on to the 45 guys. See if there's any chance of getting the supply interrupted again,' said Steven.

Walsh got on the radio.

'What do you want us to do?' asked Mick.

'If you get the chance, kill him,' replied Steven.

'They're half a mile away,' said Walsh, reporting on the commandos' position.

'Tell them to get there as soon as they can,' said Steven. 'It's a matter of life and death.'

Walsh relayed the message and Steven slowed the vehicle to walking pace as they neared the base of the aqueduct.

'Let's go,' yelled Mick as he leapt out and others followed with the exception of Walsh who was still in touch with the commandos. 'Fuck me, are you not there yet?' Steven heard him say. 'Bunch of big girls' blouses.'

Steven was vaguely conscious of an unprintable reply as he brought the Land Rover to a complete halt and got out to look up. There was no sign of the figure they'd seen earlier but he must still be there, he reasoned. There was nowhere else for him to go.

Steven climbed the steep grassy bank leading up to the iron aqueduct and steadied himself on a short section of railing at the top, designed to restrict access to the feeder pipe which emerged from the ground to spew water into the open channel. He looked along the channel expecting to see a man hiding there but saw nothing but fast flowing water.

'Where the f—' mouthed Steven, unable to understand where the man could possibly have gone. 'There's nowhere . . . absolutely nowhere . . .' he kept reasoning, 'So how . . . ?'

Steven almost fell over backwards as a figure suddenly emerged like Poseidon from the water about twenty metres along the aqueduct. Instead of a trident, he was holding up a metal flask in his right hand. He had finally run out of air.

Steven gave the man a moment to get his breath and let the water drain away from his face before saying, 'It's all over, best give that to me.' He held out his hand. The man, who had been lying on his back under the surface, was now in a sitting position with the water flowing past him. 'Something tells me I'm still holding all the aces,' he said, making a slight movement with the flask in his hand.

Steven started to move towards him but the man immediately switched the flask to his other hand and started undoing the cap.

'For Christ's sake man!' said Steven. 'Have you any idea what you're about to do?'

The man shook his head. 'None at all,' he replied. 'That's the way I like it. I'm a soldier. I get my orders. I carry them out. They pay me. That's all I need to know.'

'Don't you care about . . . ?'

'Don't waste your breath,' interrupted the

man. 'I've soldiered all over the world. I've seen everything one human being can do to another human being. I stopped being interested a long time ago.'

Steven knew he had to stall the man as long as possible so that the commandos would have time to put the divert back on the water supply again but it wasn't looking hopeful. 'Even if money is the only thing you're interested in, surely you've already been paid?' he said.

'In part. The rest goes into my account for Miriam and the kid when the job gets done.'

'Look, if it's a matter of money . . .' began Steven.

'And professional pride,' said the man, smiling for the first time as he started to get to his feet. 'You didn't know mercenaries had pride, did you? Well, we do. To be one in the first place you have to be good and British mercenaries are the best; that's why we get paid the best. Nice and simple. Nice and honest. No bullshit, no flag-waving, no pretence.'

'Even if that's true—' said Steven. He was interrupted by a shot shattering the silence as the man stood up and became visible over the parapet. A puzzled look appeared briefly on his face before he pitched forward to fall face down into the water. Steven climbed into the aqueduct channel and waded as fast as he could towards the figure before it floated away, his one thought the safe retrieval of the flask. He reached the body and straddled his legs across it while he reached down into the water to feel if the man was still holding the flask. He was but, as Steven suddenly realised in a surge of panic, he was holding it in both hands! He wasn't dead. He was trying to undo the top!

Steven wrenched it from his grasp and brought it to the surface as Mick and two of the others appeared on the gantry and came to help. They pulled the man—who now seemed to be dead—out of the water and tipped his body over the edge of the aqueduct to fall to the ground below with a thud.

'Okay?' asked Mick as Steven tried to ascertain whether there had been any leakage from the flask. There was no doubt the seal was broken. It was just a question of how far the top could be turned before the sealing gasket ceased to have any effect. 'I don't know,' he said. 'Did the commandos get the divert on in time?'

Mick made a gesture with his right hand that indicated it might have been touch and go.

'Then it's wait and see time,' said Steven.

They left the gantry and came slowly back down the grassy slope to the ground.

'Christ, I could do with a drink,' said Steven as he felt himself go weak at the knees as the adrenalin left his bloodstream.

'Looks like we're done here,' said Mick. 'I'll

call in the chopper.'

*   *   *

Steven, dressed in a smart suit and dark tie, stood at the window in his flat, watching the sunlight sparkle on the Thames. It was a sight that usually gladdened his heart but not this morning. He was due at the Home Office in forty-five minutes and he was not looking forward to it. He thought he could see what was coming and he was going to need all the self control he could muster. There was no way that that the establishment could let the whole truth come out so he was reconciled to a cover-up. It was just a question of degree and how much he could stomach before anger got the better of him. A slight smile played on his lips when he remembered what Lisa used to say when she sensed temper getting the better of him. Deep breaths, Dunbar, deep breaths . . .

*   *   *

Steven found the Home Secretary with Macmillan when he entered Macmillan's office. Both men seemed relaxed and smiled as he came in.

'Welcome back,' said Macmillan.

'Good to *be* back,' replied Steven automatically.

'I felt I had to come along and congratulate you personally on a job well done,' said the Home Secretary.

'Thank you, sir, but we're not out of the woods just yet,' replied Steven. 'There's still a chance that Glasgow's water may have been contaminated.'

'And that's something we have been taking very seriously,' replied the Home Secretary.

Steven thought how much like a politician he sounded.

'We've been in touch with the Scottish Executive, Glasgow City Council and Scottish Water. They're putting out a general warning that water taken from Loch Katrine may have been contaminated with faeces from grazing sheep. Steps are being taken to issue bottled water until we're sure the danger's past.'

Steven nodded.

'I take it, you'll be looking forward to some leave now?' said Macmillan. 'God knows, you deserve it.'

'I was rather hoping you were going to brief me on what's been happening down here,' said Steven. He noticed the uneasy glance that passed between Macmillan and the Home Secretary.

'About Crowe and Mowbray, I mean,' said Steven, in case there was any doubt.

'It's . . . difficult,' began Macmillan.

Oh, God, here it comes, thought Steven. He felt his cheek muscles tighten and his fingers

360

start to clench.

'They know, of course, that the trial of their biological agent has been a complete failure and that they won't be getting any money from abroad . . .'

'But?'

The Home Secretary cleared his throat. Steven thought it a nervous gesture. Macmillan diverted his gaze.

'Well, to cut a long story short, they've offered us a deal,' said the Home Secretary. 'They will hand over the antibiotic that can cure their damned agent and also provide technical details of its design and manufacture.'

'In exchange for getting off scot-free?' said Steven.

Macmillan said, 'It is a very difficult situation, Steven.'

'Professor Rees believes he could come up with an effective antibiotic on his own,' said Steven.

'There's no guarantee, and it could take time,' said Macmillan.

'I'm sure we don't have to point out to you the huge benefits of being able to treat Gulf War Syndrome after all this time,' said the Home Secretary.

'So it does exist then?' said Steven. He noticed a flash of anger in the Home Secretary's eyes but there was no follow up.

Macmillan, sensing the danger, intervened.

'We know how you feel, Dunbar: believe me, we do. In many ways we share your frustration.'

'It's just that some of us have to look at the bigger picture . . . for the common good,' said the Home Secretary. 'We can't afford the luxury of—'

Truth, honesty and decency, thought Steven, but he bit his tongue.

'Seeing each individual case in isolation,' completed the Home Secretary.

'So they are going to get away with it?'

'I don't think their lives are going to be that comfortable,' said Macmillan. 'They may escape legal proceedings but neither will ever work again professionally and they are going to find themselves—'

The phrase *excluded from polite society* sprang to Steven's lips but, again, he remained silent.

'Generally unwelcome wherever they go,' said Macmillan.

Steven heard Lisa's voice say inside his head, 'Deep breaths, Dunbar, deep breaths . . .'

Both Macmillan and the Home Secretary read the slight softening of his features as acquiescence. 'Good man,' said the Home Secretary. 'I'm sure, when you think about it, you'll come to see that this is the only reasonable course open to HMG in the circumstances.'

'Of course, sir . . . the big picture,' said

362

Steven. It drew a questioning look from the Home Secretary but once more, Macmillan stepped in. 'Now, about that leave?'

'That would be most welcome,' said Steven.

'Any idea what you'll do?'

'First, I have to go up to Glasgow. Then I'll go spend some time with my daughter.'

'Glasgow?'

'Call it . . . the small picture,' said Steven, 'and I'll need some of the antibiotic that Crowe and Mowbray have agreed to hand over.'

'I'm not sure if—' began the Home Secretary but Macmillan shot him a warning glance as he saw Steven's expression darken. 'Maclean?' he asked.

Steven nodded.

'I'm sure that, in the special circumstances, there won't be a problem,' said Macmillan.

Steven smiled. 'Then, if you'll excuse me, gentlemen?'

'Thank you again,' said the Home Secretary.

Steven paused outside the entrance to the Home Office to look up at the sky and savour the fresh air. Deep breaths, Dunbar, deep breaths . . .